Christmas at fireside cabins

JENNY HALE

FOREVER

NEW YORK   BOSTON

Forever
Hachette Book Group
1290 Avenue of the Americas, New York, NY 10104
read-forever.com
twitter.com/readforeverpub

Originally published in 2020 by Bookouture in the United Kingdom
First US edition: September 2022

Forever is an imprint of Grand Central Publishing. The Forever name and logo are trademarks of Hachette Book Group, Inc.

The publisher is not responsible for websites (or their content) that are not owned by the publisher.

Library of Congress Cataloging-in-Publication Data

Names: Hale, Jenny, 1975– author.
Title: Christmas at Fireside Cabins / Jenny Hale.
Description: First US edition. | New York : Forever, 2022. | "Originally published in 2020 by Bookouture in the United Kingdom"—Title page verso.
Identifiers: LCCN 2022019454 | ISBN 9781538723036 (trade paperback)
Subjects: LCGFT: Novels.
Classification: LCC PS3608.A54574 C479 2022 | DDC 813/.6—dc23
LC record available at https://lccn.loc.gov/2022019454

ISBN: 9781538723036 (trade paperback)

Printed in the United States of America

LSC-C

Printing 1, 2022

Christmas
at
fireside
cabins

ALSO BY JENNY HALE

Prologue

"Sorry I'm late," Lila Evans said to her three best friends, as she dropped into a chair around the table at their favorite coffee shop. Her purse and red-and-green Christmas shopping bags full of gifts landed on the floor with a thud beside her. She unwound her scarf, shaking the snow off of it, still breathless from rushing.

A solo guitar player strummed holiday tunes on a small holly-rimmed stage in the corner, singing into a microphone, his raspy voice coming through the miniature amplifier by his feet while busy shoppers grabbed coffees on their way to various festive destinations around the city. Live acoustic music was one of the perks of going to a coffee shop on Music Row in Nashville.

"My manager insisted that we all stay later on our shifts to help him keep the restaurant open longer during the Christmas season." Lila tucked the runaway strands of damp hair behind her ear, the newly falling snow having had its way with it. The rest of her chocolate-brown locks were pinned up in a messy bun, just like every day she waitressed. "He didn't tell me we were staying past our usual hours until I'd gotten there this morning." She fluttered her fingers in the air. "But I'm here now," she said with a grin. "And I've got something to show everyone."

Lila reached down into her purse, grabbing her iPad and setting it on the table in preparation for what she had to share with the girls.

"When are you going to quit that job?" her friend Edie James asked, clearly noticing Lila's exhaustion despite her attempts to hide it.

Edie knew all too well that Lila could be doing better things with her time than dealing with her disaster of a manager. But their conversation was interrupted when the barista called Edie's name.

"I got you a peppermint latte with extra whipped cream. I'd already figured when you hadn't arrived yet that you'd need to treat yourself," she said to Lila, getting up to retrieve the two oversized white mugs sitting next to an arrangement of berries and pinecones on the coffee bar beside their table.

Edie was the grounded one of the group, who kept them all under a strong reality check. She worked for a high-profile PR firm downtown, and she was constantly getting called in to work off-hours or on weekends for some big client, yet no matter where they decided to meet she was always punctual, arriving to their group meetings at the precise minute they were supposed to be there and leaving no earlier than exactly one hour later. She had a heart the size of Texas and she'd do anything for them.

"Thanks," Lila said as Edie handed her a steaming mug. "I don't know when I'm gonna quit." She shook her head. "The truth is that I don't have any better options, really. I could waitress for someone else, but I'm sure I'd face headaches over something anywhere I worked, and the tips are really good."

She'd worked at the steakhouse the entire three years she'd known this group of women surrounding her now, and she'd considered quitting at least once a day the whole time. She'd fallen into waitressing when she'd taken the first job she could get that paid decently, and she'd been stuck there ever since. She often wondered if she'd somehow missed the cosmic signs for what she was supposed to do with her life. Growing up, she'd imagined working with disadvantaged kids full time or doing something with people that would make a difference, but she just hadn't ever found her place.

"I hear you." Edie set her own coffee down and crossed the flaps of her cardigan, wrapping it tightly around herself, as if it would keep out the winter chill that danced into the shop every time the door opened.

Lila took a sip of her latte, the nutty smooth flavor of the chocolate and the pop of peppermint instantly lifting her up to a state of festivity. "How about you, Edie? How's the big pitch going?"

Edie had been given the largest account her firm had ever received. If she could get this one in the bag, she was looking at a major promotion. She hadn't divulged exactly what the promotion entailed, but she'd used the words "life-changing."

"We're really close," she said. "The client is considering us and one other." Edie pointed to the iPad. "Did you say you found us something?" she asked, sitting down and wrapping her fingers around her mug.

"Maybe," Lila replied, "but first, I want to hear how everyone's doing."

"My tyrant of an agent finally did something great. He just got me a TV network contract and I'll be styling the actors on a few of their shows," Lila's friend Charlotte Meade, professional hairstylist to the stars, said, all smiles. Then her full, glossy lips dropped to a frown. "But I'm a little worried about styling Nikki Mars—you know that actress who dates the lead singer of the Misfit Junkies? She's got that unruly mop of hair." She made a face and ran her almond-shaped manicured nails past her boutique hoop earrings, through her golden locks.

"You'll be great," Edie told her. She reached across the table and patted her arm.

Suddenly, as if it occurred to all three women at once, their gaze turned to Piper Watson, the bubbliest of them all, who'd been uncharacteristically quiet.

Lila grinned just looking at Piper, as she sat about to burst with excitement.

"I brought y'all something." Piper picked up the tattered patchwork bag that in its own cool way would be considered vintage rather than old, and lumped it on the table. She stood to dig around inside it, pushing up the sleeves of her oversized cardigan, which she'd layered with an old T-shirt for some rock band that Lila had never heard of. Her tiny waiflike arms moved a mile a minute in her enthusiasm.

Piper's earthy, eclectic lifestyle kept them all on their toes. A soap-maker by trade, she could always be found at the local fairs and flea markets peddling the wares for her company, Scented Spirit. Her company motto was *Skincare to protect and perfect the carrier of your soul.* She had such an infectious personality that she made an incredible living because anyone walking by would stop to listen to her, and she pulled them right in with her irresistible charm. She could sniff out a skeptical shopper in a second, and using her personable nature, she'd have them walking away with bags of her soaps. She could relate to anyone, and she held a wealth of information, her interests spanning everything from pop culture to holistic living.

"One for you," she said in a singsong voice, dropping a little piece of holiday-colored fabric tied with a string of twine in front of Edie. "One for *you*." She handed one to Charlotte. "And one for you." She gave a little happy squeal and bounced back into her seat. "Open them!"

Lila unwound the string and set it aside, the scrap of fabric becoming slack, revealing a small jar of lotion. She turned hers around toward the center of the table so everyone could see. "Mine says *Midnight*."

Lila opened the jar and smiled. "Lavender," she said, her favorite scent dancing into the air under her nose. "How lovely, Piper."

"Oh, I have *Rockstar*," Charlotte piped up, opening the lid and taking in the scent of it. "It smells like coconut. I *love* it." She dipped her finger into the shimmery cream and spread it over the back of her hand. "It sparkles." Her eyebrows bounced up and down. "Thank you."

"I made them last night," Piper said, beaming, her pointy, delicate features alight. "It's my new all-natural lotion line. I'm planning to pass some around after my yoga class tomorrow and also at the farmer's market this weekend. I've made around two hundred samples so far."

"Such the entrepreneur," Edie told her as she held hers up. "I'm so proud of you."

Piper reached over and gave Edie a hug.

Once Piper let go of her, Edie showed hers to the table. "Mine is aptly named *Focus*."

"What does *Focus* smell like?" Charlotte wanted to know, still rubbing *Rockstar* cream on her hands and wriggling her fingers to show off its shimmer.

Edie unscrewed the lid and wafted the scent toward her. "Mint." She blew a kiss to Piper and thanked her.

They all *ooe*d, making Piper bounce elatedly in her seat.

Once they'd all settled down, Edie turned to Lila. "Okay, I can't stand it anymore. Dish. Where are we going?"

Lila had known Charlotte, Piper, and Edie since she'd moved to Nashville three years ago—they'd found themselves in the same apartment complex. Lila's mother had died tragically in a car crash just after Lila's birth and her father had passed away of cancer when she was twenty, so these women were the closest thing to family she had. Wanting to live the dream so badly, she'd chased a guy to Nashville, hoping to start a family of her own one day, and when the relationship hadn't worked out, her three friends had convinced her to stay in the city. That same year, the four women, all single, formed a group to support each other, and that's exactly what they'd done.

For the last three years, during the holidays—when being single was the hardest—they spent a week together in December, filling their time with laughter, and strengthening their friendship by traveling to new places and visiting other towns and cities. Christmas was their favorite time of year. But for Lila, it was a bit more than that. Every day that went by was one day further away from the last time she'd given her dad a hug, and if she let herself think about it, she'd crumble. Just once, she would've loved to sit in a circle with her family, cherishing their time together and making the most of every moment, but she hadn't gotten to do that. So instead she valued the trips she made with her girlfriends. Having never really settled anywhere, those trips felt like home.

But this year, she was starting to worry about how many more trips they would get to take together. As luck would have it, Lila's lease was up right before the Christmas holiday and she had just weeks to decide if she wanted to stay or not. And with her friends also moving on with their lives, it was only a matter of time before they all went their separate ways and her little family, as she liked to think of them, would disappear.

"Okay," Lila said. "Now, Edie, I know you've started dating someone, and Piper, you've got so much going on right now with house hunting in Colorado…and Charlotte, I'm sure your schedule is going to be full with your new network deal—"

"Just show us already!" Piper said, sending her little air kisses.

Lila had been feeling down because it seemed as though an era was coming to an end—no more traveling, no more constant support from her close friends. Everyone else seemed to be progressing in life, but she was treading water, stuck in her current situation with no plans for anything else. Her heart ached with loneliness at the thought. So she'd called them all to the coffee shop today for an emergency meeting. She had an idea—one last celebration.

"We can take a trip in early December instead of right at Christmas like we usually do, since everyone's going to be so busy during the holiday. I say we pack up a tree and our gifts, and get rooms in cabins in the country about a two-hour drive from here. It's a sort of 'staycation.'" She brought her iPad screen to life and turned it around. "Look at this gorgeous retreat tucked away in the Tennessee hills."

She began scrolling through the photos of the main cabin, with double stone chimneys and a wide front porch framed by log railings and rocking chairs. The smaller cabins for rent sat nestled in the snowy hills, and the local market looked like it had been snapped right out of a movie set.

"It's called Fireside Cabins. It's family owned and the whole place is filled with the history of local battles and early settlers. There are hiking trails and farms down the road offering horse rides, loads of shops on Main Street, a Christmas fair . . . and there's even a coffee shop in town," Lila said, biting her lip through an enormous smile while the other ladies looked on in interest.

"I knew you'd find us something!" Charlotte said, bending down to reach into a small shopping bag she'd kept beside her chair. "I was so confident that I made these. I'm in!" She tossed each of them a T-shirt with *Girls' Week* emblazoned on the front in sparkly red-and-green script.

"Count me in." Edie ran her fingers over the lettering of the T-shirt.

"Definitely," Piper said.

"I'm glad you all approve—I knew you'd like it! I already booked it, putting it in all of our names—since the site said we could cancel

at anytime. You should get a text with the confirmation in a few days."
Lila picked up her coffee and took a sip. Then from behind her mug,
she said, "Let's make this the best Christmas vacation ever." And she
knew they would. She could feel the Christmas spirit already.

Chapter One

The purple line of hills on the horizon framed the rolling landscape of fields, an endless expanse of green, dotted with spots of white from the falling snow. As they made their way down the winding road, the only indication that the area was inhabited at all was the narrow strip of gray asphalt zigzagging through the serene countryside, and the occasional red barn, perched on the hillside like a postcard.

"How many more minutes left?" Piper asked as she wriggled in her seat. "I kind of have to go to the bathroom."

Lila made eye contact with her friend in her rearview mirror. "Didn't you go at the last gas station?"

"Yes, but I have to go again."

"And you went at that market down the road—Pinewood Market."

"I know, but I drank my whole thermos of water." She groaned.

"My navigation says the local coffee shop should be just around the corner. We can stop in there if you can't wait until we check in at Fireside Cabins."

"Yes, please," Piper squealed.

Edie pointed to a tiny shack of a structure with an old farmhouse-style sign that said *Coffee* in black letters. "There it is, I think," she told them. "Is that the name of it? Just *Coffee*?"

Lila pulled the car into the narrow gravel lot and cut off the engine. Piper shot out and ran inside, while the others followed.

Putting her hands on her hips, Charlotte fanned out her long winter coat and assessed the place. "Kind of rustic…"

Lila had to admit that the online photos of the town must have been taken at a very good angle, with lots of filters, because Main Street—which had looked like a quaint Christmas escape in the photos—more resembled a tiny spot along the road. The shops were quaint, their picture windows filled with wares, but only a few folks strolled about, the sidewalks mostly empty. Perhaps it was a winter lull. There was a used bookstore, a café, a small market, and a gas station. "Let's go check it out," she said, trying to make the best of it.

She took in the simple, unsophisticated décor of the coffee shop as they stood at the entrance. It was a no-frills kind of place. A log table sat outside with a view of Main Street, but the porch was empty, buried under snow. Lila could imagine the old oak trees in the fall, set against the backdrop of the small town with the hills in the distance, and what looked like a grand farm just beyond. She was willing to bet that it would be stunning when the leaves had all changed color, a little different than the barren empty branches that now reached out toward the heavens, as if grasping for their lives.

They all walked in, and Lila found herself standing in the center of a cramped and dark dining area dotted with only a few odd customers. A stone fireplace flickered, the fire only dancing when the door to the place was open. It had an old, bare wood bar that stretched across the wall in front of them, and there was nothing by the register or on the tables to let anyone know it was Christmas. Encased in thick shellac on top of the bar were old guitar picks and sheet music, clearly paying homage to Music City. A soft bluesy country music track hummed above them. And a sad, forlorn Christmas wreath, which might have been alive last year, hung from the center wall above the bar. The barista standing under it didn't appear to be full of festive spirit either. He was about their age, as rugged as a lumberjack, and staring at them with a frown and piercing blue eyes.

His gaze landed on the sparkly lettering of the T-shirts Charlotte had made, which they had all put on over their long-sleeved shirts. Then his head turned to the side and he leaned over to look past them, the skin between his brooding eyes wrinkling. "Can you shut the door, please?" he asked, as if he was bothered by their mere existence. "It gets cold in here."

"Oh!" Lila jumped to follow his command. "Sorry." She turned around and grabbed the doorknob, shutting out the view of her old Volvo with the giant Christmas tree tied to the top, and wondering what he thought of it. She closed the door just as Piper joined them from the bathroom. "We saw your sign outside. Is that the name of this place?" Lila asked, making light conversation.

"Sure," he answered.

"Sure?" Edie contested his answer, clearly put off by his lack of manners and obvious annoyance that they were even there. "So the coffee shop doesn't have a name?"

"The locals don't need a name. Do you, Johnny?" he called over to a man in bibbed overalls, who was reading the paper with a mug in his hand.

"Nope," he yelled back.

"Charming," Edie said under her breath. "Like Prince, but coffee. Marketing nightmare..."

"We're vacationing here," Charlotte told the man behind the bar, but he didn't seem fazed by it, so she just went ahead and put in her drink order.

The barista huffed condescendingly at Charlotte's selection as he grabbed a cup.

Lila asked for her usual latte and then plopped down into one of the chairs, ready to get their vacation started. The coffee shop wouldn't be the height of their Christmas merriment, certainly, but it was at least warm and the fire was nice.

"I read an article about this place last night when I was researching the area to get ideas about things to do this week, and it suggested that someone mysterious owns it," Piper whispered into the center of their circle once they were all settled, one eye on the barista who still wasn't giving them a minute of his attention. Piper was a walking celebrity aficionado by accident, due to her love of music and reading; she knew anything and everything about music. She could give you endless strings of concert dates, celebrity musician sightings, and song lyrics.

Piper stretched her long arms out onto the table casually, her beaded bracelets tapping together. "No one knows who the owner is for sure. The article I read said all the transactions have been made under the pseudonym Brian Brown, but no one believes he exists. There are no records of anyone in this area with that name. If you ask the barista, they say he won't utter a word about it. Maybe he's undercover or something. Or famous."

Lila tried not to be conspicuous while she stole a look at the guy behind the counter to whom she'd just given her drink order. His face was strikingly attractive, with dark hair to match the shadow of stubble and those bright blue eyes. He had a resigned look on his face while he reluctantly frothed the latte he was making. Then suddenly he made eye contact and her blood ran cold.

"Hey, I don't have any almond milk for your latte," he said to her, in a way that made it seem like he was resentful at having to use his energy to speak. "All I've got is real milk."

Lila got up so they didn't have to yell across the dining area. "You're a coffee shop and you don't have an alternative to dairy? What if I was allergic?"

He frowned. "Are you?"

"No, but still."

With his eyes on her, he picked up the jug of whole milk and tipped it, letting it glug into the frothing cup as if to spite her. When he'd finished topping off the espresso in her cup, he said, "Lids are at the back," and slid it toward her, nodding to a small stack of supplies at the end of the counter.

"Well, if we're going the dairy route, I want whipped cream," she said, sliding it back to him.

"It's extra. Twenty cents."

"No, it's not. Because I ordered an almond milk latte, which you have on your menu." She pointed to the wooden sign with the list of drinks on the wall above the bar. "And if you're out of ingredients," her words came out syrupy sweet, "no matter what I'd ordered, you should give me some whipped cream as a consolation for making me take a drink I wasn't prepared to have." Just before he denied her, she added, "But none of that matters because you charge an extra twenty-five cents for almond milk when I only got dairy milk, so you actually owe me a nickel." She scooted the cup a little further toward him. "But we'll call it even."

Those blue eyes glistened with interest for a moment, and she had to work to keep herself steady, but then it was gone, his face irritated and smug again. He unenthusiastically added whipped cream onto the top of her latte, but the can was empty, causing it to spit out all over her and the cup. Lila jumped back with a squeal, brushing the white globules off her coat as he handed her cup back.

"Anything else?" he asked.

"That's all. Thank you," she said sarcastically, rolling her eyes and returning to her friends. "I don't think he's anyone famous," Lila said quietly, disgust on her face. She glanced back over at him once more.

Charlotte leaned forward. "Even though he is pretty cute."

"Definitely not," Piper said with a chuckle. "Famous, I mean. As for the cuteness factor, he's got that going for him." She tucked her long white-blonde hair behind her ear and reached for her coffee.

"So tell us about your date, Lila," Charlotte piped up, changing the subject. "I'm dying to know what Kyle was like!"

Lila made a face. "I'll never trust your blind date suggestions again," she told her friend.

Charlotte burst into laughter.

"I can hardly match my Tupperware lids to the correct bowls on a regular basis, and that guy had me dangling from the edge of a mountain. I had to put all my faith in staying alive with these little color-coded hooks jutting out from the rock, and the tether that I prayed I'd clipped on to it correctly. Never again."

She should have seen the red flag when he told her to be sure to have cash for the parking.

"You aren't coming to pick me up?" she'd asked, while drawing her lip-gloss across her lower lip in preparation for what she thought would be a romantic evening. She hadn't worn lip-gloss in ages. She'd bought the new shade especially, since this was the first date she'd had since she and Razz had broken up a few years ago.

"I'm playing hockey with some guys after, so we should drive separately," he'd told her.

She'd thought they were going to spend a nice dinner talking and drinking wine, not climbing a mountain where her life flashed before her eyes with every placement of her fingers. She couldn't believe it when he'd said that was what they were doing.

She had almost canceled right then, but she remembered how Charlotte had told her that she had to give people a chance if she ever wanted to find Mr. Right. Charlotte had also said that every new relationship began with a first step (even a step onto a mountain, apparently). Lila knew she should try, but it wasn't easy. Ever since her breakup with Razz, she'd found it hard to get close to men. She just never felt herself with them. She knew it wasn't healthy to close herself off, but she couldn't help it.

"I nearly plummeted down the mountain," she continued as the barista brought her the drink she'd ordered. His eyes narrowed at her statement, but he didn't interject.

"He took you mountain climbing?" Charlotte asked, horrified. Her idea of danger was realizing she'd lost her Bloomingdale's coupon while holding the last pashmina on the clearance rack. "I'm so sorry."

"Thank you," Lila said to the barista.

He eyed Charlotte and then looked back at Lila curiously before he retreated to the bar. Lila ignored him and settled in, telling the girls everything about the date and sparing no details. It was what they did. They shared all kinds of stories with each other, especially the ones about their once-nonexistent love lives. That was how their little group was born.

"I can't believe it," Piper said. "You don't take a girl on a mountain climb for a first date. That's ridiculous. This guy Kyle is clearly inexperienced."

Edie, who'd been quiet the whole time, cut in. "I agree with Piper," she said. "It's a ludicrous first date."

"I think you should give him another chance," Charlotte said, sticking up for him. "His date option wasn't great, and he's not good at romance, obviously, but he's really nice. Once you dig down to his underbelly…"

Lila shook her head emphatically. "No way."

"Let's ask the guy behind the bar what he thinks," Piper said, playfully putting them all in cringe-mode.

"That guy?" Edie whispered. "He definitely looks like the mountain-climbing type. That's not a neutral party."

"If we're giving out second chances, let's see if he'll warm up to us. Maybe we'll just give him a nudge. Excuse me," Piper said, getting his attention. She waggled her finger for him to come over. "Would you settle something for us?" When he was standing by them, eyebrows raised skeptically, she asked, "Do you think it's okay to take a woman mountain climbing on a first date?"

His gaze swept across the table. "It depends on the woman," he said bluntly, before giving them a condescending look. He headed straight back behind the bar and began wiping down glasses.

"What did he mean by that?" Lila asked.

Charlotte leaned over to her. "Maybe he meant that it's okay if the woman is the outdoorsy type."

"I think I should ask him," Lila said, feeling a little annoyed that he'd suggest she wasn't the "right" kind of girl when they were his customers, buying coffees, and trying to enjoy themselves on vacation. "I hope he wasn't being a jerk. If he was, we need to spread a little Christmas cheer to this guy." She got up and headed over to the bar once more.

"Hello again," Lila said, forcing a smile.

The man's hands stilled, the glass and towel in his fingers unmoving as he looked at her expressionless, clearly waiting for whatever it was she had to say.

"I'm Lila Evans," she said, as he continued to stare at her. "What's your name?"

He gazed at her a tick before answering, "Theo." He resumed wiping the glass, set it upside down onto the shelf behind him, and grabbed another from the line of dripping glassware.

This guy's attitude had to be bad for business. No wonder the coffee shop had barely a soul in it. Perhaps she should give him a wake-up call and suggest she was going to complain about the service.

"Well, Theo, I'd like to speak to the owner."

He put his items down and leaned on the bar with both of his strong, masculine hands, his face overly close to Lila's, his unique scent of soap and spice making her heart patter with nervousness despite herself. "I *am* the owner."

She heard Piper gasp over her shoulder.

Still nearly nose-to-nose, she replied, "You haven't exactly given us a warm welcome. And where's the holiday cheer? You don't have a Christmas tree. Or candles, or a garland, or Christmas music…"

"No," he stated, righting himself.

"I think you need some festive sparkle in here. Candy canes. A few red bows," she offered, knowing she was winding him up. "I'm aware that you're a guy, so you could make it…more casual if you didn't want bows."

"You think guys like any of that stuff?"

She squared her shoulders and looked him directly in the eye. "Depends on the guy."

Charlotte stifled a snort of laughter and Edie quietly shushed her.

Lila expected Theo to be ready to throw them out, but instead, his sapphire eyes remained locked with hers in challenge and the corners of his lips rose ever so slightly, offering the hint of a grin. She'd gotten him, and he seemed to like it, giving her an unexpected flutter. But just as soon as the look came over him, it left. He cleared his throat and turned his back to her, moving to rearrange the mugs on the shelf behind him. And when he did, she realized that she hadn't been breathing until then.

Chapter Two

"Well, that was weird, wasn't it?" Edie said from the backseat, as Lila drove them further into the Tennessee hills to their vacation home for the next week. A flurry of snowflakes escaped from the blanket of clouds in the sky, the car tires shushing through the wet roads that would most certainly be a sheet of ice come sundown.

"Definitely," Lila replied, the memory of Theo's sort-of-smile lingering. "But we've got our own coffee machine at the cabin, I'm sure, so it'll be nothing but Christmas vibes all around from here on out."

They were moments away from Fireside Cabins now, described online as *a home away from home, a place of serenity that will have you wishing you could stay forever.* Lila couldn't wait until they were all nestled inside their own little hideaway, making mugs of hot peppermint cocoa in their red-and-white striped socks, hanging ornaments on the Christmas tree to the tune of festive classics. As was tradition, she'd packed the wrapping paper, bows, and all her favorite decorations. Charlotte had been in charge of the wine and snacks, Edie was bringing cookies and chocolates, and Piper, of course, had stockings chock-full of bath bombs, bubble bath, soaps, and lotions, and the most delicious-smelling Christmas mulberry candles.

"I'm so excited," Charlotte said, clapping her hands.

"We're almost there." Lila rounded the last turn.

This week was Lila's favorite of the year, and she was determined to make it the best trip yet. Christmas had been especially difficult for Lila—and every December the holiday reminded her of just how alone she was. This vacation had been Lila's saving grace through her breakup with her boyfriend, Razz Malone. Razz was the nickname he'd gotten when he was a boy because of the loud dirt bikes he used to ride. He'd razz the engine just to hear it growl. She'd known him since they were kids, and his entire life he'd had his heart set on becoming the next country music superstar.

She and Razz had taken all the savings they had, which was about nine hundred bucks in total, and headed to Music City to follow his dreams. What she hadn't anticipated was that the strain of living in his van during all the gigs he played, trying to make enough money for them to live on and surviving on pennies, would begin to tear them apart when she'd thought it would make them stronger. And then he'd hurt her in the worst way, leaving her for someone he barely knew.

As she matured, she realized that they'd become two totally different people. While she used to love his playful nature, she began to resent it when she was pulling double shifts and he wouldn't help her pay the bills, taking the money he'd earned from gigs and staying out with his new friends in the bars downtown, forgetting all about her. He didn't help her establish friendships as a couple, or work with her to find them a modest place to live where she could relax after a long day's work. And after a while, she started to wonder if he had ever really been in love with her at all. He never asked how her day was or what she'd been doing, and as he spent long nights out with his friends, it occurred to her that she was alone.

After only a few weeks together in Nashville, she'd found him in the van they shared cuddling up with the stylist he'd hired for his first video shoot, and it was then that he'd admitted he was moving on. In that instant, he'd broken her heart and cheapened all the years they'd been together, making Lila feel like she'd tagged along on the move to Nashville rather than making the journey by his side. Ever since, she kept waiting to hear his name on the radio, but to this day, she hadn't. If she were a betting woman, she'd guess that if she looked hard enough for him, she'd find him in some old honky tonk, still playing every night and never once thinking about her.

In the aftermath of the breakup, she vowed to never put herself in that kind of position again, and instead she put all her energy into her friendships. This wonderful group of women was something she didn't know how she'd live without. But she might have to learn how. Charlotte's new job with the TV network was going to require a considerable amount of travel—so much that she'd already mentioned the possibility of moving to California, where the network was located. Piper would soon be too busy with work and house hunting in Colorado. She was considering going back to school there so she could take a few business classes, since her career was building so quickly, and expanding her soap company. And Edie had met someone special—a man named Jarod. That was why Lila wanted to make this year even more special and have one final Christmas blowout together with her best friends.

Her navigation announced they'd arrived, and Lila pulled her Volvo to a stop outside the main house, all of them taking a moment to take in what was in front of them.

"Did we make a wrong turn?" Charlotte asked, as they all stared at the eyesore of a cabin.

Lila cut the engine and they got out of the car, the four of them speechless for a second as they tried to make sense of the fact that the main cabin and the grounds surrounding it looked absolutely nothing like the online photos.

"Where are... the front steps?" Piper asked, pointing to two cinderblocks covered by weeds and stacked in front of a sloping front porch, the boards rotted in places and gone altogether in others. One of the windows next to the front door was cracked, duct tape covering it to keep the elements from seeping into the house. All the brown-painted trim was peeling and in need of a good sand and stain.

"The owner told me in an email that the website was a little dated, and she needed to get some new pictures taken but I had no idea that the photos misrepresented the property entirely... I'm so sorry," Lila said, feeling terrible. It had been her who had found this place and booked it. They'd just had a bizarre experience at the coffee shop to say the least, the town was cute but definitely not enough to keep them entertained for an entire week, and now this place was falling apart.

"There was no way for you to know," Piper replied, consoling her.

"We paid our hard-earned money for this." Edie's expression was serious as she waved her hand, as if to showcase the sad line of frost-coated shrubbery, barely surviving in a bed of wet mud. "I'm going in and demanding that we get a refund. I'd rather go back to Nashville and stay at a hotel where we can drink twenty-dollar-a-glass champagne at a rooftop bar. There's no way we're having our vacation in these conditions."

Edie marched up the cinderblocks, wobbling on an unsteady step, the other women filing in behind her. They gathered around the door and Edie knocked. When no one answered, she knocked harder, exhaling in frustration.

The door finally opened, and just as Edie opened her mouth to say something, she stopped.

An old woman with a kind smile and bright green eyes was standing on the other side, and from the look on her face, she was positively delighted to see them. She clasped her hands against her large bosom and peered out at them tentatively, as if the mere sight of them would bring her to tears.

"Hello," she said warmly as a tabby cat snaked through her legs, purring before it jumped down from the porch and scurried across the yard. "I'm Eleanor Finely. I'm so happy y'all came to Fireside Cabins today. I've been working hard to get things ready for you. Let me just grab my coat and I'll show you to your cabin." She waved them in. "Come inside and get yourselves out of that dreadful cold."

Lila led them in. The house didn't feel much warmer than outside, despite the fire in the old stone fireplace. Next to it was an upholstered chair, an open book with a pair of reading glasses on its arm, and a wadded afghan in the seat. The interior was traditional cabin décor—all wood with beautiful, bucolic charm—but the cushions and throw pillows were dated, and there wasn't a shred of Christmas to be seen. What was with this town? Did nobody celebrate Christmas?

"What should we do?" Piper whispered to Lila. "That woman seems so happy we're here." Her expression reminded Lila of the way a child looked up to a parent, except she wasn't exactly sure what to do herself. "Maybe we can hike the trails and hear about all the history in the area?"

Lila shrugged in response and eyed Edie.

Edie laughed quietly at the ridiculousness of the situation, putting her hands up as if to say, "I have no idea."

"Let's just take a look at our cabin," Charlotte whispered. "Once we're on our own, we can decide our next move." She quietly shushed them as Eleanor came swishing down the hallway in her coat and hat, carrying a set of keys.

The elderly woman slipped on a pair of boots lined up next to the door. "Follow me," she said, heading out to the front porch. "Watch your step," she warned as she stepped over a broken board. "I'm planning to get someone to fix that once the weather clears up."

There was a lot more to fix at this cabin than that one loose board, but Lila smiled politely at her. "We're excited about the nature trails," she said, trying to stay upbeat.

"Oh, I'm so sorry, dear," Eleanor said. "They're closed due to so many downed branches."

"*All* of the trails?" Edie asked.

"We had a storm about a year ago…" Eleanor added.

"A *year* ago?" Edie glared at the others.

Charlotte elbowed her lightly, clearly feeling sorry for the old woman.

"Yep," Eleanor said. "My cat Presley is the only one who walks them now."

"Is he named after Elvis?" Piper asked.

"Actually, yes. My late husband found the cat as a kitten when it was curled up inside his dress boots, which he'd left outside the front door by accident. They were blue and suede," she said with a grin.

They crossed the yard through the icy cold to another cabin, taking a steep path up the hill. When they got to the top, Lila couldn't take her eyes off the sweeping view in front of her. She could see the town down below, and the endless expanse of hills that surrounded it. With the newly fallen snow, they glistened under the rays of the sun that had only briefly made its appearance. The porch on this cabin was at least intact, and two rockers made of woven branches flanked the modest doorway. So far so good.

Eleanor unlocked the door, opened it, and handed Lila the keys.

Minimally decorated, it was at least clean and orderly, unlike the main house. The women wandered through the rooms to find beds with matching quilts in blues and yellows, the edges pulled back to reveal crisp linens.

"I saw that you brought a Christmas tree on your car," Eleanor said, raising her eyebrows in happiness. "How festive." Folding her hands as if in prayer, she said, "Once you get it decorated, I'd love to see it." She took in a deep breath, as if her kids had just come home from college and her house was full—the way she liked it. "Well, I won't keep you," she said in her southern drawl as she opened the door. "I'll let myself out. Just come on over if you need anything."

Once Eleanor had gone, they began bringing in their luggage and all the Christmas decorations they'd brought.

"Hey, Lila," Piper said, as she set a box down in the living room. "I've got the topping already made for my apple pie cinnamon pita chips."

"I can't wait." Lila stood in the kitchen, warming her hands. "Let's make them tonight." Lila loved Piper's recipe. Her friend rolled pita bread in butter, cinnamon, and sugar and then topped it with her own homemade apple pie filling before toasting it to a warm crisp.

"The topping is in the cooler bag next to you and the pita bread's in the grocery sack beside it. Want to stay in for a second and warm up? All you have to do is top the bread with the mix and slide them into that toaster oven over there." She waggled a gloved finger toward the counter behind Lila.

"Of course," Lila said, excited to get the vacation started. They'd nibble on sweet treats, have a little coffee and cocoa, and decorate like crazy. She adored this time with her favorite people. Christmas was hard for her once she'd lost her dad, but these moments eased the sadness.

"Awesome. We'll grab the last few things from the car."

Lila washed her icy hands, grabbed the container of topping, and opened the lid. Piper had minced apple and coated it in a delicious sauce. The cinnamon and nutmeg smelled absolutely incredible. She perused the kitchen, looking for utensils and baking sheets. When she found what she needed, she got out the bread, spooned on the apple pie mixture, and slid it into the small toaster oven on the counter, pressing on the button. But when she tried to adjust the heat, it wouldn't work.

"I'll have to stay with it," she said over the bar, as they all came back in and Edie closed the door. "It only has one working setting, and I don't want it to burn. "Anyone need a cup of coffee to warm you up, since I'll be in here?"

Piper, Edie, and Charlotte all stopped what they were doing and raised their hands, making Lila laugh. "Okay, then. Four coffees coming right up!"

"I brought caramel to squirt in them," Charlotte said with excitement in her voice. "And whipped cream."

"Perfect." Lila clicked on the coffee maker. When the light didn't turn on, she checked the plug, wriggling the cord. "I think the coffee pot is broken," she said. "But I'll figure something out."

She'd have to get crafty. She grabbed a pot and filled it with water, heating it on the stove, planning to do a makeshift French press with the coffee filter basket and the pot of water. While the pita bread toasted and the water for coffee boiled on the stove, she checked the rest of the appliances. She opened the fridge and, to her relief, found it clean and in working order; the main oven and stovetop were all working too. "The smaller appliances aren't great, but I think we can make it work for the week with what we've got," she said, feeling hopeful. "We just need to add a little of our Christmas cheer in here. Everyone okay with a little extra effort?"

They all agreed.

"It definitely isn't the lap of luxury," Lila continued, "but we don't have many alternatives way out here. And I couldn't in good conscience let down Eleanor—did you see how happy she was that we were here?"

"We can make the best of it," Edie conceded.

Charlotte walked over to the corner of the living area, pausing next to a stone fireplace that stretched all the way up to the beamed, vaulted ceiling. "I think we just need to bring a little sparkle to Fireside Cabins. Let's get the tree. And then we can make our famous peppermint bark!"

"Yes!" Piper said. "Maybe we can make a gift basket for Eleanor with baked goods and a few of my soaps. By the way she greeted us, she looks like she might need some cheering up."

Lila couldn't help but think the whole town needed a little sparkle and cheering up. Her mind went back to Theo, that hint of a smile haunting her, despite how hostile his welcome had been.

"Maybe tomorrow I'll bring Theo a plate of goodies and we can go for coffee, since we don't have a working coffee maker," she suggested.

Piper raised an eyebrow. "He doesn't look like the cookie type," she said.

"He might throw them at us." Edie laughed.

That was a real possibility, but there was something in his sapphire eyes when he looked at her that made her want to learn more about him. "We'll never know until we try, right?" she said. "Now, let's get this Christmas party started."

Chapter Three

In an hour, the four women had completely moved into the place and started decorating. Every Christmas, they all brought their own decorations, having an unspoken contest to see who could bring the most. They'd gotten the tree into its stand and watered it, found a stack of firewood on the porch out back and started a fire, covered the sofa in cream-colored oversized-weave throws for all four of them, turned on both the lamps, and had the Christmas music playing. Piper lit the mulberry candle while Charlotte organized all the ornaments for the tree.

Lila, who was in charge of the mantel, stepped back to view her progress while nibbling on an apple pie cinnamon chip. She'd covered the stone surface in greenery that Piper had picked up at the farmer's market and nestled bunches of red berries into the foliage. She'd set four weighted brass stocking hangers at equal distance from each other and hung each of their stockings. Piper had brought one that could've been in a Dr. Seuss book: long and narrow, striped with red and green. Lila's was a creamy knit with wooden buttons securing the fold at the top. Edie's was a Christmas patchwork stocking, and Charlotte's was the color of champagne and made entirely of faux fur. Lila assessed the layout then switched the position of Piper's and her own, so the longer stockings were on the outside and the shorter ones were above the fire.

The oven beeped to signal it had preheated, and Edie slid in the sugar cookies she'd prepared before the trip, then dug through the last of what was in the cooler, putting the rest of the items in the refrigerator and freezer. "Wonder if there's a cooling rack..." she said as she rooted around in the cabinets.

"I've totally stocked the bathroom with products," Piper said, spritzing the air with her all-natural gingerbread room spray. "I made us all butter rum bath bombs that fizzle." She smiled and danced around as if they'd all just won the Christmas lottery, and then misted the scent over near the tree.

Everything was looking, smelling, and feeling very festive—just how they liked it. In this sparse little cabin in the middle of nowhere, they'd managed to create a Christmas wonderland that felt so warm and cozy that Lila already knew she'd have a difficult time leaving it. They'd worked hard and, despite their rocky beginning, it looked like things were going to be okay here at Fireside Cabins.

When the cookies had finished baking, their vanilla scent mixing with the other mouth-watering flavors in the air, Edie brought them over along with an enormous charcuterie board, full to the brim with various aged, buttery, spicy cheeses, an impressive assortment of salamis, Turkish apricots, roasted almonds, in-shell pistachios, and an array of flatbreads, some with a splash of brandy, sweet onions, or dill. She put them on the low chest that doubled as a coffee table. They'd all settled in now, having washed up and changed into their Christmas pajamas, with big warm sweaters, and woolly socks.

Charlotte and Piper carried glasses of red wine into the living room and Lila switched on the white lights of the Christmas tree, sending a romantic glow through the room that shimmered off the glass of the window. When she stopped to admire it, she noticed the lone lamplight coming through that one broken window across the yard over at Eleanor's cabin.

"I wonder why Eleanor's out here all alone," Lila said, sinking down into the sofa, Edie handing her a glass of wine.

"I don't know. It's awfully spooky over there," Charlotte said with a shudder, before she pinched a sugar cookie and took a bite.

"Should we invite her to the cabin tonight?" Lila asked. In all the years they'd been doing this, they'd never invited anyone else into their little circle, and she could see the mix of emotions on their faces. But Lila knew all too well the feelings that being alone on the holiday could bring, and she couldn't relax with Eleanor on her mind. "It's Christmas, we've brought so much life to the cabin, and she's all alone in that drafty old house."

"It wouldn't be the Christmas spirit if we didn't at least extend the offer," Edie said, siding with Lila. Charlotte and Piper agreed.

"I'll go ask her," Lila said, popping up and setting her wine on the old trunk. "I'll be right back." She grabbed her coat and scarf from the rack beside the front door, and slid on her boots.

"Be careful," Piper told her as she plunged herself into darkness.

The snow had started to fall, little flakes drifting down from a jet-black sky. The only sound was her boots crunching against the weedy grass underneath her feet as she paced across the yard as quickly as she could. She jammed her hands into her pockets, pushing herself against the wind with every step, the breeze blowing through her thin candy cane–covered pajama bottoms.

She was in a full shiver by the time she got to the door and knocked. But luckily, Eleanor's voice came from the other side more quickly than she'd expected.

"Hello? Who's there?" she asked from behind the closed door.

"It's Lila."

The locks clicked as she unbolted them and then the door opened. "Is everything all right?" she asked, worry deepening the lines around her eyes. "Do you need me?" She opened the door wider to reveal her long flannel nightgown and oversized slippers. She had her reading glasses on her nose and her hair pinned back at the sides.

"Everything's fine," Lila reassured her. "We decorated for Christmas and made some snacks and cookies. And we wanted to invite you over."

The old woman's hand flew to her chest in surprise. "Oh my goodness. Thank you so much for offering." She seemed genuinely touched by the gesture. "But I wouldn't want to impose..."

"You won't impose. I wouldn't be on your porch right now if we didn't want you to be there. We'd like to have you." Lila moved her long coat to reveal her pajama bottoms. "You don't even have to get dressed. Pajamas are just fine."

"That's so very kind of you..." Her gaze darted around the room. "I should have something Christmassy for y'all. Let me bring over a box of chocolates my friend sent me, and I'll grab my coat too."

"Okay, sounds good."

"Come into the house, out of the cold while you wait," Eleanor said, ushering Lila inside in a rush. Presley shot up the stairs.

She seemed eager to get herself together, and Lila was glad she'd asked her. It didn't seem right for an elderly lady like Eleanor to be all by herself way out in the hills on an icy winter's night. Especially as she and her friends were there to celebrate the holiday. Since this was most likely the last time they'd all get together, they should mix things up a little bit, do things they hadn't done in holidays past. Their *last* holiday... As Lila stood alone, waiting for Eleanor, with a pang she looked around the entryway of the old cabin, and it occurred to her that this could easily be her own fate one day. She hadn't met that one person in life she wanted to share her world with, nor had she found a place to put down roots.

Eleanor bustled into the entryway with her coat, and when Lila met her gaze, again she saw herself in the old woman's eyes, and the back of her neck prickled in fear. She pushed aside the uncomfortable thought as they headed out and crossed the yard back to the cabin, opening the door to a waft of buttery smells from the cookies filling the air around them.

Eleanor stood in the center of the main room in her nightgown, coat, and boots, gripping her little tin of chocolate. "Oh my goodness, ladies," she said, blinking rapidly as she seemed to fight back emotion. "Y'all have outdone yourselves! This is the most beautiful sight I've ever seen." As she said it, her words broke, and she seemed completely overwhelmed. Tears welled up in her eyes.

Lila and her friends had become quite skilled and efficient at their little ritual of organizing their festive vacation spaces, and after three years of practice they could throw a place together in about two hours. Lila had always marveled at the beauty of their decorating, but this was the first time she'd really *seen* it for what it was. It had to be a magnificent sight, coming from the main cabin in the shape it was in.

"Come on inside and settle in by the fire," Lila told her gently.

Taking a jagged breath, Eleanor slipped off her boots and coat, placing them by the door. She padded over to the sofa and took a seat, still looking around in wonderment. "This feels like a dream," she said, her eyes wide. "I wish I could still decorate for Christmas, but my back is bad, and being by myself, it's just too risky to climb up on things..." A cloud drifted over her face for a second, just long enough for Lila to notice before she cleared it.

Charlotte picked up the plate of cookies, offering her one. "Have you lived in this area all your life?" she asked, clearly trying to ease Eleanor's emotions.

Eleanor took a cookie, the answer spreading across her face in the form of a smile. "I moved here in my twenties. Chased a boy all the way to Tennessee from my little hometown in Macon, Georgia. And when we weren't together anymore, I liked it so much here that I never left."

Lila perked up. She knew all too well what it was like to follow a guy to another state. She'd moved from her hometown in Richmond, Virginia to Nashville doing that exact same thing. But she hoped Eleanor had experienced the happy-ever-after she never got.

"Did you leave him?" Lila asked, wondering how close their similarities were.

She gave a sad chuckle. "He left me."

"How long ago?" Piper asked, before sipping her glass of wine.

"Two years ago," Eleanor said, her face somber. "His name was Chester. We were together for sixty years before he passed. Heart attack."

Edie threw her hand to her chest. "Oh, I'm so sorry."

"It's okay," she said, looking around. "You know, I've been thinking of selling this place, but I just can't do it. This was ours—mine and Chester's. We never had children of our own and this place was like our baby. We nurtured it, raised it from a little possibility to what it is now. What it *was*, actually... It hasn't been the same since Chester left."

Lila's own wounds of loss and loneliness surfaced easily whenever she encountered another person who shared a similar experience. She longed for the chance to talk to her father—her rock—just one more time. She missed him terribly. For so long, it had just been the two of them, and once he was gone, the emptiness ate at her every single day. Not just the void she felt from his absence, but the emptiness her innocence had left behind once it had withered away. The innocence of those moments when she'd skipped down the steps toward her car, leaving her father waving in the doorway, and said, "See ya!" as if they had forever—those were the moments she'd never get back. If she'd only known, she'd have run back in and thrown her arms around him one last time. With no sisters or brothers, her friends were the saving grace she'd always needed.

Eleanor could definitely use a few friends, and suddenly, Lila felt purpose in their trip. There was a reason they'd stayed.

Charlotte, who'd gotten up to get another glass, returned and filled it from the bottle of wine they had on the table. "Did you ever want kids?" she asked, handing the glass to Eleanor.

"We'd talked about having kids, but we just weren't ever blessed with any." Eleanor's eyes misted over. She hid it with a big gulp of wine. Setting her glass down, she shook her head as if shaking the thought free. "I had dreams for this place when Chester and I bought it." She brightened. "If I close my eyes, I can still see children running through the hills from cabin to cabin, collecting arrowheads and other mementos." She smiled. "But God had a different plan for us."

Lila could understand perfectly. She adored children, and as she grew older and hadn't found someone to settle down with, the thought of adopting a child would flutter through her mind. But she wanted to be sure to have a job that would allow her a ton of time with a little one—she didn't feel like she was in the right place in her life. She'd done a few humanitarian trips, helping underprivileged youth, and she'd tutored kids who were struggling in school, but it hadn't been enough to fill the void for her.

"But Chester and I made enough memories of our own with just the two of us," Eleanor continued. "Did you know that one time I was helping a man reserve a room and we found out it was for Meryl Streep? She stayed in this very cabin while she shot a movie. She was here for an entire week."

"That's amazing," Piper said, her eyes wide.

"We've had all kinds of interesting people stay. Authors on retreats, historians researching the battles of the area, a couple of musicians... But enough about me. I don't want to take up your whole night. You need to enjoy this gorgeous Christmas spirit y'all have created. Y'all should be celebrating." She opened up the tin of chocolates she'd brought. "These are from France," she said proudly. "A friend of mine sent them from her travels abroad. I've always wanted to go to France—over the years I'd saved the information about hotels and flights and everything—but never have."

Lila selected a ganache-filled cluster. "Why not?" she asked before popping it into her mouth, the creamy raspberry center and crunchy dark chocolate exploding with flavor.

Eleanor looked down at the assortment of chocolates, as if she were considering whether or not to tell them her answer. She shook her head, clearing her throat, evidently uncomfortable. "Chester and I had the money at one time to travel like that, but we always said, 'one day' for those kinds of things. We never realized that the day we were waiting for would never come. Never wait to do the good stuff," she said, her chest filling with air as she pushed a smile across her face in an obvious attempt to lighten the mood. Then she changed course. "What have we got on the agenda tonight, ladies?"

"We usually put on a Christmas movie the first night," Charlotte replied. "Want to join us?"

Eleanor finished her wine and stood up. "Thank you, but I should be heading back. It's nearly my bedtime, and you girls have more fun things to do than babysit an old woman like me."

"It's really fine," Piper said. "We'd love you to join us."

Eleanor yawned. "It's all right. Y'all enjoy yourselves. I'm going to head back and get some beauty rest."

"Would you like me to walk with you?" Lila offered.

"I'll be just fine," she said. Eleanor scooted the tin of chocolates to the center of the table. "Y'all can keep these. I'll never eat them all." She went over to the door and put on her coat and boots, the four women following her to say goodbye.

"We were going to grab a coffee tomorrow and plan what we want to do this week," Lila said. "Is that café at the edge of town the only place to get a coffee out here?"

"I'm afraid so," Eleanor said.

"Okay, I guess we'll go there then. Will you come with us?" Lila asked.

Eleanor's eyes grew round. "Oh, no. Thank you, but I'll pass." Then she leaned in as if she were telling them insider information. "The new owner's a nightmare."

Edie laughed. "Yeah, we've met him."

"Good luck," Eleanor said as she opened the door. "And thank you for tonight." She headed out into the snowy darkness, the door swinging shut behind her.

"I feel terrible for her," Charlotte said, twisting a gold curl, frowning with worry.

"I know," Edie replied. "How long has she lived in that condition all by herself? I feel like we should spend more time with her, but she wouldn't stay tonight or get coffee tomorrow, and I really doubt she'd be able to keep up on our adventures this week. What should we do?"

Lila went over to the window just in time to see Eleanor making her way to the main house. She stayed there until the elderly woman had gotten inside. "We'll come up with something. Let's think on it and talk about it tomorrow." She closed the blinds. "There's nothing else we can do tonight, so why don't we just try to enjoy ourselves? We have a Christmas movie to watch."

"Yes!" Piper said, clapping her hands. "We need popcorn."

"We absolutely need popcorn," Edie agreed. "Even if we're not hungry, it's a tradition."

"She's right," Piper said, nodding emphatically. "Traditions are important. This trip is all about creating memories, right? Let's do everything all the way—no skimping! Did anyone bring some?"

All of them looked around at each other, shaking their heads.

"I'll run out to the market and grab us some," Lila offered. "It's just down the road." She grabbed her coat and purse. "Y'all decide on the movie."

Lila stood in Pinewood Market, the shop that sat a few minutes from the cabin. She walked down the chip aisle, looking for a box of popcorn, her eyes on the selections when she hit something.

"Oh!" she squealed with a jump. Only when she looked up did she realize the thing she'd hit was Theo's chest. He shook his head, irritated. "I'm sorry," she said. "I wasn't paying attention. I was looking for popcorn."

He reached around her and grabbed a box, handing it to her.

"Thank you," she said, their solitude making her nervous for some reason. He didn't respond, turning his gaze away from her to view something on the shelf beside him.

But when she started to take a step toward the checkout, he took one too, the two of them moving together awkwardly, which only seemed to bother him more. As they both walked toward the counter, they passed the refrigerator section and he stopped, pulling out a gallon of milk.

Trying to make light of the situation, she pointed to the glass. "Hey, don't you need to grab an almond milk?" She offered an uneasy grin.

His eyes were like daggers. "Nope. I'm good," he snapped, storming off toward the register.

Lila hung back until he'd bolted out of the shop, the door slamming shut with a thud behind him, leaving her stunned, standing in the middle of the dairy aisle.

Chapter Four

When they all entered the coffee shop the next morning, Theo was sitting behind the counter, reading a book. He wore an open flannel shirt that revealed the shape of his chest through the tattered T-shirt he had on under it. As they walked across to him, he turned the book over on the bar, the pages spread to mark his spot. Trying not to be discouraged by last night's odd encounter, Lila leaned in to see what it was he was reading. But he tossed a towel over it. Had he done that just to annoy her?

"Hello again," he said, his face already set in an irritated scowl.

"Hi there," she said, her tone overly friendly to spite him.

He didn't move from his chair behind the bar. "How may I help you?"

"Well, this is a coffee shop. So we'd like to all get coffees and then sit and enjoy them in a pleasant atmosphere. Is that possible?"

He shrugged. "I'd say it's possible, but it boils down to your expectations."

"What do you mean by that?"

Piper and the others went to find a table, evidently wanting to avoid confrontation.

"I didn't waltz in to someone else's establishment requesting mistletoe and Christmas bows. So maybe, if you don't find yourselves in a 'pleasant atmosphere,' it's because your expectations are out of whack."

Lila narrowed her eyes at him.

"What's your order?" he asked, not meeting her gaze.

"You know, she's really easy to talk to," Edie called over to Theo from the table. "Lila doesn't have a mean bone in her body."

"I'm not much for talking," he clipped over his shoulder, barely even attempting to look her way. He cleaned the espresso machine, the spout hissing as he wiped it down. "Just give me your order."

"Four peppermint lattes. For *Christmas*."

"What?" he asked over an exhale. "That's not on the menu. We don't even have peppermint syrup."

"No almond milk and now no peppermint syrup?"

"Like I said, your expectations might be out of whack."

"My expectation that this is a full-service coffee shop?"

"You ask for something up there," he said, pointing to the limited menu, "I make it. Full service."

She noticed that there was now a piece of tape over the almond milk option—was that to keep them from coming in? "We'll take vanilla," she said, rolling her eyes.

She gritted her teeth, debating what to do next. They needed some local tips, but this wasn't exactly the local she wanted to talk to. Yet looking around the shop, he was her only option, and they didn't want to arrive somewhere only to find out that it was closed or not worth visiting. While he prepared their drinks, Lila ran over to the table and swiped the handful of pamphlets and maps they'd gotten at the gas station on the way there. Edie's head swiveled, undoubtedly to see what Lila was up to.

"Which of these do you recommend?" Lila asked, spreading them out in front of Theo.

"Why are you asking *me*?" He snapped the plastic lid on top of a coffee and set a second latte on the bar, grabbing another cup.

"Because you live around here. You know what's good and what isn't."

"And you trust my opinion?" His voice was sarcastic and deadpan, but she didn't let it outwardly affect her.

One of the traits that made her great at her job was being able to read people's responses—it was what had made her stick with it for so long. She had a unique ability to determine whether they were up for a chat or not, if they'd become impatient waiting for their food, or wanted to talk for hours. She was almost always right, and while she was rolling the dice to think this guy was anything other than a total jerk, she wanted to try to dig down under that hardened exterior. This time though, she just couldn't quite get a read on anything.

"Yep, I trust you," she challenged. Maybe he'd surprise her.

He smirked. "Do the ropes course." He pushed toward her the pamphlet with the photo of a rope bridge that extended above a tree-lined valley. "You should have everything you need after your rock-climbing date."

She held up the pamphlet and read the title: *Your next extreme adventure awaits*. So much for thinking he might have a little kindness in his heart. "Is this where *you'd* take a girl on a date?"

"Depends on the girl."

"Oh, enough of this," she snapped. "What would you really suggest?"

"For your day out or for a date?"

"Both," she replied.

"Neither answer would impact your little group there." He slid the fourth latte toward her. "Your coffees."

"You seem to have some preconceived notions of who we are," she noted. "But you don't know us at all."

He locked eyes with her. "Likewise."

She bristled, her talent for reading people hitting a wall with this guy. "I'm gonna sneak a Christmas wreath on your front door when you're not looking," she teased, allowing herself one last lighthearted little jab at him.

He completely ignored her.

He wasn't going to ruin her vacation. So she gathered up the pamphlets and maps, pinning them under her arm as she grabbed two of the lattes. Charlotte got up and took the other two to the table.

When Lila sat down at the table, she looked over at Theo but his back was turned to them.

"I worry you might be giving him too much credit, trying to have any conversation with that guy at all," Edie said, her voice quiet.

"I don't know," Piper replied over her paper cup as she held it in both hands. "He's kind of dreamy in a rugged sort of way..."

Charlotte laughed, rolling her eyes. "You think everyone's dreamy. We need to focus. What are we going to do today?"

Piper held up one of the pamphlets. "We could tour the Pinewood Christmas tree farm. You can ride horses, roast marshmallows, and drink fresh mulled cider by the outdoor fire pits."

"Oooh," Edie said, looking on. "That sounds amazing. And it's better than the barista's rope suggestion," she said, a little more loudly than she should.

"I'm up for it," Charlotte said, holding up her latte and then taking a sip. "Let's do it."

Once the plan was made and they'd finished their coffees, the four women stood up, gathering their coats and winding their scarves around their necks. Lila turned around and called, "Wanna go horseback riding with us?" to Theo, just to bother him. The last thing she actually wanted to do was spend any more time with this guy, but she was enjoying dishing out comments to make him squirm. Charlotte gave her a playful punch on the upper arm.

He stared at her from behind his book.

"What?" she questioned him. "Are you scared to ride a horse?"

"I'm working," he said, his chest filling with a frustrated inhalation.

"So if you weren't working, you'd go?" she asked, putting him on the spot as she backed herself toward the door with her friends.

"Why do you need to go to the Christmas tree farm anyway?" he asked across the room, changing the subject. "You already have a tree. I saw it tied to the top of your car."

"Maybe I'm considering buying some charitable donations," she said, looking around the space pointedly before her eyes landed on him.

Theo shook his head and turned his attention back to his book, dismissing her suggestion. The girls erupted into giggles as they burst through the door and into the winter cold. Flakes of snow fluttered down around them, settling on Lila's shoulders and in her hair.

"You're so funny," Piper said, squeezing her eyes shut with her laughter. "You're gonna drive that man crazy. You'd better be nice to him. We've got a whole week here and I'd like to be able to get coffee," she teased.

Lila laughed and got into the car. But as she pulled away, she looked through the glass door at Theo and found he was looking right back at her.

Chapter Five

"Wow, look at this place," Charlotte said with raised eyebrows, as Lila pulled the car to a stop in the main lot of the tree farm and got out.

Christmas music played loudly over speakers. A brightly lit neon sign creating a festive archway into the farm flashed *Merry Christmas* in red cursive script. On either side of the sign were the biggest Christmas trees Lila had ever seen, dressed in white lights and towering above the backdrop of the snow-dotted expanses in the distance. The lot was lined with rows upon rows of perfect holiday trees.

Off to the side, separated by rail fencing, was the horses' pasture. A white horse leaned over the fence, the bells around its neck jingling with its movement as it took carrots from a couple of kids, who were all bundled up and laughing with the attendant. The woman with them held a basket full of vegetables with a sign that said, *Feed the horses. $2.*

Opposite the horses was a wide stone patio, full of rocking chairs dressed in ribbon, and in the center a fire pit roared with life, people standing around it, some warming their hands while others held iron skewers dotted with marshmallows over the flames.

"I see our first stop," Edie said, pointing to a barn-like structure, its greenery-draped doors open wide to reveal walls covered in wine bottles, with a small bar inside. The sign read, *Winetasting! Kick back and sip a little Christmas.* They walked over and entered the barn, the space heaters working overtime to keep them all warm. Written on an A-frame chalkboard was the message, *Local Pinewood Hills Christmas wine available by the bottle.*

"We should get some," Lila suggested.

"Oh, fine. You've twisted my arm," Charlotte kidded.

They all took a seat at the bar and the woman working came over to greet them. She smiled from under her rancher's cowgirl hat.

"Welcome to the Pinewood Christmas Tree Farm. Would you like to sample or buy by the glass?"

"Why don't we sample," Lila suggested, consulting the others.

"That sounds like a great idea," Piper told her, rubbing her thin stripey-mittened hands together.

The others agreed, so the woman behind the bar handed them a list of wines. "We do six different wines in our tasting box, so take your pick. They start with the lightest and sweetest at the top and get darker and bolder as the list goes on. I'll give y'all a second to look over the list. My name's Tori if you need me."

As they perused the options, Lila took in the festive decorations around her. The wine bottles on the walls had tiny sparkling red ribbons tied around them with bells at the ends. The tops of all the cases were draped in a fresh pine garland, the scent of spruce meandering through the floral and citrus aroma of the wine. This place just felt like Christmas.

"You know what we ought to do," she suggested, causing the others to stop their wine-selection chatter. "We should get Eleanor a Christmas tree for her house."

"Oh, I love that idea," Piper said, leaning on her hand heavily, her elbow perched on the bar.

Charlotte set her menu down. "Did you see her almost tear up, talking about her husband?"

Lila nodded. The whole idea of decorating a tree for their new friend felt so right. Christmas could be a lonely time for people who were on their own. Lila certainly understood that. With her husband gone, Eleanor must feel so isolated.

"The problem is that the house needs a lot more than just a tree," Edie cut in.

"Well, we can't fix everything, but we can at least do something to lift her spirits," Lila said.

"We could get her a couple of gifts too," Piper suggested. "I can make her some soaps. I have all my essential oils with me."

"That's so kind of you," Lila said, the Christmas spirit filling her.

"Let's decide on our wines and while we try them out, we can brainstorm ideas for what to do for Eleanor," Edie said. "I vote the Honeypot Vine as our first one. Can't go wrong with a dessert wine."

Lila grinned. "I second that!"

They ordered a bottle to share, and Lila sat back with her glass, feeling content. There was something about helping Eleanor that made her feel like there was a bigger reason they hadn't demanded their money back and left. The only other time she felt this way was when she was helping children, because helping people was what made her come alive. Every day around her shifts at work, she met with disadvantaged kids through a program in Nashville. Sometimes she took them shopping for things they needed; other times, she helped with their homework.

Her favorite memory was from last year, when she took a little girl Christmas shopping for her mother. The child had met Lila for math tutoring, but she'd broken down into tears, unable to focus, telling Lila that it was just her and her mother, and there were three gifts under the tree—her mother's entire savings—all of the presents with the little girl's name on them.

"My mom works so hard and she isn't going to get anything," the girl, Amber, had said through her sobs.

They stopped what they were doing, went down the street to a gift shop in town, and Lila told Amber to choose any three presents she wanted to give to her mother. The store wrapped them up for her and Lila had charged them on her credit card, and even though the prices were more than she would've spent herself, she never wavered from her excited smile for Amber.

Later, Amber's mom sent Lila a thank-you letter through the volunteer program, telling her how it had been the best Christmas she'd ever had, the first time in fifteen years she'd gotten a gift.

Lila had felt whole, like she was doing what she was put on earth to do. Helping Eleanor felt like that too.

She sat back and took a long sip of her wine, the sweet nectar with notes of orange blossom and wildflower honey coating her tongue and making her feel really festive. Christmas was bittersweet for her, but like the wine, the sweetness outshone the rest today.

"My name's Rex, and I'm here to be your personal rodeo cowboy tour guide," a four-foot-nothing young boy about five years old said in a thick southern accent, as he stood in front of the women with his hands on his Wrangler jeans–clad hips, his miniature cowboy boots covered in dust.

They all looked at each other, biting back their smiles. Lila had to, otherwise she'd gush all over this freckle-cheeked creature of pure cuteness.

"The first thing ya gotta do is grab 'em by the reins," Rex said. "They know it's comin', so it ain't a big surprise and they'll be happy about it." He took the reins of a copper-colored horse and clicked his tongue to get the horse to step over toward him, which it did, only causing the women to grin more over the little boy. "Now, I've already gotten this here girl saddled up. I need to fix a few things on my saddle somethin' bad, but I don't have the tools. Y'all got a good one, so don't worry."

Rex dragged an overturned wooden crate to the side of the horse. "The next thing ya gotta do to make sure you have a good ride is mount the right way. I'ma show you how, just as soon as I get each one of y'all your horses."

He headed over to a snow-white horse saddled up and ready to go. Rex clicked his tongue again and walked it over to them. "Who wants to ride Phantom? Before ya answer, I'll tell ya a secret about her."

"Oh my gosh, he's the cutest thing I've ever seen," Piper whispered to Lila.

"All right," he carried on, "here's the thing about Phantom. She's a little older and she's decided she's gonna take her sweet time, so if you want to go slow, she's your girl. Who wants her?"

All four of their hands shot in the air.

"Well, nah, I reckon you're gonna have to take turns if y'all want her." He turned to the horse. "Hear that, Phantom girl? They all like you the best." He patted her nose and she pawed the ground with her hoof, making a snorting sound. "She's glad y'all like her too," Rex told them.

"I think the brunette over there should have Phantom, Rex," a husky voice said from behind them. "I've heard she gets a little nervous about outdoorsy activities."

Before she even turned around, Lila knew exactly who'd uttered that comment. She pursed her lips in disapproval as Theo walked into the horse ring, carrying a saddle and a blanket. He seemed taller and more substantial than he had behind the bar, his biceps showing through his flannel shirt when he slipped off his coat and set it on the bench.

"Theo!" Rex said, breaking his horse-guide character and suddenly turning back into a five-year-old, wrapping his arms around the man excitedly. Theo set down the saddle and lifted him up, wrinkling his nose playfully at Rex.

Lila was frozen in place, trying to snap her gaping mouth shut. Rex actually *liked* this guy? How? He was as cold as ice with seemingly everyone he came in contact with, except this little boy... She'd never seen Theo smile until now, and when he did, he was incredibly handsome. His blue eyes sparkled as the edges of them creased with happiness. His smile was like coming home after a long trip—despite all the other warning signs, suddenly she wouldn't have minded if it were directed at her.

"I'm on my lunch break, so I thought I'd stop by," Theo told Rex. "Where's your daddy?"

"He's tendin' to the folks in the tree lot 'cause he's down a worker, and when he's finished he can't come over 'cause he has to do the plumbin' tonight."

"He's working tonight?"

"Yes, sir. He's fixin' the crop sprinkler for Bud Simmons. At five o'clock."

"So he's got you on horse duty," Theo said, chuckling at him affectionately.

"Yup, and I made him pay me more than my chore money."

"A businessman. I like it."

Theo set Rex down and approached another horse that was white with gray spots, picking up the saddle and a pad and placing them over the horse's back, securing the straps. "Phantom's good for beginners.

This one—Maisy Jane—on the other hand is the fastest at Pinewood Farm. She's won twenty blue ribbons in her young life."

"Then I'll ride her," Lila said, defiant, something in her wanting to prove to Theo that she wasn't entirely made of Christmas sparkle.

"This is the horse *I* ride," he stated, meeting her eyes.

"Well, today *I'll* be riding her."

"Suit yourself." He pulled one of the crates over to Maisy Jane and gestured for Lila to come over. Ignoring the ogling eyes of her friends, she complied, stepping up onto the box, gritting her teeth to hide the jolt of nerves that coursed through her. "Grab the reins above my hand," Theo said. "Then put your foot in the stirrup there."

"You leadin'?" Rex asked him.

"Just for this," Theo replied. "Let's double up. You get the others and I'll take care of this one, since she needs a little extra help."

Lila shook her head in disapproval, but she couldn't deny the zinging excitement she had at being in such close quarters with Theo. She placed her foot in the stirrup, trying to make her movements as fluid as possible to give him less to say, and swung her leg over the horse's back, mounting and then realizing it had a double saddle. Had he planned to ride with her all along?

"Take your foot out of the stirrup a minute," he said.

When she did, he inserted his own boot, and before she could say anything, he'd mounted the horse behind her, his arms around her to hold the reins, making it difficult to breathe properly, her heart beating a mile a Christmas minute. "Have fun," he said to the others before calling something to the horse.

At his command, Maisy Jane took off, running and causing Lila to squeal, blowing her hair back, the scenery rushing past her in a blur as they bolted through the open gate at the back and out into the hills. She snapped her eyes shut as panic swelled within her, her body lifting slightly in Theo's grip. She'd never been on a horse in her life. They were going too fast. How should she hold on? What if she fell? She clenched the saddle with all her might.

But then Theo's chin was on her tense shoulder, his arms holding her securely, his calm voice at her ear. "I've got you. Just relax, breathe in the fresh air, and open your eyes. They'll adjust."

Her heart slamming around in her chest, she did what he said. He was right. Suddenly, she was acutely aware of the smell of pine, the purple hills in the distance, and the snow-covered ground that stretched out in front of her as far as she could see. It felt like she was flying, floating on air. There wasn't a single sound except for the wind in her ears, as the horse galloped through the fields in a giant circle on the outskirts of the farm. The air was so clean here, the miles of unspoiled beauty abundant and wild. A stream meandered down the hill, creating a little waterfall that gurgled at the base. It was incredible. She imagined what it would be like to grow old with someone out here, away from the hustle and bustle of the city, sitting on a porch swing, watching the sunset...

Before she knew it, they were making their way back into the horse ring. Maisy Jane slowed to a trot as she snorted, finally stopping and giving Lila a chance to get her bearings. They came to a stop by the box, and Theo dismounted, holding his hand out to help her down. Despite the calm he'd created on their ride, she was still shaking. She took his hand, his grip tender and gentle as he guided her to the ground.

The others were all on their horses, walking slowly in a circle with Rex at the front, chattering away.

As Theo let go of her hand, he called out to Rex. "I've gotta go," he said, unbuckling Maisy Jane's saddle. "I'm gonna grab a sandwich from your mama and head back. Does she have any of her famous chicken salad at the store?"

"She made a whole bunch this mornin'! I helped her fill the cold boxes in the store before we opened."

"She pay you for that too?" he teased, giving Rex a wink.

"Nah, she told me it was good practice to help a lady."

"She's right," he said, tucking the saddle under his arm. "Catch ya later." His gaze went over to Lila and then, as quickly as it had landed on her, it skittered away.

"I'm just going to say it. What the heck was that?" Charlotte asked, as they came upon the country store on the farm's grounds. It, too, was a barn-style building with shelves full of southern fare, and it had a cozy dining area with red-and-white checkered tablecloths and bunches of Christmas foliage in the center of every table.

"What?" Lila said, still thinking about Theo's voice in her ear. That was not the way he'd sounded all the other times she'd heard him talk…

"The coffee guy who whisked you away into the hills of Tennessee. What was *that*?" Charlotte repeated as she browsed the baked assortment of cookies and bites—vanilla cream cakes, butter rum balls, double-stuffed peppermint brownies—all hand-wrapped in cellophane with sticker price tags that had $1.99 written on them in ballpoint pen.

"I have no idea." Lila shook her head, still trying to make sense of it. She grabbed a chicken salad sandwich to see what all the fuss was about. "Did you all have fun on your rides?" she asked.

"I did," Piper said, picking up a plastic bowl of salad and inspecting its contents before cradling it in her arms as she decided on the drinks. "But not as much fun as you had with your sexy cowboy."

Lila laughed.

"How adorable was that little Rex?" Piper continued.

"He was the cutest," Edie said on her way up to the register.

When they had all unwound their scarves, taken off their coats, and settled at one of the tables with their meals, Lila tried to get Theo out of her mind. "We should surprise Eleanor with the decorations," she suggested. After the tasting session and a few full glasses of wine, they'd bought all kinds of greenery for Eleanor, and they couldn't wait to surprise her. They'd been able to leave the items they'd bought with the family who owned the farm until the end of their visit today, and while they were riding horses, a few of the guys were tying the tree they'd picked out to the top of Lila's car.

"Oh, that's a great idea," Charlotte said, squeezing a pack of mayonnaise onto her open sandwich. "Maybe two of us could bring her to our cabin while the other two decorate her living room as a surprise."

"I'll decorate," Piper said.

"Me too," Lila agreed. "Edie and Charlotte, would you two entertain her while we're in the house?"

"Oooh! I could offer her some PR as a Christmas present and tell her I'd like to take some new photos of her, to update the Fireside Cabins website," Edie cut in. "You said she knew she needed some more recent photos."

"I could do her hair and makeup as my gift," Charlotte said. "I'll get her ready for the photo shoot and take my time."

"Perfect," Lila said. "Think she'll fall for it?"

"We'll just say we wanted to do something nice for her for Christmas," Piper said. "And then we hope she'll go for it."

"Oh, I'm so excited," Piper said with a giggle. "Let's go grab a few ornaments and some lights and get the car. Time to spread some Christmas cheer."

Chapter Six

"We bought way more greenery than we needed," Lila said with a chuckle as she stood in the living room, still out of breath after hiding the tree from Eleanor and then dragging it with Piper all the way to the house through the snow.

Eleanor had fallen for their plan hook, line, and sinker. The girls had told her that Piper and Lila wanted to keep shopping at the Christmas tree farm but Edie and Charlotte had gotten cold, so they'd come home. They'd said that they'd love her to keep them company and then Edie suggested the photo shoot. Eleanor wasn't quite sure about that and it had taken a little convincing, but Edie promised it would be worth it to take a new photo while they were there visiting because then she'd have it at the ready if and when she updated the website for Fireside Cabins.

"We'll find a place for it," Piper called to Lila, filling up a glass at the kitchen sink with the water for the reservoir in the tree stand. She came back in, and poured it into the stand under the tree in the corner of the room.

Lila stretched a piece of cedar garland along the broken window, trying to figure out how to hide it. "I wish we could do something for the rest of the house too," she said. "I worry about all her cabins being empty. Did you see how many people were at the Christmas tree farm? Those are potential customers for Eleanor."

"With all this land," Piper said, "she could retire if she sold this place, and it's a goldmine for the right investor. Do you think she should sell it?"

"I think on paper, yes," Lila replied. "But she's all alone and she has so many memories here. Even updating it might be a delicate subject, let alone selling it."

"You're right," Piper agreed. "Can you come over and help me string these lights?"

"Absolutely." Filling up Eleanor's home with happiness was important to Lila because she knew all too well what it was like to need to hold on to the memories. And if a few Christmas lights could bring back the joy of this house for Eleanor, then Lila would do whatever it took.

They'd worked at light speed, and Piper and Lila had finished decorating the living room before Eleanor came back.

They'd created quite a bit of merriment: the mantel was dripping in wide swags of spruce greenery held up by bright red glittered Christmas bows, their ribbons cascading down in waves, the flames in the fireplace shimmering off their sparkling surface. The enormous tree in the corner was decorated in reds and whites with crystal snowflakes that sent a buttery glow through the room, the white lights dancing off the hardwood floors like fireflies. They'd found a few candles and lit them around the room, wrapping the bottoms in fresh pine they'd cut and wired together to make candle rings. They'd decided to hang wreaths in all the windows, tying big gold bows that filled the center to hide the cracked window. They'd even put out a bowl of milk for the tabby cat Presley, who would come out of hiding and brave strangers in his house just to have some, they discovered.

Piper had texted the other two women to see if they could get Eleanor outside, pretending they wanted to take more pictures for the photo shoot. Then she sneaked into the cabin to grab some of the cookies and Christmas snacks they'd brought with them, along with wrapping paper, bows, and a handful of her soaps and lotions to wrap up under the tree.

Lila set out the final bowls of candy canes and plates of macaroons, Piper's apple pie pita chips, chocolate fudge, and Lila's vanilla bean cookies, and Piper gave a last nudge to arrange the stack of beautifully wrapped gifts in silver-and-red paper under the tree. When they'd put the finishing touches on everything, Lila texted Charlotte and Edie to let them know they were ready, and then she ran around and switched on a couple of lamps, turning off the overhead light for ambience.

"Let's go meet them on the front porch," Lila said, excited.

They went outside just as Eleanor and the other two were crossing the lawn, confusion already spreading across the elderly lady's newly made-up face. With professional hair and makeup she looked about twenty years younger. Her skin was softer, her cheeks pink with blush, her hair combed into a soft wave. She had on a blouse under her open coat and a pearl necklace.

"You look amazing," Lila said as she made her way to the porch.

"Thank you," Eleanor said, touching her new hairstyle. "I had no idea I could ever look like this." She gave a thankful nod to Charlotte. "What are y'all doing here on my porch? I thought you were out shopping."

"Well, we *all* were. Charlotte and Edie told you a little fib." Lila opened the door. "You see, we hated to leave you over here by yourself

when we were hogging all the Christmas excitement in our cabin..."
She led Eleanor into the living room.

Eleanor stood in silence, her lips open just slightly as she took in
all the festive decorations. She didn't move but her eyes glistened,
tears spilling down her cheeks. She placed her fingers over her mouth,
clearly still in shock.

"Merry Christmas," Lila said.

Eleanor turned her streaming eyes toward the four of them. "Y'all
are like a group of Christmas angels," she said. "You have no idea what
this means to me."

She wobbled on her feet, needing to sit down. Lila helped her to the
sofa. With jittering hands, Eleanor motioned for them all to take a seat.

"I've been by myself for two years now, and Christmas is really
hard on me. I never thought I'd find myself out here all alone." Her
lip wobbled, but then she turned toward the Christmas tree, and it
subsided. "Y'all have brought life back into this place."

Lila felt a surge of purpose and affection for Eleanor.

They stayed and chatted with Eleanor for quite a while before she
started to look tired. The sun had gone down, plunging them into the
kind of darkness that was only possible in the depths of the countryside.

"We still have a little greenery left," Lila said when they'd gotten
back to their cabin. "What should we do with it?" She walked over and
stretched it out on the kitchen counter. Suddenly, it hit her. "I could
sneak over and decorate the coffee shop door." She put her hand over
her mouth to stifle her giggle.

Edie nodded. "That would serve him right for racing you around
today like you were some sort of jockey."

Lila laughed, but inwardly she couldn't get her mind off it. It was
the first time she'd really been surprised in a while, and she actually

enjoyed it. So much so that she wouldn't mind riding with him again sometime.

"I'll toast to that," Charlotte said, clinking her glass with the others.

"I'm gonna do it," Lila told them, grabbing the leftover garland and then putting some scissors and wire into one of the boxes they'd used to bring the decorations home from the farm.

"I wish we could be a fly on the wall when he sees it!" Piper said.

Lila slid on her coat. "I'll be right back." She grabbed her purse and phone and ran outside to her car. She drove right off, not even letting the car warm up, the winter cold giving her a shiver from her head to her toes.

Merging onto the main road, the sharp turns caused her to have to grab the supplies to keep them from sliding from the passenger seat onto the floor. The dark sky above was an endless expanse, the clouds hiding any hint of a star. As she drove, she thought about how much Theo confused her. He went from ice cold when they'd first met to whatever that was during their ride, and then he'd left again, barely even making eye contact. She'd never met anyone so difficult to read.

When she arrived at the coffee shop, she pulled up along the edge of the road and cut off her lights, not wanting to draw attention to herself. Cinching up her scarf against the biting wind, she snatched the garland and the box of supplies from the passenger seat and got out of the car, quietly closing the door. Then she walked across the small gravel lot, the darkness wrapping around her with the frigid cold of night. She tossed the decorations over her shoulder and blew air into her mittened hands to try to keep warm.

As she approached the coffee shop door, she had to check to make sure she wasn't seeing things. She stopped in front of it, unable to slow her whirring mind.

There, on the door, was a Christmas wreath, and at the bottom it had a big red bow. Unexpectedly, hope swelled within her. Had she worked her very own Christmas miracle?

The crunch of gravel behind her registered just as she heard his voice. "May I help you?" he snapped.

The hope she'd felt evaporated in an instant at the harshness of his voice. "I was just bringing this over to you," Lila said, holding out the garland. Like always, she couldn't read him at all, and the last thing she wanted to do was to make a fool of herself. "We had extra when we finished decorating."

He stepped up to her, closing the space between them. "And so you thought you'd bring it to me when the shop is closed?"

"Uh…" she said breathlessly, unable to find her words. She was usually quick on her feet, but her head was a jumble as she looked into his piercing blue eyes. "I was going to decorate your door as a surprise," she said honestly, once she'd found the ability to speak again.

"Well, I don't need it decorated anymore." His tone was such that she couldn't tell what he meant by it. Was he telling her he'd done it *for* her? Or was he telling her to go away?

"I see that." She took in a steadying breath.

"I hate surprises," he said, brushing past her to the door and putting his key in the lock.

Lila's cheeks burned with unease, his brusque reaction stinging her. It was Christmas. And if he didn't want her coming around, perhaps he shouldn't have taken her on that ride. But at the very least, she was his customer. She deserved some common decency, surely.

She strode up behind him. "Tell me why you put that wreath up," she demanded.

He opened the door and flicked on the lights, not answering.

"Tell me," she pressed him, coming in behind him.

He shut the door, the two of them standing in the empty coffee shop. "Trudy was getting rid of it and told me to take it home—I live upstairs." He pointed to a small stairway at the back of the shop. "Trudy couldn't bear it dying on her."

"Trudy?" she questioned.

He took in an annoyed breath, as if she were supposed to know the answer. "Trudy Johnson, Rex's mother. She and her husband Judd own Pinewood Farm."

"Oh," she said, the word withering on her lips. So he hadn't gotten the wreath for her . . . "Well, here's some more," she said, holding out the greenery. "We don't need it, and your customers might like it." When he didn't take it, she put it on the bar. "Why don't you like surprises?" she asked, as he headed over to the staircase at the back.

"Because sometimes they can rip your heart out," he replied, heading up the steps. "Lock the door behind you when you leave." His voice sailed down the stairs, echoing in the empty space between them.

Chapter Seven

"Should we go to the coffee shop this morning to see the look on Theo's face?" Edie said to Lila as they all sat around the kitchen table having a big, over-the-top vacation breakfast like they always did—eggs, sausage, bacon, an array of muffins and biscuits, fruit, and cheesy homemade grits. She passed Lila the butter for her biscuit.

"Maybe not," Lila replied, still rattled by the conversation, or lack thereof, that she'd had with Theo last night, the whole thing leaving her totally confused. She finished preparing her biscuit and nipped another piece of bacon from the plate in the middle of the table.

"Yeah, you're right," Edie said. "We shouldn't start our day with Mr. Sourpuss barking at us because we wanted to spread a little Christmas merriment."

"I wonder what he thought when he saw it," Piper said, looking around the table as she delivered mimosas to everyone. "He's so mysterious. Doesn't he know that he'll probably sell more coffee if he's actually pleasant to talk to?"

"Unless it's just us he doesn't like," Charlotte said.

Lila stiffened at the thought.

"He didn't seem that way with Rex at the farm yesterday. Did you see how the little boy responded to him?" Charlotte continued.

"Why wouldn't he like us?" Piper asked. "We haven't done a thing to him."

Lila shook her head, wondering if Charlotte was right. Theo had been awfully friendly with Rex, and he'd even hung a wreath on his door for the little boy's mother, yet he barely even cracked a smile whenever he looked at her, and then that intense reaction to being surprised—what had he meant by that? But then she remembered the softness of his voice as he'd said, "I've got you," and how tightly he'd held her on that horse ride, his big hands gripping her firmly, keeping her safe. It didn't make any sense.

"What are you thinking about?" Edie asked. "You look like you're solving an algebra problem over there."

"I don't know," she replied, not entirely present in their conversation anymore.

Edie leaned into her view. "You don't know what you're thinking?"

"Hm?" she said, swimming out of her reverie. She needed to get to the bottom of it. Suddenly she couldn't stand it. Theo couldn't just treat her like that. "I forgot the box of scissors and stuff at the coffee shop. I'll go get them."

Piper's knife and fork stilled in her hands, as if she were dialing in to Lila's inner thoughts. "We could all go get them."

"No, I'll go," Lila said, getting up. "I'll be back in time for our day out, but I want to talk to him."

"What happened last night?" Edie asked, following her with her eyes as Lila slipped on her shoes. "I know we'd all turned in by the time you got back, but I'd expected you to run and jump on all our beds, waking us up and telling us what you'd done. You've been quiet this morning—it's not like you."

"I'll fill you in later. But I can't until I talk to Theo."

They all sat around the table silently looking at her, and she knew what they must be thinking. Why was she rushing away to talk to some guy instead of spending quality time with the people who knew her best? But she wouldn't be able to enjoy her vacation until she got to the bottom of Theo's reaction.

"I swear," she promised. "I'll be fast."

Lila strode through the snow that was now piling up beneath her feet, through the coffee shop door, the Christmas wreath swinging as she closed it behind her, and past a few people sitting at the tables with their coffees. "Hey, Johnny," she called to the overall-clad man in the corner she remembered from their first visit.

Johnny didn't look away from his paper, but his hand went up in greeting.

The closer she'd gotten on her way there, the more she'd realized that no matter what Theo's issues were, he had no right to be so rude to her. And the more she'd considered this, the more frustrated she'd gotten.

She went straight up to the bar and glared at Theo, her eyebrows raised in anticipation, just hoping he'd figure out that he owed her an apology. When he didn't say anything, she dropped her fingers down on the bar and squared up to him. "What's the matter with you?" she asked quietly, so as not to disturb his customers.

His expression didn't change from the blasé one he'd had when she'd first walked up, and that just angered her even more.

"Well, right now, the matter is that you aren't ordering your coffee, since people are waiting behind you." He looked past her and apologized to the woman who'd come in after her.

Lila stepped aside. "You can order," she said, to the lady's inquiring stare.

The woman squinted up at the menu on the wall. "I'll have a double-shot espresso with...What dairy substitutes do y'all have?"

Lila let out a huff of sardonic laughter.

"I just got some new ones," he said. Theo rattled off a few selections of various milks: coconut, oat, cashew, soy—but no almond. A thud of disappointment mingled with the frustration Lila already felt, while she waited, inwardly gritting her teeth. She'd gotten all her courage up on the way over and now it was slowly withering away.

Eight o'clock in the morning must have been the busiest time for Theo because someone else stepped in line right after the woman, and then two more people came in and waited at the side for their to-go orders. Surprisingly, business wasn't too bad for the coffee shop with no name.

Once there was a lull in customers, she addressed Theo again, her initial surge of adrenaline having completely subsided as she'd waited. "Look, I won't stick around and bother you, but I just want to know, what have I done to make you so angry with me?"

There was a crack in his cool demeanor, and a flash of something she couldn't identify flickered in his eyes for a second, but he wouldn't answer.

"What was that during the horse ride yesterday?" she continued, exasperated by his silence. "You knew we were going to the farm. If you wanted to avoid me, why did you come and then offer to lead the ride?"

He grabbed a rag and moved down the counter, wiping coffee rings from the surface. She followed him.

"I'm glad you did," she said gently. "I just don't understand what changed between then and last night." She leaned over the counter, demanding his attention. "Why did you go through all the trouble to get your saddle, find me, and take that ride? I want to know, Theo."

His lips parted as if he was going to say something, but then he snapped them closed.

"Tell me," she pressed.

Finally, he said, "Sorry. I had a momentary lapse in judgment at the farm. I won't let it happen again."

Another customer came in and Theo went over to take the order.

Her heart sank. So the only time Theo had shown her anything other than hostility had been a "lapse in judgment." She couldn't deny the unexpected hurt it caused her, but she wasn't going to spend the rest of her vacation worried about some random guy who very clearly didn't want to be around her, who she would never even see again after this trip.

"Okay," she said, nodding in complete understanding now. She turned around and walked out, deciding right then and there that she wouldn't be coming back to his shop. This was about spending time with her friends on probably their last Christmas trip together. There was no way she would allow Theo to distract her from that anymore.

"I think we should try the bakery first," Piper suggested, pointing to the tiny storefront with the red-and-white striped awning as they walked down Main Street. After her confrontation with Theo, Lila had suggested they all get ready and take a walk in town, hoping the icy winter air and poinsettia-filled sidewalks would put her back into the festive mood. Then they could figure out their big outing for the day.

The town's little Main Street was perfectly preserved from its original construction at the turn of the century—one tree-lined avenue with a string of independent businesses and shops running along its edges.

They peered past the Christmas trees in the main window of Gingerbread Mama's Bakery at a line of caramel apples sitting on the counter to cool.

"Oh my…" Charlotte said, as she squinted at the menu through the glass from outside. "They have pear brûlée-filled donuts with a sugar glaze. If I go through those doors, I swear, I think I'm going to gain ten pounds."

"Well, I'm absolutely game," Piper said, tugging on the long vintage door-pull and dragging Lila inside, the others following.

"Of course Piper doesn't mind," Charlotte teased under her breath. "She's like a hundred pounds dripping wet."

Lila laughed but was distracted, immediately overcome with the sweet scents of caramel and chocolate. She browsed the display tables of treats—containers of peppermint bark, bourbon almond chocolate truffles, and salted caramel buttercream buttons—all adorned with mistletoe and holly, every table draped in swags of fresh pine. A Christmas tree, filled with sugar cookie dough ornaments, glistened in the corner.

"I already know what I'm getting," Edie said, pointing to a tray behind the rounded glass display case piled with raspberry lavender dark chocolate bites.

"Have we walked into heaven?" Piper teased. "I'm getting one of those too."

"Me too," Charlotte said, peering down at her phone and typing. "Let's make it an even four."

An older woman with a bright smile and a flour-covered apron greeted them. "Hey there," she said as she rang them up. "I'm Carol. Y'all grab yourselves a table and I'll bring them out to you."

Lila paid for them all and they crossed the small space, taking the only table with four chairs.

"Work," Charlotte said as she sat down, when Piper looked questioningly at her phone. "My agent wanted to know where I was. Like I can't take a week for myself." She slipped her phone into her bag, turning her attention to the treats coming their way.

"These go amazingly well with espresso," Carol said, as she grabbed their chocolates with a little square of parchment, dropping far more than four into their bag and bringing them over to the table. "I keep thinking I should get an espresso machine..."

"Maybe you could partner with the local coffee shop," Edie suggested.

Carol bit back a look of disgust. "Maybe..." she said, in a way that Lila could tell really meant, "Not on your life."

"I know that the owner isn't the most personable..." Edie continued.

"Definitely not." Carol passed them all paper napkins with *Gingerbread Mama's* written in curling green and red for the holiday season. "Y'all from out of town?" she asked, clearly moving on to a more pleasant subject.

"Just a few hours' drive. We're staying at Fireside Cabins for the week," Lila replied.

"Eleanor is just the sweetest woman," she said, shaking her head affectionately. "Has she told y'all the best shops in town yet?"

"Not yet," Lila replied.

"Well, there's Wishful Thinkin', a shop full of collectibles that's owned by my sister Arlene, so you know I'm gonna mention that one first," she said with a warm grin. "And if you want some vintage charm, you can get glass-bottle Coke and classic treats like ice cream floats and banana splits at Americana. And one of my favorite places is Imagination Books. They sell everything from rare novels to local indie authors. You never know what you'll find in there."

"Well, our day just got a lot more interesting," Piper said.

Just like Lila had hoped, this little trip into town had melted away the toxic atmosphere created by Theo. This was what she would focus on from now on, she told herself, as she soaked up the festive vibes and made the most of being surrounded by her friends.

With their arms full of shopping bags, the others had gotten cold and returned to the cabin, but Lila had wanted to stay out a little longer, swept away by the selection of volumes in Imagination Books. She'd settled in one of the oversized chairs tucked away in a corner of the shop under strands of white lights, and switched on a little reading lamp next to her, as she sat with the pile of books she'd gathered from the eclectic grouping of shelves that lined the walls. She promised her friends she'd be fine, relishing the time she could spend in that adorable shop. She told them she'd walk home, and only be about thirty minutes behind them, but she'd ended up taking almost an hour, arriving home with a bag of books under her arm.

"Don't be angry," Charlotte said with her hands held up, standing beside her suitcases when Lila opened the door to the cabin. "My agent called. One of the stylists on set at the network is sick. They need me to fly out to LA immediately to take over for him."

"Right now?" Lila asked in disbelief, setting the bag of books down with a thud and shrugging off her coat, already realizing that was a stupid question given the fact Charlotte's bags were packed.

"Yes, I'm so sorry. They've already sent a car to pick me up. It should be here any minute. Just keep my Christmas decorations until I get back. Piper said she'd take them down for me and box them up when y'all leave." A car horn honked outside and Charlotte opened her arms for a hug, Edie and Piper coming into the entryway to say goodbye. "I'm so sorry, Lila. I really wish I didn't have to go, but this is huge," Charlotte said. She gave Lila a squeeze.

"I totally understand," Lila told her, as regret sank in. What else could she say? She did understand how important this was for Charlotte, but it stung to know her friend wouldn't be there for the rest of their last trip together. Now she wanted to kick herself for wasting her precious time with Theo.

There was another honk, and Charlotte gathered up her things and opened the door. "Have fun!" she said over her shoulder, before hurrying out and leaving them in silence.

"And then there were three," Edie said with a sad smile.

"It's okay," Piper replied, trying to lift their spirits. "We'll have a great time for Charlotte, and we'll show her all the photos when she gets back."

"You're right. I say we make a deliciously festive drink, go into the living room, and decide what our big adventure will be today," Edie suggested.

The three of them made mugs of mulled cider, put on their fuzziest socks, and gathered on the sofa. Piper turned on the radio, "I'm Dreaming of a White Christmas" filling the room and instantly lightening the mood as they all relaxed. Edie pulled out the brochures and Lila searched the area for Christmas activities on her iPad.

"There's a wreath-making class twenty minutes away…" Lila said, scrolling through her feed. The holiday images of the quaint town lifted her spirits. Pinewood Hills was a sleepy little place, but there was a certain charm to it. It managed to keep its quiet streets secluded from the growth in surrounding areas, and the more time Lila spent there, the more she felt like it was a reprieve from all the craziness that went on in the rest of the world. It comforted a piece of her that she'd never realized needed comforting.

Edie wrinkled her nose. "We've got our share of greenery at the moment. What else is there?" She wrapped both hands around her mug.

"Laser tag, and there's a movie theater..." Lila scrolled down a bit more.

Piper chewed on her lip. "It feels weird already without Charlotte and she's only just left."

"I know," Lila told her. "That's why we have to find something really fun to do, to take our minds off of it. Plus, we want to make her incredibly envious when she sees our pictures, since she left us, right?" she teased, making her friends laugh. "Oh wait," she told them, clicking on a link. "We couldn't do it until dark, but there's an enchanted forest." She read the description aloud: "'Find your Christmas spirit among millions of holiday lights as they tower above you, scattered along the trees tucked away deep in the forest of the Tennessee hills. Keep warm with hot cocoa stations along the way or follow the peppermint road to our bakery, restaurant, or Santa's toy shop.'"

Piper sat up straighter. "That would be fun."

"I think so too," Edie said. She turned around the pamphlet she'd been reading. "We could do this during the day. It's a tour of Christmas confectioneries." She turned the leaflet back around to read them the description. "They've got something called a Sugarplum Christmas Bomb, peppermint chocolate drops, and...Oh my goodness."

"What?" Piper asked, excited.

"They have fried homemade banana bread dipped in chocolate and rolled in powdered sugar," she replied with wide eyes.

"I can feel my hips growing just hearing you read that," Lila said with a laugh. Then, suddenly, she sharpened her hearing. "What's that noise?"

Piper and Edie stopped and listened.

The hum was getting louder. It sounded like the groan of an old creaky door. Piper got up and turned off the Christmas music, the three of them craning their necks in an attempt to hear the noise better.

"It sounds like it's coming from your bedroom, Edie," Lila said. She stood up and the other two followed her down the hall. The closer they got to the room, the louder the sound—now a thunderous banging and clanking—all of them looking at each other in alarm.

Tentatively Lila pushed open the door. "Oh no!"

It looked as though a spring rainstorm had cropped up in Edie's room, the ceiling gushing with water, the light fixture swaying from its electrical cord while water poured out around it.

"Grab your coat," Lila said, taking both Piper and Edie's arms and dragging them down the hallway. "We need to get out of here until we know it's safe. The water's too close to the electrical work." They snatched their coats and handbags from the hooks by the door and plunged themselves into the freezing cold, the ice on the cabins glistening under the dull light that peeked through the clouds.

"Let's go tell Eleanor, so she can get a plumber in right away."

The three women ran across the large expanse of yard between their cabin and the main house, which was so frozen it was like jogging over a solid rock. They knocked wildly on Eleanor's door.

When she opened it, Eleanor looked filled with worry, her hand over her heart, her eyes wide. "What's wrong?" she asked, nearly breathless.

"Edie's room is flooded, and there's water pouring from the ceiling," Lila told her.

The elderly woman looked past them toward their cabin. "Oh, no." Then out of nowhere, she started to cry.

"Are you okay?" Lila asked, putting her arm around her. They all stepped inside the musty cabin onto the tattered entry rug, and Piper shut the door behind them against the cold wind.

Leading Eleanor to the sofa in her living room, Lila sat down beside her. Piper and Edie sat on the other side, and Piper took Eleanor's hand.

"My body's failing me, and I can't do the handiwork I used to do. I've paid for questionable work on this place... I had a leak in another cabin and I just closed it off. It was going to cost about seven thousand dollars to repair. Fireside Cabins are aging. I'm not getting renters anymore, except for the odd few. The last couple that came requested a refund, and I can't blame them. I'm so sorry that I misrepresented what I had to offer." She sniffled. "I just don't have the money or the manpower to keep the cabins and grounds at their best, but without renters, I never will." She drew in a deep breath and let it out in a painful sigh, wiping her eyes.

"What are you going to do?" Edie asked, handing her a tissue from the box on the table beside the sofa.

Eleanor blinked her tears away, dabbing under her eyes. She took in another deep breath and straightened her shoulders. "I'm going to try to find a plumber, and then I'll see what I can do about replacing your things, Edie." Her lip wobbled.

"Don't worry, I can cover the cost of anything of mine that's been ruined," Edie said. "Let's focus on getting the leak fixed."

"I don't even know what that'll cost... And where will you sleep?"

"It's fine," Edie replied. "Charlotte had to leave for work, so I can have her bed."

"We need to see if we can get a deal from a local plumber," Piper said.

"What if we did before and after photos and I gave him free advertising? It's what I do for a living," Edie told Eleanor. "I could even offer him a couple of commercial television spots. I can make a few calls to people I know in the business. They're usually fine doing a favor for me here and there."

"The only plumber I know is Judd Johnson," Eleanor said tearfully.

"Yes, that's right," Lila said. She remembered the conversation with Theo and Rex about his daddy. "He does irrigation or something, along with the farming, right?"

Eleanor nodded. "He's got so much going on with the farm and the business already though...I don't feel like I could ask."

"I know someone who might," Lila said, a pinch forming in her shoulder. "But I'm not sure if he'll help us..."

"Who is it?" Eleanor asked, and the hope in her face sat like a cinderblock in Lila's stomach.

"Theo from the coffee shop." She braced herself for Piper and Edie's eye rolls.

Eleanor grimaced. "He's a recluse and doesn't really mingle with the locals. I went in once and he was less than cordial."

"Want to try to talk to him, Lila?" Piper asked.

"I can try, but I'm not promising anything."

Chapter Eight

"Back so soon?" Theo said when Lila approached the bar, as he loaded chocolate croissants into the front window at the register. His lips were set in their usual straight line of annoyance.

"Something's happened and I need your help," Lila said, happy the coffee shop had emptied out. This was going to take some time, so she needed his attention. "And you don't have to talk to me to do it."

"What is it?" he asked, the aggravation leaving his face but his expression remaining guarded.

"You know Eleanor Finely down the road, who owns Fireside Cabins?"

He stared at her, still holding one of the croissants he was loading.

"A pipe burst in one of her cabins and she doesn't have the money to pay a plumber. I was wondering if you could talk to Judd Johnson for me. I heard you mention that he has a plumbing business. My friend Edie would offer free PR and take before and after pictures for advertising if he'd help us."

"I doubt pictures of a wet rug will help his commercial farming irrigation business." His words came out harshly, but a hint of compassion showed on his face. Looking at him wrestling with his emotions, Lila wondered why he was putting up such a wall.

Her shoulders slumped. "I know Christmas might not be a big deal for you, but it's the season of giving and I can't bear to see Eleanor in tears like she is. I want to help her, and if I can't find someone, then I'll find a way to pay for it myself. I'll pick up extra shifts at my restaurant if I have to."

Interest flickered across his face. "You own a restaurant?"

"I'm a waitress." She lifted her chin proudly.

He finished placing the pastries in the display case and closed the sliding door at the back, the whole time looking thoughtful. Grabbing a rag, he walked around the bar to wipe off the glass. Lila put her hand on his bicep, ignoring the electric current that shot through her when he stopped in response.

"Please help her," she begged.

His jaw clenched as he peered down at her. Then, surrendering, he said, "I've worked with Judd before and he's taught me quite a bit. We replumbed this entire shop. I'll lock up this afternoon and take a look at it, and either fix it myself or call Judd for you."

Lila squealed, and in pure joy at being able to help Eleanor, she threw her arms around him. In all the movement, his hands found her waist and he broke out into a reluctant smile that took her breath away. Together, they stopped still as if they both had to get their bearings. The smile that had emerged lingered on his lips as he looked down at her, and in that moment, she felt like she was finally able to see him for who he was behind that wall he'd worked so hard to build.

Lila gazed deeply into his eyes.

He let go of her and turned away, and she considered whether his reaction was some sort of defense mechanism or something else. "Theo," she said, with no idea of what she planned to say but not wanting the moment to end.

His gaze shifted over his shoulder and he turned around.

"Thank you for helping Eleanor."

He nodded, not saying anything else.

"Oh, look!" Piper said to Edie and Lila. She grabbed their arms and skipped down the frosty path, past rows of decorated Christmas trees, up to the glittering carousel in front of the confectionery shop. Tinkling music sailed through the air as kids and their parents climbed aboard the giant horses, or piled into the curling-edged sleighs of the carousel.

"I can hardly keep up," Eleanor called to them, slowing them down.

"Oh, sorry," Lila said. "Being with Piper is like having a child," she teased. "I suppose we'll have to ride the carousel for her."

"I'm young at heart." Piper reached out and took Eleanor's arm, giving her a squeeze. They'd convinced Eleanor to come out with them after telling her that Theo was coming over to fix the leak and they'd all chip in money for her ticket. It had been about an hour's drive out of town down the snow-filled winding country roads, but Eleanor had assured them that it was worth it.

"This would be a wonderful place to bring a child," Eleanor said, waving at a little boy who was giggling atop one of the horses. She took in a long, wistful breath. "I always wanted someone to buy their famous Sugarplum Christmas Bomb for, even though it's heart-stoppingly huge."

"I read about that," Edie said. "What is it?"

Eleanor tipped her head back in amusement. "Ah, well I won't spoil the surprise. You'll have to get one for yourself to see."

"The suspense is killing me," Piper said. "Let's get one right now."

"Well, dear, if you can be distracted from the carousel this easily, wait until you see what's inside."

They went up to a pair of enormous cherry-red double doors with men dressed as nutcracker soldiers on either side. With gloved hands and pristine uniforms in red and gold, they opened the doors in unison.

"Oh my goodness," Lila said, stunned.

The floor was made of clear glass, covering thousands of different kinds of candies. A path of chocolates wrapped in a rainbow of cellophane snaked along the center of the room, twisting and turning, leading to different areas of the confectionery. To their right, a row of workers in bright white chef's suits, and tall hats with holly pinned to them, stirred gleaming silver pots of melted chocolate in various shades, and beside each of them were displays of skewers with different treats on the ends for dipping—marshmallows, peppermints, white chocolate squares, coconut-covered nougat, toffee—all of them arranged in the shapes of Christmas trees. Behind the chefs was a waterfall of chocolate, the smell of buttery, creamy fudge filling the air.

Lila had to tear her eyes from it to take in the rest of the place. To her left were tables of children decorating their chocolates with all shapes and sizes of candies, while Santa's elves buzzed around with silver trays offering them options. Straight ahead was an enormous spiral staircase leading to the second floor, the entire roof of the place a peak of glass, showing off the electric blue sky. The temperature was still low enough to retain the little piles of snow that had settled on the edges of the roof, giving the whole place a magical feel.

"Let's head upstairs," Edie suggested, pointing to a sign that said, *Chocolate rum cocktails this way.*

"Apparently, upstairs is where all the grown-ups are," Piper said.

"What else is up there?" Lila asked Eleanor.

"The tasting rooms with wine and chocolate pairings, and the café where you can get your Sugarplum Christmas Bomb. Shall we go?"

"Absolutely," Piper said.

"Mind if we forego the stairs? The elevators are just over there." Eleanor pointed to an elevator sliding smoothly upward as kids pressed their foreheads to the glass, their eyes round with excitement.

"Not at all," Lila replied.

They waited their turn for the elevator and took it up to the second floor. The view from the top was incredible. What Lila hadn't realized until she'd seen the aerial view was that the rainbow path spelled out the word *chocolate* in curly script. Eleanor was right: this would be an amazing place to bring a child. Lila could just imagine bringing her own children here one day. If she allowed herself, she could picture being a mother so easily in this quaint little town—pushing a stroller down Main Street, stopping in at the market to get local veggies for dinner, reading children's stories in the little pillowed area at Imagination Books... Lila pushed the thought away. She was far from being at the stage in her life where she'd have a husband and children.

The doors pinged open and they stepped out into another magical space: a line of booths offering different experiences. The first had a red-and-white striped awning, with tables full of gifts wrapped in festive paper and enormous ribbons. A chalkboard sign by the doorway said, *Surprise your loved ones and yourself with a mystery chocolate bundle!*

"Should we all buy a little one to put under the tree?" Lila said. Then she explained to Eleanor, "Normally, we take our trip just before Christmas Eve so that we're there for the big day, and then we all wake up on Christmas morning and open our presents, but we couldn't make it happen this year, so we're going to open our gifts the night before we leave."

"You don't have families to visit?" Eleanor asked.

"Nope. I don't have any relatives. My mother died just after I was born, and I lost my dad to cancer when I was twenty."

"Oh my dear…" Eleanor laid a gentle hand on her arm.

Lila smiled in gratitude at her gesture. But she didn't want to think about being alone because it would remind her that her dad wouldn't be there for yet another holiday, and the ache that came with that settled upon her like a sack of bricks when she let it. "The others live so far away from their families that they don't travel to be with them every year," Lila continued, shifting the focus to her friends.

"I usually go to see my parents in San Diego on Thanksgiving," Edie explained. "That's when my brothers prefer to visit, because they want to spend Christmas at home with their own kids."

"And my family lives in Portland," Piper said. "But my parents travel over Christmas so we usually get together for other holidays. Last year, we all flew home for my nana's birthday."

"Want to be an honorary member of our little club?" Lila asked.

"I'd love to." Eleanor's eyes shone with happiness.

"Everyone pick something," Edie said. "It's on me."

Lila chose a narrow, rectangular mystery chocolate bundle, with gold wrapping and a deep red bow.

After they'd chosen their presents, they filtered through the rest of the booths, sampling their signature peppermint chocolate drops, little squares of the fried homemade banana bread the brochure had promised, and all sort of confections—all free for tasting. Finally, they ended up at the café.

"I barely have room for anything else," Piper said, rubbing her thin torso through her red suede vintage fringe jacket, which she'd fashionably paired with an oversized knitted cream scarf that now hung loose over her shoulders. "But I have to try that Sugarplum Christmas Bomb. There's been way too much hype around it to leave without experiencing it."

"I second that." Lila nodded toward the white tables with bright green umbrellas set up to shield them from the sun coming in through the glass ceiling.

They went in and took a seat at one of the tables. Not long after, a waitress came over. "Welcome to the Sugarplum Café," she said, placing a gold-wrapped candy on the appetizer plate that sat in front of each of them. "Take a minute to look over our menu and let me know if you have any questions. I'll be right back with some hot cocoa and a glass of water for everyone."

"I'll never have enough space in my stomach for the Christmas Bomb if I eat this," Piper said, holding up the gold-foiled sweet.

"I agree," Eleanor said, "but you need to at least open it. There's a little message inside every one."

Lila unwrapped hers, revealing a butterscotch candy. She set it on her plate and spread the wrapper out to read her message. "Mine says, *When faced with a choice, choose to believe. It'll change your life.*"

"Ooh," Edie said, squinting her eyes in contemplation.

The more Lila thought about the statement, the more she realized that she'd spent her whole adult life believing in everyone else but herself. She'd believed in Razz, in her friends, in the kids she had worked with, but what was true about her? What was she capable of? She'd never tested her limits to see. She'd always taken the easy route: staying in a city she wouldn't have necessarily chosen for herself, taking a job that her boss himself had said could be filled by any warm body as long as they were willing to undergo the training. What did *she* really want in her life?

Just then the waitress returned, setting down mugs with a candy cane protruding from a pile of marshmallows. "Are you ready to order?" she asked.

"I think we'll all do the Sugarplum Christmas Bomb," Piper said.

"*All* of you?" the waitress asked. "You could probably share."

The three of them consulted Eleanor.

"Oh, go on," Eleanor urged them. "Why not get your own? You only live once, right?"

Piper turned back to the waitress. "Four Christmas Bombs then." Once the server left their table, Piper said, "I love my fortune! My message says, *Trust in yourself and you'll reach your dreams.*" She hugged it to her chest. "Maybe my expansion of Scented Spirit will be a good move. I needed to hear that right now."

"Mine says, *Take time for yourself and you'll find love on the horizon.* Maybe things will go even further with Jarod," Edie said. She lifted her hot cocoa to her mouth and took a sip before turning to Eleanor, who was already misty-eyed. "What does your say?"

She read her message. "*Take time to look around you to see the goodness in people. There are angels everywhere.*" She smiled at each one of them. "That is so very true. I am sitting with a table full of them right now."

"Aw," Piper said, patting her hand.

As they fell into conversation, Lila pondered the message in her candy wrapper some more, and she couldn't get it out of her head. She wanted to tell herself that it was just a cute Christmas note for kids, which didn't really mean a thing, but the words kept rolling through her mind.

"Here we are," the waitress said, pulling Lila from her thoughts.

The woman set down a dish the size of a small fishbowl in front of each of them. It was full to the brim with vanilla ice cream, which sat on something bright purple and crumbly. Piled high on top of the ice cream were so many different toppings that she could hardly focus on one at a time.

"What's in this?" Lila asked the waitress.

"We start building it with our sugarplum pie. It's chopped almonds, figs, sugared blueberries, and our house-made sugarplum filling baked into a buttermilk pie crust, warmed and placed below the ice cream and then topped with candied blueberry truffles, white chocolate cubes, brown sugar graham cracker wedges, sugar cookie morsels, and finished with a drizzle of our famous sugarplum syrup plus a big dose of whipped cream and a cherry." The waitress handed her a spoon. "Enjoy," she said with a grin.

They all dug into their own personal bowls. Lila took a bite, the warm spicy crunch of the pie mixing with all the toppings and the cold vanilla like a burst of holiday cheer.

"I can't believe how good this is," Piper said, as she savored the last remnant on her spoon before going back in for more.

"You're not lying," Edie agreed.

They all looked at each other and laughed, and Lila took in the moment. As she considered what she believed in and what she wanted for herself, still unable to get that message out of her head, she knew one thing for sure... What she wanted was to create a life where she could be around the people she loved most. In the end, that was what it was about for her: people. She was so happy to be with her friends, both new and old.

Chapter Nine

Wearing a pink Santa hat with a white fur trim, Lila stood beside Piper, next to a post with festively painted arrows pointing in different directions: *Peppermint Road, Ginger Avenue, Sugar Drop Lane, Cocoa Court.* Under the sea of lights glowing above them, she gave a bright smile and squeezed Piper around the shoulders as Edie snapped their photo.

"Let me see," Lila said excitedly, as she grabbed Piper's arm and ran over to Edie to peer over her shoulder at the shot. "What a great picture!"

"Definitely a keeper," Piper agreed. "Text it to us, Edie."

With the winter darkness taking hold by five o'clock, Lila and her friends decided to have dinner at the enchanted forest they'd read about earlier. It had worked out because Theo had called and said he had another commitment, and wouldn't be over to work on the plumbing until around seven.

"Which way to the restaurant?" Lila asked.

Edie unfolded the pamphlet they'd gotten when they'd arrived, revealing an enormous cartoon map. She tapped the path they needed to take. "Looks like Sugar Drop Lane is a straight shot. So I guess we follow those lanterns." She pointed to the trail of flickering lanterns that lined the winding track through the woods. Every single tree was bound with sparkling lights, from the roots to the tips of their bare branches. Peppering the snowy hills, between the glittering trunks of oaks and pines, were fully decorated Christmas trees. Holiday music filled the frosty air.

Lila closed her eyes to take in the icy aroma of winter and the sounds of laughter as children ran along the different paths, running through mazes of brightly lit hedges or roasting marshmallows by the fire pits that dotted the bare areas on the hills.

"Look." Piper's whisper caused her eyes to snap open.

Suddenly, a familiar face caused her to home in on one particular peal of laughter. Rex threw his head back, giggling as—to Lila's complete surprise—Theo swung him up on top of his shoulders, and handed him a giant paper stick of baby blue cotton candy. Lila felt as though her feet were glued to the path, her breathing shallow as she witnessed the softness in Theo's face, the way his eyebrows rose and his hefty chuckle when Rex grabbed his cheek to hold on. Theo's elbows were pointing out, his hands clasped behind Rex's back, talking a mile a minute to the little boy.

Excitedly, Rex pointed to Santa's Toy Shop with his free hand, his other clasping the cotton candy. "Let's look at them toys in there," Rex said.

"All right, but then we need to head home and get you a burger, or your mama's gonna have a word or two with me. It's dinner time." Theo walked Rex over to the shop's entrance and Rex wriggled down his back, running inside.

"Come on, Theo!" he called through the door from the center aisle.

Theo laughed, stepping in, the door closing behind him.

"Hey, Lila," Edie called.

Only then did she realize her friends had moved along down the trail, and Lila was standing in front of the toyshop alone.

"Sorry," she said, catching up with them, her mind spinning.

"Was that Theo with little Rex?" Piper asked, threading her arm through Lila's as they walked.

"Yeah," Lila said, still struggling to find words.

"I didn't know he was capable of smiling," her friend teased.

Lila grinned, but she'd barely heard her friend; the kind look Theo had given Rex and their banter burned into her mind. Why was he so different with her?

"They've got wine on the menu," Edie said, reading the back of the pamphlet as they neared the restaurant. "I'd say we all need a glass, yes?"

"Definitely," Lila said, trying to shift her focus back to her friends. "Wine would be good…"

"The old cast iron pipes were full of corrosion, and that, mixed with the cold temperatures, caused the pipe to split and burst," Theo said to Eleanor once Lila and her friends had gotten back, all business. Lila viewed him with a new lens after seeing him with Rex earlier. "It's just a matter of replacing the pipe, but I want to warn you that you might be facing this issue throughout all your plumbing on the property if it's the same age as this."

Eleanor nodded, fear sweeping across her face.

"I could get it done faster if I had some help, but I don't think we'll find too many volunteers, so if you're okay with the room being torn up for a few days, I can work on it every evening after I close the shop."

"What if I worked the shop for you?" Lila offered.

She immediately took stock of Edie and Piper's reactions, having not consulted them at all, but they both seemed so worried for Eleanor that they didn't flinch.

Edie's phone rang and she stepped out of the room to answer it.

When Theo didn't reply, Lila asked Piper and Eleanor if she and Theo could have a minute.

"Of course, dear. We'll be in the kitchen," Eleanor replied.

Lila pressed her hand against the dated wallpaper and stepped over a waterlogged pile of clothes to reach Theo. "It might be fun to learn how to make all the coffees, and it would free you up to come here for more than just the evenings," she continued. "I could learn how you make the drinks during the busy times, and then you could leave me there when traffic is lighter."

He glanced at her, unsure.

"I'm a waitress. I know how to take orders and be nice to the customers. Are you nervous that I'll show you up, and they'll all be asking for me?" She gave him a grin. "Or even worse, there might be an actual name on a sign out front. I've got ideas already…"

He pursed his lips in disapproval, but she could tell by the twitching at the corners of his mouth that he was hiding his amusement, giving her a flutter.

"Come on," she said, putting her hand on his arm to drive it home that she was serious.

He moved, brushing her fingers with his hand. Before she could catch her breath from the lightness of his touch, he'd stepped away.

"Okay," he said.

"What?" she asked, barely able to form a coherent thought as she looked into his eyes. But then she scrambled to harness this because she wanted answers. She wanted to know why he was so cold every

time they were together. He seemed to hide his emotion like some
sort of rare jewel, as if it could be stolen from him. She reached out
to touch his arm again. Immediately, she could see him start to pull
back. "Don't," she said.

He stopped moving, his silent question forcing her to say more.

"I like it when you let your guard down," she said honestly.

He pulled away again.

There was an underlying emotion lurking, which screamed to her
that Theo was struggling with something. And maybe, she figured,
since she'd been the one to notice, it was her job to help him figure
out whatever it was that had him so closed off. She'd dealt with her
own issues of not knowing her worth after Razz had hurt her, and she
understood what it felt like to move through her days while holding
on to a secret pain and fear that she couldn't be enough for someone,
suppressed for the benefit of everyone else.

"Why won't you show me who you really are?" she pushed. He
didn't answer. She reached for his hand, but he wouldn't let her take it.

"You don't really want to know," he said, but instead of barking
at her like he usually did, his words came out wounded. "You came
out here on your week's vacation, looking to have fun, and then
you're going to go back to your regular life, wherever that might
be. But this *is* my life. This is it. And something tells me that when
it comes to dating someone, you'd want more than the guy at the
coffee shop."

"How do you know that? You're presuming a lot of things." Then
she tilted her head up to directly address him. "I think you're scared."

"What?" he asked, walking away, his usual annoyance returning.
"I'm not scared of anything," he said, but his eyes told a different story.

"What is it?" she asked. "Why won't you let your guard down?"

"I don't need to explain myself," he snapped, a frantic scramble for a response swimming across his features. Her questioning had clearly hit a nerve.

"You're terrified to feel something, and you're hiding behind your anger and that coffee shop instead of facing whatever it is," she ventured.

"You don't know anything," he spat.

"Don't I? By the look on your face, it sure seems like I do." She strode over to him, forcing him to stay by blocking his path to the door.

"Hey," Edie said, suddenly coming into the room.

The two of them flew apart, Lila's heart slamming around in her chest.

Piper and Eleanor followed Edie back into the room.

"You know the client I'm trying to win for my firm?" Edie said, biting her lip, clearly so worried about the phone call she'd just had that she hadn't even noticed Lila and Theo's reaction when she'd come in. "They want an emergency meeting tomorrow before their CEO flies to Vail for the holidays. I have to present. He wants to make a decision before Christmas."

"What does that mean?" Lila asked.

"I know it's getting late, but if I want any time to prepare, I have to leave tonight." Edie paced back and forth. "I offered to help Eleanor with photos and that free PR..." she worried aloud.

"It's fine," Lila soothed, trying to absorb the blow that another friend was leaving. "Theo can do the job and he agreed to it without any PR."

"I feel terrible," Edie said, her face crumpling with dejection. "First Charlotte, now me." She held up her phone. "I have to find a rental car company somewhere nearby, but I doubt I'll have much luck."

"We'll figure something out," Lila told her. "Worst case, you could take my car..."

"I could always come back to pick you up. But let me look for a rental first."

"I have an extra car," Theo said. "If you take Lila's, I'll either loan her one that can be returned later, or I'll find another way to get her home."

Edie turned her goggling eyes toward Lila.

Then, as if something occurred to him, he asked Lila, "Where do you live?"

Was Theo putting himself in a position to *have* to see her again? "California," she said.

But the shock that registered in his expression made her unable to keep her poker face. "Just kidding," she said. "I live in Nashville."

He let out a nervous exhale. "Glad it's at least in the state. Probably should've thought that through before I offered."

"No need for all that," Eleanor cut in. "I hardly ever drive anymore. You're welcome to use my car as your own, any time you need it, until your friends can come back for you. It's the least I can do to repay you for all your help."

"Thank you, Eleanor." Lila was grateful for the offer, but she couldn't help the regret that bubbled up at having lost an opportunity to see Theo again.

"This is awful to say, but I think we might need to just call off the Christmas trip this year," Piper said. "With Edie having to leave and Charlotte already gone, it just doesn't feel the same. And now the cabin will be torn to shreds with repairs... It makes the most sense if we all get in the car together and go home."

"I agree," Edie said, shaking her head with resignation. "I don't want to, but I think we've been given no other choice."

"Except that Theo would be forced to work all day at the coffee shop and then all night on the plumbing, since there wouldn't be anyone to take over the shop for him," Lila said.

Piper chewed on her lip.

That familiar feeling of being alone slithered through Lila. "What if I stay behind?" she suggested. She didn't want to go home. She'd managed to have people she loved around her every holiday, and that had kept her from falling apart. If she went back now, she'd be alone, and she'd have to think about how much she missed her father and how she wished she had a family of her own. The more she thought about it, the more she realized that she felt she was needed here, like she had a purpose. And if she couldn't be with her best friends, this was where she wanted to be.

"I don't want to abandon Eleanor. The last thing I want is for her to spend her holiday alone," Lila said. "I can work in the shop for Theo during the day and keep Eleanor company in the evenings. I'd love to learn about all the history on the grounds. The website said there was a ton of it here, and we haven't had a chance to hear it. I'll bet Eleanor has a wealth of stories... I want to stay."

"You sure you want to do that?" Edie asked.

"Yes. It'll be great for Eleanor."

Edie gave a knowing nod. "Yes," she said. "It'll be great for *Eleanor*. You'll be wonderful company for her." She put her arm around Lila. "And I couldn't help but notice you and Theo when I came in," she whispered.

So she *had* seen... Lila shook her head to tell her it was nothing, but she knew her friend understood.

"Okay, Piper," Edie said. "Let's see if we can bag up my wet clothes and get them into the car." She turned to Lila. "Want us to leave the decorations? I could come back to get you, and we can take them down then."

"I can take them down—it's no problem," Lila said. "It'll be nice to have them all up."

"I feel terrible leaving you," Piper said.

"I think she'll be just fine," Edie said with a smirk.

Edie was both right and totally wrong, Lila mused. While she might be trying to make the best out of a bad situation, there was a hole in her heart that they'd never really get to have that final vacation, sharing gifts and laugher, making memories they could cherish forever. Charlotte, Piper, and Edie were like her sisters, and an era was coming to an end. At this rate she probably wouldn't ever get to have another Christmas with them—they'd barely managed a few days together *this* year, and given how their lives were moving in different directions, it would only get harder. Lila wondered how long it would be before they abandoned their regular coffee dates and quit hanging out completely, struggling to snatch a quick hour together. She'd be completely alone, without her best friends or any family, in a city that wasn't hers. What would she do with her life?

If anything could be said about this Christmas, it was full of surprises, that was for sure. Hopefully, there wouldn't be any more. Her heart might not be able to take it.

Chapter Ten

Eleanor's house was lit up this morning before the sun rose. The lamplight created a glow from inside as Lila knocked on the door. Presley the cat greeted her and rubbed once across her leg before darting off into the snowy surroundings.

Lila had come over earlier than she'd originally planned, just to take some time to be with Eleanor. Her eyes stung with lack of sleep, all night her body caught between the desperate need for rest and the wild, constant thoughts that rushed through her mind, not allowing her any peace. She kept thinking about how her friends were moving on with their lives, yet she felt stuck, like she was running in quicksand, being left behind.

"Good morning," Eleanor said when she answered the door. "Come in. Do you want some breakfast?"

"I'm on my way to the coffee shop in a bit to help Theo out," Lila replied.

"I've made biscuits and eggs," Eleanor said. "I'll whip up a sandwich and wrap it in some cellophane for the road."

"Thanks." Lila grinned gratefully at her. "I just wanted to stop in and see how you were."

"I'm fine, dear," she said, but the cloud of worry that overtook her when she said it told a different story. She sat down in her reading chair by the fire, which was lit already.

"You sure?" Lila asked, setting her coat on the arm of the sofa and taking a seat.

"Do you ever feel like you have no idea where your life is going?" the old woman asked with a sigh.

Lila couldn't help laughing. "Sorry, it's not funny. I'm laughing because I know *exactly* what you mean. In fact, I've been feeling the same thing myself."

"I thought that by this age, I would be settled, looking back on my life and knowing I was finally in the place where I could live out my years in comfort and security."

"Do you think anyone really gets to have that?" Lila wondered aloud.

Eleanor contemplated her question before replying, "I think some do."

"Then how do they get that lucky?"

Eleanor smiled. "'Lucky' is the key word there. I think we all have paths we take in life, and as long as we've prayed for them and tried to do what's right, we are on the correct one. But contentment isn't a guarantee. I guess, during those times when things seemed to be moving faster than I could keep up with them, when this place was buzzing with activity and I had Chester by my side—I suppose I thought I'd manage to become one of the lucky ones. But then it all just fell away…"

"Yeah, I get that," Lila said. "I've always wondered why I had to lose my parents."

"Oh, you poor girl," Eleanor said, reaching out for her.

"I'm okay," Lila said. She got uncomfortable whenever people tried to console her about the loss of her parents. Over the years, she'd tried to figure out why, and finally it occurred to her that she'd worked so hard to be strong all her life that if she accepted their loving embraces, she feared that she might crumble to the ground. But sitting there with Eleanor, it became harder to fight, and the tears rose up without warning.

Eleanor wrapped her in a warm hug, squeezing her gently. Lila put her head on the old woman's shoulder and took in a jagged breath, the feel of Eleanor's arms around her making her feel safe.

"Thank you. For the hug," she said, pulling back and wiping her eyes. "I feel like you just get me."

"Maybe we are lucky, the both of us," Eleanor said. "Perhaps we've come through so much so we could understand each other." Her eyes filled with tears. "I never had a daughter. And you never had a mother. And here we are." She suddenly grinned, giddy, and put her hands on Lila's face. "What a way to start this day," she said.

"Crying?" Lila asked with a laugh and a sniffle.

"No," she chuckled. "We started our day by finding a person who understands us. Maybe it's the first day of our happy ending."

"I like that," Lila said, giving Eleanor another squeeze.

"Hold this," Theo said at the café, having resumed his unsociable behavior, thrusting a bunch of lavender into her hands, the stems filling her nose with their floral aroma. His gaze landed to her and then skirted away before tending to another customer. He was supposed to be teaching her how to make all the signature lattes, but he'd been so busy with a bunch of to-go orders that it had been more piecemeal than lesson. She figured that worst case, she could ask him to write down the recipes.

Even if he was being ornery as usual, Lila was glad to be at the bustling coffee shop this morning. She'd slept with the Christmas lights on last night, feeling isolated way out there in the cabin on her own. Before she'd gone to bed, Eleanor had called and offered a different cabin for her, but she'd declined, not wanting to make more work for the old woman. She said she'd be just fine. But the old wood in Edie's room had started to smell musty from all the leaking water, and she'd been afraid to light a candle so late at night for fear she might fall asleep with it burning.

"Stuff the lavender into one of those mesh bags over there," Theo told her, wagging his finger at a stack of small steeping bags. He had the same look of irritation at the process of soaking lavender that he'd had when she'd asked him for almond milk. It was as if making anything other than a plain cup of black coffee bothered him.

He hadn't mentioned what had happened yesterday yet this morning, and with the way the shop was buzzing, he definitely wouldn't get much of a chance to. He turned away from her to ring up another customer.

Lila grabbed a mesh bag and did what she was told, while Theo handed the customer her change. "I've got a pot boiling in the kitchen," he said over his shoulder to Lila. "Drop the bag into the water, reduce it to simmer, and set the timer for three minutes."

Lila went back into the kitchen where a pot of water steamed on the stove. She released the bag of lavender into it and turned down the heat just a bit. Then she set the timer as he'd said. A wooden spoon sat nearby and she used it to stir the lavender water, watching the little bubbles fizz up from the bottom, thinking about when she'd first come in this morning.

She'd allowed her happiness to show when she'd walked in, looking forward to spending some time with Theo despite how up and down he could be, but he had been quiet. She had purposely left Eleanor's in time to come in a few minutes before opening so she could give him a chance to talk to her with just the two of them there, but he'd busied himself unpacking boxes in the back room, barely glancing in her direction. Then he'd gotten straight to work, training her, beginning with a caramel crunch latte and then rushing over to the first customers waiting at the door. As she stirred the lavender, she tried to guess what had caused his silence.

She set the spoon down and went out to see if Theo needed her, still thinking about him when—bam!—she slammed right into his chest. "Oh!" she cried, stumbling backward. Theo caught her, his strong hands steadying her in a flash.

"Sorry," she said.

"It's fine." He hurried past her, avoiding eye contact.

"You know, if you end up driving me home and you're this quiet, it's going to be a long journey..." she teased.

He finally looked over at her. "I'm not being quiet," he said.

"So what do you call this silence then?"

He pursed his lips. "Working."

She offered a challenging look. "Wanna see working? I'll show you working. Take over the lavender boiling." She walked back into the front and stood by the register.

Theo poked his head through the kitchen doorway. "But you don't know all the—" A customer came in so he stopped talking, gritting his teeth and retreating to the kitchen.

An elderly woman lumped her handbag onto the counter. "Y'all got just plain coffee?"

"Of course," she said with a smile.

The woman looked around the shop. "Theo's been itchin' to get me in here. He told me I should pop by sometime, but I can make my own coffee just fine in my housecoat at six in the mornin'. I don't need to be runnin' the streets for it."

Her candor gave Lila a burst of pleasure. "I totally understand," she said, shooting a grin over to Theo, but he moved out of sight. This woman was the type of person she could spend hours talking to—she could already tell. "What's your name?"

"Adele." The lady looked Lila up and down.

"Adele, it's nice to meet you," Lila replied. "Are you going to settle in and relax with us, or are you in a hurry?"

"I was gonna take it home with me."

"Well," Lila said, "you're more than welcome to stay by the fire over there for a chat, but I'll make your coffee in a to-go cup so if you need to head out, you can take it with you. How does that sound?"

Adele nodded. "That would be wonderful, thank you."

Lila grabbed a paper cup and filled it with the coffee that Theo had brewed this morning after she'd come in. "Are you all ready for Christmas?" she asked the woman as she snapped the lid on the cup.

"Nearly. I've still gotta get a gift for my grandson Rex."

"Rex from the Christmas tree farm? I met him the other day," Lila said, while hunting for the correct buttons on the register to ring up the order. "He's adorable."

"Yes," Adele said, perking up, clearly keen to talk about her grandson. "He's such an old soul. I have no idea what I should get him for Christmas."

"You know, we rode horses with little Rex, and he was such a delightful host," Lila told her. "He mentioned that he needed some tools to fix his saddle. Maybe you could find him some... That'll be three seventy-five," she said, proud of herself for ringing it up correctly. Luckily the register was similar to the one she'd used at work.

"Oh, like a little leather tool kit or somethin'?" Adele asked, getting excited as she handed over her money.

"Yes, exactly!" Lila put the bills into the cash holder at the bottom of the register and handed the woman her change as a line began to form, the next customer grabbing a paper coffee menu to make his selection.

"Thank you so much for the idea." Adele gathered her bag and cup. "You have a lovely Christmas, okay?"

"Yes, ma'am."

The woman stopped. "What was *your* name, dear?"

"Lila Evans."

"It was so very nice to meet you, Lila. I'll have to let Theo know how great an employee he's hired. You know, I've been waitin' for him to get a little help. He works so much…"

"Yes," Lila agreed, glancing over to the kitchen door, but Theo wasn't there. "Everyone should have a break now and again."

"He's been here almost a year now and he barely sees anyone," Adele said, speaking around another customer who was picking up a to-go order. "The locals don't like him," she whispered. "And they won't believe me when I tell them he's the kindest person someone could ever know."

Lila got the waiting customer's name and checked the bags lined on the counter for his order.

"The only reason we met him was because he inquired with Judd about having his plumbin' repaired when he first began renovatin' this place. He's such a lovely person if you can break through to him. Rex adores him."

Lila knew her hunch had been right. Theo had so much more to offer than what he'd shown her. She'd witnessed the way Rex reacted to him, how the child let his guard down, leaving his little grown-up persona behind and acting like a kid, allowing Theo to pick him up. She loved seeing the interaction between those two. "I can see why

Rex adores him," she said, her thoughts slipping out before she'd had a chance to consider saying them aloud.

"How long have *you* been here?" Adele asked, pulling her from her musings about Theo.

"Only a couple of days." She rang up the to-go order, easily finding the correct buttons on the register this time. She handed over the bag. "Thanks for coming in," she told the man who'd been waiting for his order.

He waved back to her on his way out the door.

"You should come to the town Christmas fair tomorrow night. Judd's hostin' it."

"There's a fair tomorrow night?" She immediately wished the vacation with her friends had worked out this year. Charlotte, Piper, and Edie would've loved to go.

"Yes. It's tons of fun. There's a Christmas parade, the local merchants set up tables at the farm, and there are all kinds of booths and rides. They've started settin' up the Ferris wheel today, actually." Adele took a step back toward Lila and whispered dramatically, "You should try to get Theo to go."

Lila chuckled, looking once more at the empty kitchen doorway, surprised that he'd left her alone this long. "I suppose I could try," she said. "But I'm not promising anything."

"It would be good to see him let loose."

Lila couldn't imagine Theo letting loose, but one thing was for sure—she definitely would like to be there if and when he did. She didn't have a chance to think about it too long before the other to-go orders came in.

"I'll see ya," Adele said on her way out the door.

"Sorry Adele Johnson held your ear for so long," Theo said, when she'd rung up the last customer for the moment. He was holding a silver pitcher of what she assumed was the lavender water. Two customers who'd been sitting in the dining room threw away their trash and left, leaving just the two of them in the shop.

"I didn't mind. It's good to talk to your customers," she said with a rebellious smile. "You might actually get to know someone if you do that."

"What if I don't want to know anyone?" He set the pitcher to the side and turned back to her.

"So you enjoy being an outsider? I can't think of anything worse."

He shrugged. "It's not the first time I've been an outsider."

"You were invited to the town Christmas party at the farm," she said. "I heard."

Lila cocked her head to the side. "You did? What else did you hear?"

"Enough to know that Adele Johnson just wants to meddle in my business."

Lila threw back her head and laughed. "She seems like a lovely woman. She was only inviting you to be neighborly."

"Look around. Do you think I moved *here* to be neighborly?"

Lila wondered exactly why he had moved to Pinewood Hills, but she was more focused on the farm's Christmas party.

"I dare you to go with me to the party tomorrow night," she said, ignoring his question. In truth, she hoped he would because she couldn't bear another night secluded in the cabin all by herself. "You know you want to."

He stared at her. Then he shook his head and turned his back to her.

"You're avoiding the question." She moved around his shoulder and tried to make eye contact, causing him to lean back, but the smile playing at the corners of his mouth only encouraged her. She went over and grabbed the small stack of receipts, holding them up in front of him. "These are my sales this morning. Whoever sells the most coffee today decides whether you go to the party tomorrow night."

"Let me take a look at those," he said, plucking them out of her hand. He flipped through them. "These were called in before you got here. They're mine."

"But I made the coffees and rang them up."

It was clear by the little sparkle in his eye that he enjoyed it when she challenged him.

"What are you worried about?" she said. "It's my first day and you're a seasoned pro at this. Surely you'll win…" She smiled deviously.

"Fine," he said. "But the tabs start now so we're even."

"Done." She held out her hand to shake on it.

When he shook her hand, she could've sworn there was affection in his grip, as he held it just a tick longer than he should have.

Chapter Eleven

It was nearly closing time. Lila had learned how to make every single drink on the menu—the only two that she still needed to use her cheat sheet to create were the triple-spice cappuccino and the ultra-filtered ristretto, and she had to wonder if he'd added those to the menu just to wind her up. Despite Theo's less-than-warm demeanor, Lila had had a ball working in the shop. She loved the opportunity to speak to so many wonderful people, and she enjoyed the chance to feel like she was a part of the community in a way. She and Theo had rushed to the register each time, both of them trying to be the first there to ring up their sale, and they'd made drinks at light speed. Not to mention the food orders—Lila could bag a couple of croissants in less than a second.

She put her hands inside the pocket of her apron, fingering the wad of receipts and wondering if she'd made enough sales to win the bet with Theo. They'd both been so busy trying to beat each other that they'd barely spoken the whole day, only sharing the odd stubborn grin, neither of them backing down.

"Ms. Witherspoon," Lila addressed a woman who she'd made conversation with earlier when she served her. "I just wanted to bring you a blueberry muffin on the house to say congratulations on your daughter's pregnancy. I know she's thrilled."

"Oh, thank you!" Ms. Witherspoon said with a wide smile. "That is so very kind of you."

Lila moved back to the bar, taking in Theo's disbelieving expression.

"I'll buy the muffin. I owe you three fifty," she whispered to him.

"Fine, but why did you offer her free food anyway?"

"Well, for one, it's a nice thing to do. But for another, it's the oldest trick in the book."

Like clockwork, Ms. Witherspoon came up to the bar to say goodnight and thank Lila again. "That muffin was the most delicious thing I've ever eaten," she said with wide eyes as she wrapped her scarf around her neck. "I would die for the recipe so I could make them."

"Well, I can't divulge the secret recipe," Lila replied, "but we've got a fresh batch right now. They'd be so great to take home to your family on this cold night. We're selling them for three fifty, but if you get a half-dozen, they're only two dollars apiece."

"Oh, yes!" she said. "I'll get twelve."

"Excellent." Lila elbowed Theo playfully as she put on a pair of gloves to retrieve the muffins. "Would you like any more coffee to go with them? It might be a nice after-dinner treat—we do have decaf."

"Do you sell coffee by the pot?" Ms. Witherspoon asked.

"We have a traveler's box for ten dollars."

"Done. I'll take it."

"Perfect. I'll get it all wrapped up for you." She winked at Theo and he rolled his eyes, but this time he allowed himself a little chuckle.

Lila danced into what had been Edie's room, where Theo was on a ladder, with his head and arms inside the hole he'd cut in the ceiling to repair the plumbing. His checked shirt was raised just slightly as he reached up, showing off the muscles in his torso, and Lila struggled to focus on anything else.

He'd come over straight after work, and she'd promised to fix him dinner if he got started right away. She didn't want him to have to be working through the night. He'd agreed and grabbed a change of clothes so he wouldn't have to eat while covered in sheetrock and water. With a casserole in the oven, Lila had begun tallying their receipts to see who'd won their little selling competition today.

"Guess what," she said, watching him work.

"What?" he returned, his focus still on the pipe as he twisted a wrench back and forth.

"I sold exactly eighteen dollars and thirty-two cents more than you did today."

He ducked out of the hole in the ceiling.

"Ms. Witherspoon won the contest for me." She waved a wad of receipts in the air.

"And I should trust your math?" He went back to the pipe without a reaction, not mentioning the town Christmas party. With a grunt, he pulled a large, rusty length of pipe out of the ceiling and climbed down the ladder, setting it on a tarp he'd brought in. Only then did he make eye contact.

"Of course you should trust me. I ring up bills and calculate tips for a living." She tried to ignore the fact that he had a five o'clock shadow which made him look incredibly handsome, despite his dirty clothes. There was something irresistibly rugged about him. "So that means you're taking me out tomorrow night."

He wiped his hands on his jeans and picked up a section of new pipe. "I don't go on dates," he said, on his way back up the ladder.

Lila shoved the receipts into the pocket of her jeans. "Why not?" she asked, stepping over the old pipe and looking up the ladder at him.

He twisted the new pipe into place. "They're useless."

"Useless? So you mean to tell me that meeting people and enjoying the company of others is *useless*?"

"Yes."

The timer on the oven went off, signaling the casserole had finished cooking.

"Dinner's ready," she said, wanting to continue the conversation.

That was the most ridiculous thing she'd ever heard. Lila couldn't imagine how she'd have gotten through the last few years without the companionship of others. The loss of her parents was more than anyone should have to deal with, and the fact that Theo would so flippantly say that being with people was useless made her blood boil. She could see now that getting Theo to enjoy himself was going to take a lot of work.

"I'm at a good stopping point for the night anyway," he said from the ladder, pulling her back into the present moment. He climbed down, his neck and face full of dust from the sheetrock that he tried unsuccessfully to brush off. "Do you mind if I jump in the shower really quickly?"

"No problem," she said, still wanting to shake him by the shoulders. If it killed her, she was going to change his mind. But she had her work cut out…

"What is all this?" Theo said, pulling her attention to the doorway, her breath catching on the sight of him in his fresh clothes and bare feet, his hair clean and wet from the shower.

His gaze swept across the small table, which she'd set with a tablecloth she'd found in the kitchen drawer and one of the candles that Piper had made burning in the center. Their plates were dressed with the dinner she'd prepared, and beside them, she'd placed a bottle of wine and two glasses.

"Practice," she said.

He walked around to her side, and to her surprise he pulled out her chair, although his expression seemed to show irritation. He sat down. "If you're expecting white tablecloths at the town Christmas party, you're in the wrong place."

"I'm not expecting that," she said. "But tonight isn't the Christmas party. It's dinner. You've worked a long day and you get to share a meal with a nice person." She batted her eyelashes playfully, that slight grin forming at the corners of his mouth before he straightened it back out.

"I know how to treat a person on a date," he said. "I just don't choose to go on dates." He sat down across from her, the flame from the candle showing off flecks of silver in his blue eyes.

"Why do you think they're useless?" she asked, resuming their conversation from before.

"Because I prefer to be by myself."

She picked up her glass of wine, the rich taste of it evening out her mood a bit. "And why is that?"

He scooped up a forkful of casserole and took a bite, not answering.

"You're not going to tell me?"

"Will it improve your life in any way if I gave you a reason?"

"Maybe not," she said, "but it might improve yours."

"*Me* telling *you* my thoughts would improve my life? I don't need therapy, thanks." He took another bite.

"Letting someone in isn't a bad thing," she told him gently. "I'd listen if you'd let me." When he didn't respond, she decided to change the topic. Perhaps she was asking too much of him right now. "I haven't seen Eleanor yet tonight. Wanna go with me later to have a visit?"

"No," he said quickly.

"Why not?" Her shoulders slumped in defeat. She couldn't get him to budge on anything. Then suddenly, she remembered that Eleanor had called him "a nightmare." She leaned in toward him on her forearms. "You've met Eleanor, yes?"

He focused his attention on his plate.

"I'm going to go out on a limb and say that you might not have been very nice to her when you met, am I right?"

He chewed slowly, but she thought she could see the guilt in his face.

"You treated her like you treated us when we came in, didn't you?"

"I had a lot going on, all right?" he snapped. "I'm not proud of it."

She smiled warmly at him. "And now you're fixing her broken plumbing for free, and that's really kind of you."

He took a long gulp of wine from his glass, clearly reflecting on something.

"She's a lovely woman, and I'm sure she'd welcome you with open arms," Lila pressed. "*And* it would give you a chance to apologize for not being at your best when she came in."

"Why do you care what she thinks of me?" he asked seriously.

She shrugged, unsure herself. "Maybe it's because I feel like we all have something to give to ourselves and others. You just need a little push."

"Why, though? Why do you feel that way? I really just want you to leave me alone and go back to wherever you came from."

His words stung Lila, but she wouldn't be deterred that easily.

He grabbed his napkin from his lap and set it on the table, standing up. "You're so frustrating," he said, running his fingers through his hair.

She put her fork on her plate and got up from her chair. "Well, I don't have to be frustrating," she said, standing behind him. "Come with me to Eleanor's."

Carefully, she threaded her fingers between his, and an electric current ran through her when he caressed the palm of her hand with his thumb, confusing her and making her struggle to keep focus. He turned around and faced her, still holding her hand. She thought she saw that vulnerability flash in his eyes and then he closed up again.

"You're so frustrating," he said again, "because I like...how thoughtful you are and how you see the best in me, even when I try not to allow it." He shook his head. "I don't want anyone in my life right now, but...I can't stop thinking about you."

"I want to know you, but I don't even know your last name," she said with a little laugh. "Mine's Evans. Lila Evans. What's yours?"

He let go of her hand. "I, uh... I don't tell anyone who I am."

"You won't tell me your last name?" she said, wrinkling her nose in utter confusion. Why wouldn't he tell her that? Then something Piper had mentioned when they'd first gotten there came back to her; she recalled her friend saying the owner was mysterious and signed all the transactions for the coffee shop as Brian Brown. "Who's Brian Brown?" she asked.

"What?" he asked.

"Is your name Theo Brown?" she asked, confused.

"No..." He got his dish and pushed the leftovers into the trashcan with his fork, setting his plate in the sink.

"Are you in the witness protection program or something?" she asked playfully. But then she sobered. "Wait, *are* you?"

"No," he said, clearly amused despite the fact he'd rather not be. "I don't tell just anyone my last name. Look, are we going to see Eleanor Finely or not?" He grabbed her coat and handed it to her.

"That's because your last name is Wolfersnauzerrobertsutzen," she teased. "And you don't know how to spell it. I can just call you Theo W."

He rolled his eyes, slipping on his own coat.

She opened the door. "Maybe it rhymes and you don't like the way it sounds. Theo Brio? It actually has a nice ring to it…"

He stepped out the door and closed it behind them.

"Maybe it's Theo DiCaprio, and it's so close to Leo that everyone gets you confused with the famous actor."

"Will you stop?" he asked on their way down the stairs. A grin broke through and he shook his head. "You're ridiculous."

"*I'm* ridiculous? I'm not the one who won't tell his date his last name."

"We're not on a date," he said, exasperated.

"Then why did you stay for dinner?"

"You're obsessive," he said, trying to hide his laugh.

"I'm optimistic. There's a difference."

"You're crazy," he teased.

"Maybe, but neither you nor your coffee shop have a name. Kind of weird if you ask me…"

"Is there a better name for a coffee shop than Coffee? Why does it have to be something else?" he challenged.

"You want to draw people in, give them a *feeling*." She touched her fingers to her thumbs in the meditation stance, making him chuckle. The truth was, she did get a feeling whenever she was in there, and she thought they could convey it to others. Lila felt friendship and camaraderie, coziness and good cheer—even when he was in one of his foul moods.

"People will come if they want coffee."

"What if you named it..." She stopped and faced him. "Theo's Coffee? Make it more personal."

He shook his head.

"Or more eclectic, like *Dairy Coffee—we don't do almond milk?*"

He cracked a smile.

"You could call it Something Different! That's a great name for your coffee house." She gave him a big, cheesy grin. "Because the shop *and* its owner are definitely...different."

"What's wrong with the shop the way it is?"

"You actually want my opinion?" she asked.

"Not really, to be honest," Theo replied.

"It needs character. People don't want just coffee. If they did, they'd make it at home. They want the atmosphere. What are you offering them that they can't get in their kitchens?"

"I'm plenty busy with just the coffee." He started walking again, taking a path that led between two barren maple trees.

"Right, but it's mostly to-go orders," she said, keeping pace beside him. "What about creating a spot where the community can come and take a load off? You want to keep your customers coming back for more, give them something they can't get anywhere else—you. And on the rare occasions when you allow me to see your personality, I have no doubt that if you let them in on who you are, your shop would be standing room only."

"What if I like it the way it is?"

"Don't you want everyone to know about your shop? Don't you want people to—"

He froze, his jaw clenching. "No," he clipped. Then he pulled ahead of her, his feet crunching on the frozen grass, his strides too big to keep up with. Confused, she jogged to catch up with him, but that only seemed to make him speed up more.

"What did I say?"

"Nothing," he said, shutting her down, but she wasn't budging.

"You're right," she said straight back to him. "I said *nothing* wrong. You work in retail, but you don't want to talk to anybody. You sell a product, but you don't take time to market it or provide everything the customer needs."

"Look, there's a reason I am the way I am, and nothing you say is going to change it."

"Tell me the reason then," she demanded.

"Something happened…" He snapped his mouth shut, turning his gaze toward the tree line as he clomped away from her.

"You can't just stay closed off forever."

"Says who? You? Because you know what I've dealt with? You know what it's like to *have* to create a different life for yourself, whether you wanted it or not? I don't think you do."

When they got to the porch of Eleanor's house, Lila was out of breath and still wondering what had just happened between them. Theo stomped up the stairs and she stopped him just as he knocked on the door.

"What in the world is the matter?"

"You don't get it at all! And you don't need to. Just butt out."

She flinched, needing a minute to get her bearings again. "Something is clearly eating at you, and you can't possibly go through life like this. You'll never survive it."

He turned away from her, but she stepped in front of him.

"My parents died," she said. "I don't have a single person apart from those three girls I walked into your shop with who gives a hoot about me, and I don't love my job or even know what I want to do in life, but never have I let any of it eat at me until I treated others the way you're treating me right now. Whatever happened to you isn't who you are, and I pray that you figure that out sooner rather than later, because in the meantime, you're wasting a whole lot of precious moments."

Eleanor opened the door, slicing through the moment. "Oh, hello," she said cautiously, when she registered that Theo was at her door.

"Hi, Ms. Finely," he said calmly, having clearly worked to get himself together. "I just wanted to come by with Lila to tell you that I'm sorry if I wasn't hospitable when you came into the coffee shop. I'm not the greatest at..." He looked over at Lila. "I'm not great at being friendly with people right now." His chest filled with air and then he let out the breath. "But I shouldn't have taken out my own frustrations on you. I'm sorry."

"Oh, dear, that's just fine. Thank you for the apology, and thank you for offering to fix the pipe out in the cabin." She ushered them in. "It's freezing. Why don't you two come on inside and warm up."

Lila pushed aside the hurt and irritation she'd felt on the doorstep and went inside. A little flutter of happiness floated up inside her once she was in the cabin. Eleanor had tidied up, all the Christmas lights were glowing, and the tree glistened in the corner. The gifts Lila and Piper had wrapped up were still sitting under the tree.

"The fire's dwindling," Eleanor said, hurrying herself over to it. "Let me get it going for us."

"I've got it," Theo said, as he picked up a couple of logs from the hearth and threw them onto the fire, making the flames crackle and hiss.

"Thank you so much," Eleanor said. Then she clasped her hands together hospitably. "Would either of you like to have anything to drink? I've got some cider I can warm up."

"Don't worry yourself for us," Lila told her, sitting down on the sofa. "I—we—just wanted to pop over to see how you were doing."

"Same as always," she said. "Thanks for checking on me. It's chilly in here. I'm going to get myself a mug of cider to keep warm, so I'll go ahead and make three. It's no trouble. Y'all chat and I'll be back in a second." She bustled into the kitchen.

Once they were alone, Theo came over and sat down next to Lila. "I'm sorry," he said quietly.

"Thank you," she told him with a smile. "And if you do it again, I'll call you out on it every single time, so you'd better not."

He allowed a little show of affection in his eyes.

They sat together in the quiet house, the silence heavy between them.

Then Theo noticed a guitar on a holder in the corner of the room. The silence must have been getting to him because he stood up and went over to it, lifting it off the holder and spreading his fingers across the strings on the neck. He carried it over to the sofa, picking out a chord and then tuning it. Then, out of nowhere, he began to play. His fingers moved effortlessly. He strummed the tune to "Silent Night," and it was so beautiful in the stillness and hush of the cabin under the white Christmas lights that it gave Lila goose bumps.

Eleanor came in with a tray of mugs and set them down on the coffee table. "You are wonderfully talented," she said, bringing one of the mugs to the table nearer to him.

"I wouldn't say that. I play a little bit," he said modestly. "Do you?"

"Oh, no, dear. I can't play a lick. That guitar belonged to my husband."

"Hmm," he said, thoughtful.

Eleanor picked up her mug but didn't drink from it. Her eyes glistened with tears for the lost love of her life.

Lila lifted the mug to her lips, inhaling the cinnamon and nutmeg before she took a sip, savoring the delicious flavors.

"I wouldn't want Chester to see what's become of this place," Eleanor said. "My husband worked so hard to make the cabins beautiful." She shifted in her chair, moving her reading glasses from the arm where they'd been sitting to the small table beside her. She took in a deep breath and closed her eyes, a soft smile on her lips at the memory. "The grounds were so pretty back then. Nothing like they are today. We had endless wooden walkways that led through the woods to scenic overlooks of the hills, with little signs that told the history of the area. The whole trail was covered in wildflowers—Chester and I scattered the seeds every year. Oh, it was so beautiful..." She let out a wistful sigh.

"I'm trying to keep it going," she continued, "but it's been harder and harder. There's so much to offer in this little town, but I need a miracle to draw people out here these days." She set her mug down and swiped a tissue from the box on the table. "I don't know why I'm telling you both this," she said.

"Edie works in PR. Maybe I can pick her brain to see what she'd suggest that could help boost sales."

Eleanor nodded but didn't seem encouraged. "It would take a lot. I'm clearly not great at giving people what they want these days."

"Don't be so hard on yourself. My friends and I loved it from the website, and while it wasn't quite what we thought it would be, it's still a great place to stay. We've loved being here."

"Lila, dear," replied Eleanor. "That's kind of you to say, yet everyone has left but you, and you're sitting here with the plumber because your cabin is full of water. Not exactly the vacation spot you were hoping for, I'm sure."

"She's actually sitting with a barista, if you want to get technical," Theo said, obviously trying to lighten the mood, which warmed Lila's heart. He started strumming again quietly.

Eleanor looked happier after his comment. She closed her eyes and swayed to the gentle lilt of music before taking a sip of her drink.

"We'll figure it out," Lila said. She wasn't sure how, exactly, but she was going to do everything she could to save Fireside Cabins.

Chapter Twelve

Lila stood next to Theo's old Ford truck, bundled up to her chin to keep warm. She had her hands on her hips, staring at the roofline of her cabin after their chat with Eleanor, her breath puffing out in front of her from the cold. "These cabins would be so pretty if they were decorated with Christmas lights."

Theo didn't protest, which wasn't like him. She'd expected some sort of shrugging-off, but he'd remained quiet.

"I guess it'll take more than Christmas lights to get this place going again," she carried on, but he hadn't seemed to hear her, his eyes on his phone.

"I have to go," he said abruptly, his face like stone. He ran around to the other side of his truck, getting in and starting the engine.

"I'm coming with you!" she said, climbing up inside and shutting the door. The sight of his face just now had scared her, and there was no way she was letting him go without knowing what was happening. "What's the matter?" Lila asked.

"I have five missed calls and a text from Rex on the cell phone his dad gave him to use for emergencies when he's out on the farm. He said he's lost in the woods behind his house and doesn't know how to get home."

"Oh no."

"Judd and Trudy are probably still working in the fields and aren't answering their phones. They probably think Rex is playing in the yard near the house like he always does."

Theo pulled out, hugging the curves of the private drive as they made their way through the hills and down to the main road. He was quiet, focused, both hands tightly on the wheel as the truck whooshed past the frozen evergreens, the sky an inky black without a star to be seen. Lila shifted in her seat, her feet hitting a pair of work gloves on the floor, and stared at the white beams from the headlights shining on the dark asphalt of the road.

"You seem to know Rex really well," she noted, eyeing him to judge his level of worry.

"Yeah. I give him guitar lessons."

"You're a music teacher too?" she asked, surprised.

"No. I just help Rex. I was playing my guitar when Judd was teaching me how to repair the plumbing, and he asked if I'd show Rex how to play. Judd offered to waive the charges for any future plumbing on the shop in exchange."

"Did Rex give an indication in his text about where he could be?"

"Not really." Theo's jaw clenched. He was noticeably worried. "He just said, 'Come quick. My leg is hurt.'"

"Oh my gosh." Lila clasped a hand over her mouth. "It's freezing outside. We have to find him."

"We will," he assured her, although she had no idea how he could be so certain, given the immense expanse of woods surrounding the property. "If he has to go to the hospital though, the nearest one is twenty miles away."

"So Rex is out in the wilderness, all alone in the dark?" Lila felt a swell of panic, thinking of Rex trying to manage by himself with an injured leg.

"He's too young to be by himself. Actually, why don't you text him now to let him know I'm on my way?" Theo fished his phone from his pocket, put in his Touch ID, and handed it to Lila. "Tell him we're about three minutes away."

Lila messaged Rex and waited for a reply, her heart pounding like a snare drum when the little boy didn't answer. She handed the phone back to Theo. The vast hills rolled past them, adding to the bleak darkness that surrounded the truck.

When they got to the farm, Theo parked outside the old farmhouse and bounded up the stairs to the long country porch, ripping open the screen door and then the main one with Lila right on his heels. A large pot that sat empty for the winter teetered precariously when Theo rushed past it. Lila caught it, steadying it before she went inside.

"Trudy? Judd?" he called out, his head swiveling back and forth. Theo grabbed Lila's hand and took off down the hallway, leading the way to the area of the farm open to tourists, the shimmering Christmas trees lining the path that took them through the crowds of eager shoppers, past the horse ring, and out to the Christmas tree lot where they found Judd.

"Y'all look like you've seen a ghost," he said with a bright smile, as he lifted a tree out of its stand and bent down to place it on the ground so he could tie it up for a waiting couple.

Theo leaned over and whispered in Judd's ear, and suddenly the man's face matched theirs, the tree dropping with a whooshing thud. "I'm terribly sorry," he said to the couple. "Paul!" he called to one of the workers. "Come tie their tree up for them." Then Judd, Theo, and Lila made a dash for the woods behind the house.

"I'll take the northeast corner of the farm," Judd said with purpose. "He sometimes likes to play there. I'll try to call him." He took off, pressing his phone to his ear as he ran.

"Let's go," Theo said, grabbing Lila's hand. "I have another idea of where to check." They sprinted through the field toward the side lot that butted up next to the woods. "It's not like him to leave the farm. He usually stays close. But there's a family of deer over here that he loves to watch. He always sends me photos."

Lila's fingers were already numb, and she couldn't feel her nose. She worried about how cold Rex must be by now. "Think he's watching them now?" she said, her head rotating back and forth frantically, searching for the little boy.

"I wonder if he followed them into the tree line and didn't realize how far he'd gotten." He pulled out his phone. "It's worth a shot to try to text him and ask." When he didn't get a reply, he started calling. "Rex!"

They entered the dark woods, and Lila joined in. "Rex!"

Theo kept hold of her hand as they navigated the thick brush between the trees, and he seemed to notice her trembling, squeezing her fingers in his reassuringly. "We'll find him."

They walked for quite some time, all the while keeping the original tree line in sight so as not to turn back on themselves. The air was crisp and eerily silent, the only sound coming from the snapping of twigs under their feet as they made their way further into the forest. Suddenly, Lila spotted something—a pulse of light from the icy ground. Theo rushed over to it and picked it up.

"It's Rex's phone," he said. "Damn spotty service. My text just now went through." Then a rustle from beside them caught their attention.

With a tear-streaked face, Rex came running toward them, wrapping his arms around Theo's waist and burying his head into his coat, sobbing.

Lila let out an exhale so big it felt like she'd held all the air she had in her lungs while they'd searched.

"Hey, buddy," Theo said calmly to Rex as he went to work, checking Rex's legs. "What happened?"

"I almost touched the deer," Rex said through his tears. He buried his head again, and Theo comforted him, opening his coat and wrapping him in for warmth. "And I saw two more, so I wanted to try to pet them even though I knew they'd never let me. I fell in a hole and hurt my leg." Rex reached down, holding his right ankle.

"How does it feel now?" Theo asked, his voice soothing and tender.

"It's a little better."

"Okay," he said, clearly relieved. "This is my friend Lila. She came with me to help find you," he explained.

Lila smiled at Rex as he looked up from Theo's coat. "Remember when Theo took me on a horse ride, and you stayed with my friends?"

"Yeah, I 'member." Rex wiped his tears with the back of his sleeve.

Theo picked him up. "Lila, could you call Judd and tell him we found Rex?" He tossed her his phone.

As Lila held the phone, selecting Judd's name from Theo's contact list with still-shaking hands, Theo spoke softly to Rex, telling him it would be okay and he knew the way home.

Rex sniffled, his top lip wobbling as he nodded, all traces of his earlier persona melted down to just a scared, tiny five-year-old.

"I got him," Lila said. She handed Theo his phone. "He's meeting us at the house."

*

A sleeping hound dog met Theo, Lila, and Rex inside the front door as they entered the old farmhouse, a blast of heat from the fire inside thawing them out.

"What's his name?" Lila asked, when Rex wriggled down from Theo's arms to hug his pet.

"His name's Winston," Rex said.

Winston raised his head, his ears perking up at his name. When nothing else happened, he put his snout back onto his paws and exhaled loudly, completely oblivious to everything that had just gone on.

"Oh, my baby!" Trudy cried, as she rushed toward them from the back of the house with Judd on her heels.

"He was chasing deer," Theo said, ruffling Rex's hair.

"The farm is so busy right now that we can hardly keep up. Rex is always helping, but I wish he didn't have to work with us all day. Rex, honey, you never follow those animals into the woods, okay? Even if you get bored. You find us." Trudy's eyes glistened with emotion as she pulled her son into an enormous embrace. Judd wrapped his large arms around his little family.

"Thank you," Judd said, his emotion causing his words to break as he said them.

"It's no problem," Theo said. "Hey, if you're busy tomorrow, I don't mind taking Rex for the day. Lila and I can take him out somewhere fun." He gave Lila a small smile of solidarity.

"You can drop him by my cabin in the morning if you want to," Lila added.

Rex lit up as though it was Christmas morning. "Can I, Mama?"

"Of course," Trudy said.

Then Rex gave Theo a big hug. "Thank you for saving me," he said.

"You're welcome." Theo gave him a squeeze right back.

Lila was overcome watching the two of them, knowing that this night could've turned out so differently were it not for Theo's quick thinking. He'd been a hero in every way tonight, and from the look in Rex's eyes, the little boy thought so too.

Lila patted the empty spot on the sofa in the cabin. She'd asked Theo to come back with her, her nerves still a wreck after the whole ordeal. Now she struggled to keep her eyes open, the events of the night getting the better of her. Exhausted, she rested her head on Theo's shoulder, noticing how his chest was rising and falling steadily, and when she pulled her eyes away from it to look up at him, he offered her a brooding smile. "I'll go so you can get to bed," he whispered, getting up, but she stopped him.

"Stay just a little longer," she said. Resting her elbow on the back of the couch, she leaned on her hand. She was barely able to stay awake. She'd just close her eyes for a second . . .

She wasn't sure how long it had been since she'd drifted off, but she felt Theo slip his arms around her, pulling her gently toward him where she rested in the crook of his arm. She was so comfortable that she dared not open her eyes to ruin the moment. Then, just as she was starting to drift away again, she heard Theo whisper something to her, evidently thinking she was fast asleep.

"My last name is Perry," he said, barely making a sound with his words. "Theo Perry."

Chapter Thirteen

There was a loud pulse across the room, causing Lila to swim out of her sleep. She was increasingly aware of how comfortable she was, and the tranquility of the silence between each ping. Her body was heavy with the absolute calmness she felt in that moment, and she had to force herself to keep from slipping back into dreamland. Finally, she opened her eyes, only to realize that she and Theo were still cuddled up together on the sofa. Her head rested on his chest, his arm draped over her, his steady breathing coming to an abrupt stop under her cheek. They both shot up quickly.

"That's probably Trudy and Rex, texting," she said, running her fingers through her disheveled hair.

Theo stood, blinking as if to clear his focus, his breathing still deep and relaxed as his body coped with the jolt of waking so quickly. He yawned, stretching his arms, and then straightening his wrinkled shirt before walking over to get his phone. "Yeah, it's Rex," he said with a sleepy grin as he returned a text. "He's excited to go out with us today."

"I'll jump in the shower," she said, glad for the diversion so they wouldn't have to figure out how to interact with each other in this intimate situation. "Want to run home, and then come back and pick me up when you're ready?"

"Yes," he said, pulling the keys out of his pocket. "I'll bring you a coffee."

"You will?" she asked, unable to hide her delight over the gesture.

"Yeah." He grinned. "Back in a bit."

Lila fluffed the pillows on the sofa, smoothing out the dip in the cushions where she and Theo had awakened this morning, when Theo came in, carrying a to-go cup of coffee in each hand.

"For you," he said, handing hers over.

Lila took it gratefully. She'd jumped straight into the shower after Theo had left. They'd gotten up so late that now it was after lunchtime, and all she'd had was a couple of pieces of leftover bacon she had in the fridge. She sat down in the chair across from Theo to wait for Trudy and Rex, basking in the slip of time she had to take in the lights of the Christmas tree and drink her coffee. She took a long, slow sip, her gaze landing on Theo.

"Is this...an *almond* milk latte?" she asked.

Theo laughed. "It came in a selection of milks I ordered," he said. "I didn't order it especially." He'd never admit it; she knew that much.

"Of course," she said, biting back her happiness.

Their conversation was interrupted by a knock. Lila went to stand up, but Theo motioned for her to stay and relax.

"I'll get the door," he told her.

As Theo came in with Trudy and Rex, Lila set her coffee on the side table and stood up to greet them.

"How's your leg?" Theo asked.

"Good," Rex answered, giving him a high-five.

"I think it was just a twist," Trudy said. "He was running around the house this morning—the best sight ever." She played with the collar on his coat affectionately. "Thank you for taking him out for a bit today."

"Of course," Theo replied, and Trudy headed out, giving them a goodbye wave over her shoulder. "It's after lunchtime already. Wanna get something to eat?"

Rex's eyes lit up. "Yes, sir! I'm starvin'. Can we go to Arnold's?"

Lila sent Theo a questioning look.

"Arnold's is a local hamburger joint in town," Theo explained.

"You know what it's famous for?" Rex asked, beginning to bounce with excitement. "Horseshoe throwin'."

"Horseshoe throwing?" she repeated, to be sure she'd heard him correctly. "A hamburger place with horseshoes?"

"But not just any kind," Rex said. "They're real heavy and you've gotta throw 'em through this bull's-eye hole in the wall."

A tiny smirk formed at the edges of Theo's mouth. "We should get Lila to throw some of those horseshoes. She loves stuff like that."

"Really?" Rex assessed Lila, looking her up and down.

"Yeah—horseshoes, mountain climbing...she's real outdoorsy."

Lila cut her eyes at Theo playfully. Then she squatted down by Rex. "I'd like to play horseshoes with *you*," she said. "Will you show me how?"

"Yes, ma'am!" Rex said with a huge grin.

Arnold's was nestled into one of the hillsides just above town, jutting out of it like a wild rock. It had a stone front with chocolate brown clapboard sides, and a stout chimney that sat in the center of the old tin roof. An old 1950s neon sign outlined in Christmas greenery flashed its name out front, and an icy river rushed past them to the side of the restaurant. Theo pulled the truck into the gravel parking lot and came to a stop.

"Have you ever been bull ridin', Miss Lila?" Rex asked. "There's one at the fair. You oughta do it." Rex had been talking a mile a minute all the way to the restaurant.

"There's a bull at the Christmas fair?" Lila asked.

"A mechanical one," Theo explained, cutting the engine. "They put a Christmas wreath around the horns." He rolled his eyes for Lila's benefit, before addressing Rex. "You know, Lila and I are going to the fair tonight." He grinned deviously at her over Rex's head, and she knew he was already thinking of trying to get her on that thing. But it didn't matter to her one bit, because he'd just said he was going to the fair. She never thought she'd hear him say those words.

They hopped out of the truck and headed inside. A wave of heat from the giant stone fireplace in the center of the large space and the charcoal smell of the grill engulfed Lila. She paced across the cement floor, stopping when Rex bent down to try to pry out one of the old coins embedded in it throughout.

"You won't ever be able to get one of those to come out," a portly man with ruddy cheeks and a kind smile said to Rex, as he walked over to them. "He tries every time he comes in..." He clapped Theo on the back. "Nice to see you again, sir."

Theo nodded hello.

The man turned back to Rex and Lila. "Glad you could get this guy out of his little coffee shop. Sometimes I think he sniffs too many coffee beans because no matter how hard I try, I can't get him in here. And who wouldn't want to come?" He waved a chubby arm around the establishment, and Lila took in the wall of flat-screen televisions, the chandeliers made of antlers hanging from rafters constructed with smooth logs that reached up to the center of the stone chimney, and the enormous fresh Fraser fir tree full of rustic ornaments in the corner.

The man leaned in toward Lila as if he had a secret to tell. "We have Wednesday night football here, and we're just itching to get some new blood into our fantasy football pools, but this one won't budge. I was thrilled when I heard he'd moved into town, but then he stayed inside that coffee shop and never came out." He held out his hand. "Buddy Bennett."

Lila shook his hand. Then he reached down and offered one to Rex, who was still trying to get the coin out of the floor. The little boy refocused and shook Buddy's hand.

"Rex, have you ever heard the story of how those coins got into the floor?"

"No, sir," Rex said, still picking at one of them.

"The gold belt snakes through this part of Tennessee all the way to North Carolina," Buddy told them. "When the first owner built the original floor, he whittled out little divots in the wood to house the coins he'd found in a watering hole on the property. But kiddos like you, Rex—and I'm guessing thieves in the night as well—picked them out, so many, many years later, they were laid in concrete and glossed over with a sealer. Those coins were from the gold rush of the 1800s."

"Oh?" Lila peered down at the coins.

"Back in 1831, I think it was, people emptied their old coins into the watering hole that sat on the property to make room in their pouches for the gold they were fixin' to find. But when they got to pannin' in the river, they discovered there wasn't enough gold in there to make any of them rich, so they moved on to other places. You can still see flecks of that gold on a low day in the river outside."

Rex's eyes grew big. "Can we try to get some?"

Buddy laughed, his belly heaving like old St. Nicholas. "I reckon you can, but you might want to wait until the warmer months if you'd like to keep your fingers. It's so cold in the shade that frostbite'll take 'em right off." He reached over and grabbed a handful of menus from the hostess station. "Where'd you like to sit today—your choice."

"We wanna throw horseshoes," Rex told him excitedly.

A big smile split Buddy's flushed face. "You do, do ya? Well, I'll give you the table next to the horseshoe toss. Come on to the back with me." He started toward a small hallway on the side of the main dining area as they all followed. "How many are throwin'?" he asked over his shoulder.

"Three!" Rex said excitedly. "We're gonna show Lila how to do it, aren't we, Theo?"

Theo bit back a smile.

"All right," Buddy told them, as they reached a table next to an enormous horseshoe pit. It had old burlap bags at the bottom to soften the fall of the horseshoes, and instead of a stake in the ground for a game of horseshoes, there was a hole in the wall. "Here are your menus. I'll grab you some horseshoes."

They all took a seat as Buddy grabbed an armful of horseshoes and brought them over, hanging them on a hook at the side of their table.

"I have a suggestion," Theo said. "We should all get Mountain Burgers."

Lila scanned her menu for a description but couldn't spot it. "What's a mountain burger?"

Theo beamed conspiratorially at Rex, who giggled. "It's a secret, off-menu burger, and I promise, you'll love it." Rex snickered again. "And if you can eat it all, you get a little trophy with a real gold nugget on top."

"It's gigantic!" Rex said with a laugh.

"Shh," Theo told him, his finger over his smiling lips. "Let's let her get one and see."

"Fine," she said, ready to take the challenge. "We can all have Mountain Burgers."

"Did I hear you say you are all getting the Mountain Burger?" Buddy asked, stepping up to their table.

"Yes, sir!" Rex said, his eyes nearly squinting shut with his enormous grin.

"All right! Two adult Mountain Burgers and one kiddie Mountain Burger, coming up. What will you have to drink?"

"I'll have a glass of iced tea," Lila said.

Buddy clasped his hands together. "Perfect. And you, Theo?"

"I'll do the same."

"Excellent," Buddy said.

"Milk for me, please," Rex told him.

"Got it. Enjoy the horseshoes." Buddy headed off to the kitchen.

Theo stood up and pulled the horseshoes from their spot on the side of the table, handing one to Lila and one to Rex. "Think you can do this?" he asked Lila, as he deftly spun the horseshoe around his finger.

"Of course," she said, faking confidence. Lila held hers with both hands, the weight of the thing substantial. She dared not be careless with it. It would certainly hurt if she dropped it on her foot or something, which wasn't out of the question. She stepped up to the pit and Theo came up behind her.

"You want to hold it like this." He took her hand, making her work to hide her smile, and set the horseshoe in her palm, closing her fingers around it. "Then it's kind of like bowling, but you really have to give it a good toss when you let it go, to make it sail far enough to get it into the hole. Want me to show you how?"

"I think I've got it," she said.

"You sure? You might want me to show you."

"I can do it." She didn't really know if she could, but she didn't want to give him the satisfaction.

Lila stared at the hole, swinging her arm a few times, getting her aim. On the third swing she let go with a heave, closing her eyes as the horseshoe left her fingers. When she didn't hear the thud of it hitting the floor, she opened them and slapped her hand over her mouth as the horseshoe went into the hole. Bull's-eye!

"Dang! Lila got it in first try!" Rex jumped around, slapping his leg with his free hand.

Theo stared at Lila wide-eyed. "How did you do that?"

She had absolutely no idea. Beginner's luck, she guessed. "Skill," she said instead, with a smirk.

"Theo, you go next," Rex said. "You have to show her up."

Theo laughed, stepping up to the spot and holding out his hand while squinting one eye to focus on his shot. "I'm a champion at this," he said.

"You're all talk," Lila teased, making Rex throw his head back in amusement.

Theo's arm swung back and then forward, the horseshoe sailing from his hand and landing with a thud on the bags, short of his mark. His mouth hung open. "Hang on a minute. What?" He went into the pit and retrieved his horseshoe, inspecting it. "I need another one," he said. "There must be something wrong with this one."

Lila couldn't help the laugh that escaped from her lips.

Theo went over to the table and replaced his horseshoe with another while Rex took his spot, lining up for a smaller hole in the wall under theirs, obviously made for kids. He sunk it in the hole on his first shot.

"Yeah!" Rex danced around.

"Nice shot, Rex!" Lila took a second horseshoe. After a couple of practice swings, when she had her momentum, she let it go, and into the hole it went. "This is surprisingly easy," she said.

Theo took his new horseshoe up to the line and spent a minute strategizing. Then he tossed it. It bounced off the wall a few inches from the hole and landed on the bags. "Is this some kind of prank?" he asked.

Lila and Rex both doubled over in hysterics.

"Seriously, are you all giving me some kind of weird horseshoes?" He examined it again, making Lila and Rex hoot with laughter. He stuck his arm into the hole in the wall and pulled a horseshoe out. "I'm using Lila's next time."

"Suit yourself," she said.

Rex got another one in his hole and high-fived Lila.

Lila went up to the line. "Think I can get three out of three?" she asked Rex.

"Yes, ma'am!" Rex said with his hands on his little knees, poised to watch her throw.

Sending hers into the air, Lila got it right in the hole. "Theo's turn!" she said, offering him her flirtiest grin. This was the most fun she'd had in ages.

Theo stepped up to his spot, his game face on. He released his final horseshoe, and they all watched as it made a perfect line for the bull's-eye. But when it reached its target, one side of it was just short and it bounced out, hitting the floor.

"Come on..." Theo said.

In a fit of laughter, Rex climbed up on his chair at the table.

Theo joined him, shaking his head. "I cannot believe that just happened," he said with a chuckle of his own. "Unbelievable." When Lila took a seat beside him, he said, "I'm challenging you to a rematch later."

Just then the waitress brought out their Mountain Burgers, setting the plates in front of each of them. Lila's eyes widened at the sight in front of her. A towering display of three beef patties that bulged over the bottom bun, each of them separated by cheese, avocado, lettuce, tomato, a row of both onion rings and fries—the whole thing topped with fried mozzarella, all the condiments, and the other half of the bun, held together by a pickle skewer.

"How do I bite into this?" she asked, picking it up. Half the ingredients fell onto her plate, making both Theo and Rex laugh.

"Very carefully," Theo replied. "I've heard there's an entire avocado's worth of slices between every layer."

Lila lifted the massive burger to her lips and nibbled part of it. "It's really good," she said. Then she looked over at Theo. "Hey, you're cheating," she said with a chuckle.

Theo had taken his apart and was cutting little slices of it with his knife and fork. "Not if I eat it all," he said. "It's strategy."

"I don't think you'll need strategy. I might just let you win this one," she said with another bite of her burger.

"Like I let you all win at horseshoes?" he asked.

"You did not *let* us win! Did he, Rex?"

"No way," Rex said, his fingers a mess of mayo and ketchup. "We won fair and square."

Lila shook her head, amused, but she didn't let this little moment go by without thinking about how wonderful it was. She'd miss things like this when she went back to her lonely apartment in Nashville.

Chapter Fourteen

"Do it, Theo!" Rex said. The little boy eyed the gate full of rodeo hopefuls, who were all vying to ride victoriously on a mechanical bull dressed with Christmas bells on its horns and a wreath around its base. Or at the very least, they'd all decided to escape the cold of the fair outside for the heated tents full of fresh, hot caramel corn, s'mores-making stations, photos with Santa, and—of course—Christmas bull riding. Although with her big coat and scarf, and the area heaters positioned throughout the fair, Lila felt surprisingly cozy.

Theo and Lila had taken Rex to the fair while Trudy and Judd ran the special booths they'd set up at the farm. She'd asked Eleanor if she'd like to come with them, but Eleanor had declined politely, telling them she was far too old to spend the whole evening out in those freezing temperatures.

"My bull-riding days are over," Eleanor had said with a laugh.

"You're not really gonna ride that thing, are you?" Lila asked Theo, the bull bucking and writhing as a man in a cowboy hat and denim jacket held on for dear life.

"I have to redeem myself after the horseshoes," he said, with a little smirk that made her insides do a twirl.

When the cowboy finally lost his grip, he sailed through the air, yelling "Yee-haw!" and landing with a thud on the giant foam pit below.

Then he struggled to climb back to the side through the dense blocks of foam. Next a couple mounted the bull—a heavy-set woman and an older man. Lila covered her eyes as they took hold of the handles, not wanting to see what the bull would do to these two.

"Oh!" Rex said with excitement. "You and Theo could ride together!"

Lila yanked her hands from her face. "Are you kidding? There's no way I'm getting on that thing," she said with a laugh, ruffling the boy's hair.

"Do it, do it," Rex sang, jumping up and down. "It's fun!"

"We can't leave you all alone," she explained, feeling confident that she had a rock-solid out for this crazy idea.

"It's fine," Theo told her. "Look who's running the bull. It's Adele. She'll watch Rex." He bent down to eye level to address the little boy. "You'll sit with your grandma and watch us, won't you?"

"Yes, sir!" Rex said with wild excitement in his eyes.

"And I'll bet she'll even let you run the bull," Theo added.

"I'm not riding that thing," Lila said again, folding her arms. "A girl could fall off and hurt herself."

Theo leaned into her, that adorably rugged grin playing at his lips, the same challenge in his eyes she'd seen before, making her lightheaded. "Depends on the girl."

Lila wrinkled her nose at him but had a difficult time keeping a straight face when he laughed—really laughed. She'd never seen something so wonderful in her life. She never wanted him to stop. "Fine," she said, allowing a giggle to escape.

Rex cheered.

Before she knew it, they'd made it through the line and Lila was climbing onto the bull with Theo. "I can't believe I'm doing this," she said under her breath.

Theo put his arms around her and leaned over her shoulder. "Aw, come on. We've ridden together before. This is nothing." His cheek was next to hers, and if she twisted just slightly in his direction, she could put herself in a precarious position that, if she were honest, she wouldn't at all mind being in.

Suddenly, the bull came to life with a jolt, and both her hands flew to the handle, Theo tightening his grip on her. Rex was in the operation box on Adele's lap, doubling over already while his grandmother laughed behind him. But her view was ripped away when the bull bucked wildly, causing Theo to squeeze Lila tighter. Her body came off the saddle, making him laugh behind her. She had a unique mix of adrenaline and excitement pumping through her; Theo's lightly spicy scent of aftershave mixed with the fresh, powdery smell of soap had her heart pattering.

Then in a flash she came off the seat again, but this time the bump was so hard that she and Theo were thrown into the air, the handle coming out of her grip, the two of them landing in the pile of foam on their sides. Only once they'd come to a stop did she realize that Theo's hand was behind her head to protect her as they fell. The two of them were face to face, their bodies intertwined. Without thinking, she'd put her hand on his chest to shield herself from the weight of his body during the fall, now noticing she could feel the thumping of his heart under her fingers as he looked down at her.

Theo took her in for a second and then a smile slowly spread across his face. "See? That wasn't so bad," he said, his voice gentle. Seeing how he'd let his guard down, Lila could hardly breathe.

And she had to admit that being tangled up with Theo definitely wasn't so bad.

Theo hopped up and grabbed her hand, pulling her to a standing position.

"That was awesome!" Rex said, as they stepped off the mat to exit. He wriggled between Lila and Theo, grabbing their hands and swinging their arms back and forth as his little cowboy boots clacked along the floor. "What do ya wanna do now?" he asked.

"If you're warm enough, we could go out and ride the Ferris wheel," Theo suggested.

"I'd love that," Lila said.

They went outside and got in line for the Ferris wheel, its red-and-green lights like Christmas stars against the black sky above. As it went around, tinkling carols played underneath the laughter and merriment of the crowds.

When it was their turn, they stepped up to their seat, all three of them squeezing in with Rex in the middle. To give them more room, Theo put his arm around the back of the chair, his hand lying gently on Lila's shoulder, causing a tingle of happiness to rush through her. The attendant came around and checked the door on their seat, making sure it was closed tightly for the ride.

"I can't wait," Rex said, his eyes glittering with excitement.

The giant wheel began to turn slowly, their seat lifting and swaying back and forth with their movement. The chatter of the crowds faded as they made their way into the air, and then it was as if they were floating, looking down on the rows of Christmas trees at Pinewood Farm, the snow blanketing the tops of the hills, the thin gray roads that snaked through the small town, the flashing lights of the game booths below—it was the most gorgeous sight Lila had ever seen.

Taking it all in with Rex and Theo by her side made Lila realize how empty her life had been. She wished she had a family of her own to share moments like this with, but if she didn't, this might be the next best thing. Rex was adorable and such an easy child to love, and Lila couldn't believe how Theo had opened up tonight. It felt like some sort of Christmas miracle. And when she didn't think things could get any better, through the shoulder of her coat, she could feel Theo's fingers stroking her affectionately, making her look over at him. When she did, all her thoughts faded away at the vulnerability in his face. It was almost as if he was silently questioning her with something, but she couldn't read it. She smiled instead, and he turned back toward the view below. Something was definitely happening, and it was making her reconsider everything she'd ever thought about him.

It was late when they'd dropped Rex back home at the farmhouse, armed with a fistful of cotton candy and a teddy bear he'd won at the ring toss. Not wanting to impose, Lila and Theo had stayed on the porch. Trudy had thanked them for taking care of Rex and invited them to come by soon.

And now Lila and Theo were standing at the door to her cabin, his face barely visible in the darkness below the pines. "I had a great time tonight," she told him.

He nodded, that contemplative expression she'd seen on the Ferris wheel coming back with a vengeance. "It was a good…date," he said, the corners of his mouth twitching upward.

"Wait—date?" she said, taking the bait, unable to hide her ridiculous grin. "Did you just say we went on a *date*?"

She reached out to take his arms and playfully shake him, but suddenly lost her ability to speak when he swept her up into an embrace, looking down at her with an intensity in his eyes that she'd never seen before. He leaned in, his lips so close to hers that she could feel the warmth of his breath.

"Yes," he whispered before his lips brushed hers. Then he kissed her, his mouth moving on hers like she'd never experienced before. There was something magical about the two of them together, as if she'd been waiting her whole life to find the puzzle piece that fit exactly right. He gripped her passionately, their movements perfect complements to one another, his breath mixing with hers, sweeping her into this unbelievable moment. As his lips roamed around her own, a swarm of butterflies seemed to take over her insides, fluttering all the way into her mind, making her lightheaded. No one else had ever come close to this.

Theo pulled back, looking stunned before regaining his composure. "I, uh…" Confusion slid across his face as he shook his head. He looked back at her as if he were just now really seeing her for the first time. "I don't know what came over me," he said.

"You don't have to apologize," Lila told him. "I didn't mind." She smiled, her heart still all aflutter.

"It's late. I should go," he replied, but the look in his eyes told her something different.

"I'll see you in the morning," she said.

Still clearly processing what had just happened, he took in a long steadying breath and then found her hand, winding his fingers through hers. He lifted it up and kissed the back of it, then let go. "In the morning when you come to work, if I'm not downstairs yet, I keep the spare key to the shop on a nail under the Coffee sign. Just let yourself in and make some coffee if you want to. Then come up and get me."

"Okay," she said.

He gave her a loving grin. "See ya."

"Bye."

Lila slipped her key in the lock of the cabin and let herself inside. She shut the door behind her and flopped onto the sofa in a lovesick daze, the lights of the Christmas tree sparkling like diamonds, surprised by the emotions she was feeling. She was falling hard and fast for the mysterious coffee shop owner, and there was no going back now.

Chapter Fifteen

On her way to the coffee shop the next morning, Lila rolled down her car window to greet Eleanor on her way out of the main drive. The old lady was in her rubber boots and big coat, holding the mail, one of the letters open in her hand. Her nose seemed too red to just be cold.

"Are you okay?"

Eleanor cleared her throat. "Oh, I'll be fine, dear," she said, fluffing the paper in the air with a huff. "Just office stuff. Where are you headed this early in the morning all by yourself?"

"I'm going to work at the coffee shop so Theo can finish fixing the plumbing in the cabin."

"Ah," she said, her voice quivering.

Lila got a quick look at the letter in Eleanor's hands—some sort of overdue notice with a hefty dollar amount. "Are you really okay?"

"Yes, yes," Eleanor said, waving her off. "Go. Theo's waiting."

Eleanor turned around and started back up the drive, giving Lila no other choice but to put her window up and continue to the coffee shop. As she drove toward the fields at the bottom of the hill, glancing at the horses' winter turnout sheets strapped over them to shield them from the weather, Lila considered the paper she'd seen in Eleanor's hand. Could she not pay the basic bills for the cabins? Were things really that bad?

She stopped and put the car into reverse, easing back up the driveway. Eleanor turned around when Lila cut the engine and got out of the car to walk over to her. "I can't get on with my day until you tell me what's going on." She pulled out her phone.

"What are you doing?" Eleanor asked.

"I'm texting Theo to let him know that I'm going to be a little late."

"Please don't," Eleanor said, nearly frantic. "I need the plumbing fixed right now." She seemed completely panicked, the hand holding the mail trembling.

"We're going inside and you're going to tell me what's happening." Lila marched ahead of her while Eleanor stood still, as if her worry was causing her legs to stop working. Lila turned around. "You'd better come with me if you want me to get to the coffee shop so Theo can fix your pipes. I'm not leaving until I know you're okay."

With a resigned sigh, Eleanor followed her to the cabin.

When they got inside, Lila unwound her scarf and sat down on the sofa. Eleanor hung her coat on the hook by the door and joined her, tears filling her eyes. "I'm behind on my bills…" Her fingers shook when she rubbed her face, pressing down as if she could wipe the worry right off it.

"Is that what you had in your hand just now? An overdue bill?"

She nodded. "It's the third notice…I've paid the minimums to keep the electric, gas, and water on, but I don't know how long I can continue." She shook her hands in the air. "But it's not your concern. This is your vacation. You need to be enjoying yourself instead of pressing an old woman to tell you about her aging resort issues."

"Okay, look, don't panic. Let me think about this for a little while. We'll figure something out."

"Oh, my dear, it's too far gone. Thank you for trying, though."

"Never say never." And right then, she realized that she had a *friend* who needed her.

Theo was busy making a latte when she arrived, still thinking about Eleanor and her situation. When their eyes met, her stomach did somersaults and she couldn't wait for him to finish with the customer so she could talk to him. She'd had such a wonderful time last night that she'd slept like a baby, barely even noticing the emptiness of the cabin. She'd gotten up, had a cup of coffee and some eggs, and she'd even spent a little extra time on her hair and makeup this morning.

"Hey," he said, when she'd finished washing her hands in the kitchen. She smiled as she approached him, fumbling while trying to tie the apron behind her back. Theo turned her around and finished the bow. "So what happened with Eleanor?" He wiped down the espresso machine and tossed the rag into a basket on the back counter, before giving her his full attention, his lips gently turning upward as he looked at her.

"She's struggling."

"Oh?" Theo offered her one of his lattes with the caramel drizzle on top.

"Thank you." She took the mug between both hands, letting it warm her as she breathed in the nutty, sweet scent of it. "She doesn't want to sell but she admitted to me that she's late on her bills."

Theo sat back on the barista stool and sipped his coffee—a mug of black dark roast with no frills—looking thoughtful. "It needs a lot of work," he said, thoughts still flashing behind his eyes.

"I know," she said, shaking her head. "Every cabin needs exterior and probably interior paint. The main house needs a complete remodel.

All the appliances and lighting could be updated, the grounds need to be manicured, and the gravel drives should be paved and marked. And that's just on the surface. Look at the plumbing. I wonder how long it's been since she's had an inspection of the structures."

"Yeah…" he said, before taking a drink from his mug.

She grinned, trying to lighten the heaviness she'd created. "I wish I could give her the money. Got a job for me that will make me rich? We could overhaul the coffee shop, buy a franchise or something."

His expression turned to stone.

"I just thought it would be nice to be able to pay for repairs on Fireside Cabins for Eleanor," Lila replied, thrown by his reaction. "If I had the cash, I would. What it would be like to have all that money…" She'd completely redo Fireside Cabins, buy her friends whatever they needed, get herself a little house outside of Nashville somewhere, and maybe a new car since hers had been cutting out on her.

He laughed incredulously. "Look around." He waved his arm through the air and then settled back on his stool, taking another drink from his coffee, looking frustrated.

She wondered at his reaction. Was he insecure with his own level of income? He shouldn't worry about that, though. She hardly made bundles of money herself, even when tips were good. "I don't really want a job," she said, drawing his attention to her once more. "I like the coffee shop the way it is. And I like you just the way you are."

He set his coffee down and hopped off his stool, walking over to her tentatively. His eyes swallowed her like they had last night, but with a new intensity behind them. The action, in the light of day, seemed more real than it had in her memory of last night, and she had to work to keep her heart from pounding out of her chest.

"This is it, right here. *This* is all I have. Swear that that's okay," he demanded.

"I swear," she said, worried by his change in demeanor.

The door to the shop opened, and they jumped apart as a customer entered. Confusion swarmed Lila when she saw Theo's pensive frown. The customer didn't seem to notice though, shuffling in and lumping her purse onto the counter. She put in her order.

"I'll let Lila work on this for you," he told the woman, backing up to allow Lila space to move toward the register. As she passed him, he leaned toward her. "I'll head over to the cabin to work on the plumbing now."

"You don't want to make sure I've got things down pat?" she asked.

"I trust you." Without another look, he headed out the back of the coffee shop.

Theo hadn't returned all day. Lila was desperate to find out what his reaction that morning had been all about. He seemed like he was always on edge, battling some invisible demon he couldn't shake.

He'd taken so long that she'd tried to text him, but he hadn't answered. She'd had to pull up the hours of operation for the shop on her phone to know when to close. After setting the dishwasher in back to run all the dishes for the day, wiping down the tables, sweeping the place, she did what she could to clean the machines. As she pushed in the last chair at the back, she caught sight of a light on in his office so she went in, just in case he was there. The room was unoccupied, but she scanned it curiously. There was a little bookcase in the corner, and she wandered over to take a peek at what was on it. The shelves were full of academic books and titles she'd never even heard of. Lila pulled out one called *The Significance of Ethics* and flipped through it, an envelope from inside falling to the floor. A flash of heat crawled up Lila's face as she tried to figure out what two pages it had been hidden between. She flipped the envelope over and read the addressee: *B. Brown, P. Perry.* B. Brown, as in Brian Brown, the coffee shop owner? And who was P. Perry? It was stamped from a law firm in Nashville. Lila checked the door, holding her breath, her heart racing as she looked inside the envelope. But her heart fell. It was empty. She returned the envelope to the book and slid it back onto the shelf.

Then her gaze fell upon the filing cabinet beside Theo's desk. She really shouldn't snoop…

Leaning out of the doorway, she assessed her surroundings once more. The shop was completely empty. Quietly, she paced over and bit her lip while pulling open the drawer. She ran her fingers through the files, stopping at one labeled "Legal." Maybe the letter that went with the envelope was in there. She opened the file on his desk and scanned the contents. Not much out of the ordinary—the deed to the building, a business card from the same law firm, and a few government documents for the state of Tennessee. But at the back, a note typed on the law firm's letterhead caught her eye. It read,

Theo,

Sending this via mail since I can't get you on the phone. Everything has been tied up in terms of the old business arrangement and there's nothing more to worry about legally. No one can be charged with a crime, since we took care of it this way. You have my number if you need me.

It was unsigned, and nothing more was said.

Crime? Was Theo involved in something illegal? Surely not the Theo she knew...

Lila put it back in the folder and slid it into place in the filing cabinet. Already feeling guilty for prying into Theo's personal affairs, she flicked off the light and then locked up with the key behind the Coffee sign, before heading back to Fireside Cabins.

When Lila had parked Eleanor's car back in front of the main cabin and walked over to hers, Theo's truck wasn't in the usual spot. She went inside to see if he'd left a note or anything. Sweeping through the kitchen, she checked the counters, then moved over to the dinette table, before trying the living room and Edie's old room—nothing. She peered up at the ceiling. The hole had been patched and spackled over, all the old pipes removed. All the room needed now was a fresh coat of paint and new carpet. So he'd finished the job. Where was he? It was nearing dinnertime. Perhaps he'd gone out to grab a bite to eat. She texted him again and then went around the cabin, turning on the Christmas lights and lighting a candle, the warm cinnamon scent filling the air.

Her feet were tired from standing all day at the coffee shop, and once she'd settled into the comfy sofa and soft lighting at the cabin, she could feel the exhaustion taking over. She washed up, changed into her pajamas, and then warmed up some leftovers. Taking her plate and a glass of wine into the living room, she switched on the TV and navigated to an old Christmas film, snuggling down with her plate on her lap.

As she looked around the room, she considered the idea that being alone wasn't so bad. But the more she tried to convince herself of this, the more she thought about how much better it would be to have Theo next to her, the feel of his lips on hers lingering in her mind.

While she waited to hear back from him, she finished her food and set the plate on the coffee table. With the movie playing in the background, she scrolled through area painters on her phone, just to see how much it would cost if she were to surprise Eleanor with fixing the cabin. But taking into account the carpet too, and any painting outside of that room, she just didn't think she could swing it. Lila closed her eyes and tipped her head back, resting it on the sofa, hoping some ideas would come to her. She wanted to find a way to make this Christmas perfect for everyone. Even if it seemed impossible.

Chapter Sixteen

Lila's eyes flew open with the abrupt awareness that the sun was streaming in through the cabin window, dulling the shine of the Christmas tree lights that had been on since yesterday. She was still in the living room—had she slept there all night again? She must have toppled over from her sitting position in the wee hours, because she found herself curled up with a blanket that had been on the arm of the sofa. Fishing around underneath it for her phone, her fingers located the device between the cushions, and retrieved it to check for a return text from Theo. He still hadn't responded. She couldn't help feeling a niggling sense of unease.

Lila stood up, put last night's plate in the kitchen sink, and stepped into the shower, washing quickly. Then she got dressed, pulled her hair back into a ponytail, and threw on her boots and coat. Her worry mounting, her mind raced with questions. Had Theo been called with some kind of emergency?

Lila rushed over to Eleanor's, bounding up the wobbly cinderblocks to knock on the door.

"Hello, dear," Eleanor said. She was wearing an apron, her hands dusted with flour. "Won't you come in?"

"I will, I promise, but I'm in a bit of a hurry," Lila explained. "I wanted to see if you'd heard from Theo. Did he stop by or anything once he'd finished fixing the pipes last night?"

"No," Eleanor replied, pursing her lips and shaking her head. "Why? Is everything all right?"

"He didn't come back to the shop yesterday and I had to close up for him."

"That's odd. I'm sure he's fine, though. Please don't look so worried, dear. There's no sense in getting upset until you have reason to be. I have to keep telling myself the same thing."

Lila forced a smile and nodded.

"When you find him, I'll have some banana nut bread coming out of the oven in about an hour. You two should stop in for a slice or two."

"That sounds delicious," she said. "I'll keep you posted."

Lila got into the car, using the keys Eleanor had loaned her, and tried to take the woman's advice. The heat cranked to life, giving her a shiver after the icy air as she put the car in reverse and pulled down the long drive, making for the coffee shop.

She'd barely known Theo any time at all, yet he could send her emotions on a wild swing in a second. But in a strange way, she was sure that she *got* him. She wasn't offended by his standoffish behavior, but rather challenged to figure him out. She was convinced that if he just let her in, everything would be okay.

Lila came to a stop and got out of the car just as Adele pulled on the locked door handle of the coffee shop. She put her hand to her forehead in salute and peered through the glass window.

"It's closed," she said, as Lila stepped up to the door. "Why would he be closed?"

Lila leaned around Adele to view the dark interior, the tables all empty, the clean cups on their towel on the back counter just as she'd left them last night. "I'm not sure," she replied.

"So much for my mornin' pick-me-up. I was just gettin' used to comin' out here," Adele said, as she turned on her heel and retreated to her car. "Have a good day."

"You too," Lila called. Then she got back in Eleanor's car and headed for Pinewood Farm, not knowing where else to go.

The whole way, she teetered between total panic that something had happened and irritation that he would just disappear without a word to her. There was something about him that she couldn't put her finger on, something that just didn't seem to fit. He was a barista in a nowhere town, but she thought about the books she'd caught sight of in his office last night, and then there was that cryptic letter she'd found in his files. He wouldn't even tell her his last name...

Or had he?

A vague memory came through, but it was so fuzzy she couldn't remember what he'd said to her, or if it had been the remnants of some dream...

Her mind whirling with it all, Lila pulled up at the farm and knocked on the farmhouse door.

Little Rex swung the door open. "Hey, Lila!" he said, stepping onto the porch and wrapping his arms around her. "It's Lila, Mama," he called into the house.

"Hey, Lila!" Trudy's voice sailed down the hallway.

"Whatcha doin'?" Rex asked.

"I was looking for Theo," she replied. "Have you seen him?"

"Nope."

"Will he be coming by today? When's your next guitar lesson?"

"Not till next week."

She nodded, thinking.

Trudy came down the hallway. "Sorry it took me a minute to get to the door. I was just fixing breakfast. Did I hear you say you were looking for Theo?"

"Yes, have you seen him?"

"I haven't heard a word from him."

"Well, if you do," Lila told her, "let him know I'm looking for him."

"I've been baking like crazy," Eleanor said, placing a little dessert plate with Christmas holly painted around the edges in front of Lila. "I think it's my brain's way of choosing to focus on something I can control." She sliced a piece of warm banana bread from her loaf and set the steaming treat on Lila's plate. The kitchen table was full of cookies, fudge, cakes, and pastries, the sweet scents tickling her nose.

"You've definitely been busy," Lila noted.

"I've baked so much that I'm going to make Christmas gift boxes for everyone in town."

"Ah, that's really nice of you." She picked up a cookie and nibbled on it, savoring the milk chocolate morsels mixed into the warm buttery dough.

Eleanor handed her a fork. "So did you find Theo?"

Lila shook her head. "No. I have absolutely no idea where he is."

"That's worrying."

"I know," Lila agreed. "I don't even have a clue when he disappeared. Where would someone hide in this town? I was working the coffee shop all day, so who knows what time he finished up with the plumbing and left the cabin? Did you happen to see when he left?"

"I'm afraid I was upstairs cleaning most of the time, and I didn't pay attention."

"He could be missing and no one is looking for him," Lila fretted.

"Should we contact the authorities?" Eleanor suggested.

"I don't know his last name or anything," she said, racking her brain for that foggy memory of him mentioning it as she'd fallen asleep. What had he told her? She considered the names that had been on the envelope: B. Brown, P. Perry. Not a Theo in sight.

"Someone has to know it," Eleanor said.

"Tell me who, and I'll call them right now."

"What about Judd Johnson? He and Theo were friendly. Would he know?"

"We can ask him."

"I've got his number," Eleanor said. "I'll call." She got up and went into the kitchen, returning with her address book and her cell phone. Then she dialed the number and put the phone to her ear. "Hi, Trudy," she said. "This is Eleanor Finely. I've got Lila Evans here with me, and we're looking for Theo. Have you seen him?" She put the phone on speaker.

Trudy's small voice came through the phone. "Lila came over looking for him earlier. You still haven't seen him?"

"No," Eleanor replied.

"Hi, Trudy," Lila said. "I'm here with Eleanor. Do you happen to know Theo's last name?"

"You know, oddly I don't. Let me check with Judd. Hang on just a second."

"Hey, Lila!" Rex's voice came over the speaker.

"Hi, Rex," she said with a smile.

"I can help you," he offered.

"You can?" Lila asked, picking at her banana bread, her mind on anything but the treat under her fingers.

"Yep. I asked Theo what his whole name was one time and he said, 'Just Theo,' and when I said, 'But what's your last name,' he said, 'I don't have a last name anymore.'"

"What?" Eleanor asked, her face crumpling in confusion.

"He's weird about his last name for some reason," Lila said. "He wouldn't tell it to me either." She turned back to the call. "Thanks for your help, Rex."

"No problem."

Just then Trudy returned. "Hey, y'all, I'm back. I just asked Judd and he said he wasn't sure of his last name either, but he thought it might be Brown."

"Thank you, Trudy," Lila said, knowing it wasn't. Theo had told her that himself.

Eleanor ended the call. Then all of a sudden, Lila remembered what Piper had said about the coffee shop when they'd first arrived: *I read an article about this place and it suggested that someone mysterious owns it… No one knows who the owner is for sure. The article I read said all the transactions have been made under the pseudonym Brian Brown. If you ask the barista, they say he won't utter a word about it.*

She needed to call Piper. Maybe she had some further intel.

"Eleanor, do you mind if I head back to my cabin for a little while?" she asked, worried that she might uncover something Theo didn't want people to know.

"Not at all. Take your bread with you," she said, handing her a napkin to wrap it in. "I'll bring you a Christmas box when I've finished packing them all."

"Thank you, that would be nice," Lila replied, getting up and sliding her coat on. She grabbed the napkin and pinched the piece of bread within it, cradling the treat in her hand. "I'll let you know if I find out anything else." She let herself out and jogged over to her cabin, unlocking the door and setting the bread and napkin on the kitchen counter while simultaneously dialing Piper.

"Hey, girl!" Piper said after the first ring. "Holding the fort over there in the hills?"

"Sort of..." Lila said. "Do you still have that article you read about the coffee shop here in Pinewood Hills, by chance?"

"What article?"

"The one about someone named Brian Brown owning the shop."

"Oh!" Piper said. "Yes! It's in one of my magazines. Why?"

"I can't find Theo."

"What?"

"He's been missing since yesterday, and I'm thinking I might report it to the police—you know, just to be on the safe side," Lila said, trying not to panic herself with unnecessary thoughts about Theo being in some kind of trouble.

"Oh my gosh," Piper said through the phone.

"Yeah. But I kind of need to find out his last name before I call. No one seems to know it. I'm wondering if there are any clues at all in that article." She explained to Piper what had happened, catching her up on all the details.

"Here, I've got the article now. Let me read it aloud to you," Piper told her. "Stop me if I say anything that might help." She began to read. "*The obscure coffee shop hides on the back of a hill in the small town of Pinewood Hills, Tennessee. You haven't heard of it? Don't feel bad. Not many have. The aging little village has more than meets the eye with its Christmas festivities, but it's the coffee shop that we feel will garner the most interest. Its mysterious owner, Theo, is known for his lack of hospitality and run-down premises.*

"The townsfolk will tell you it's just a ploy to keep tourists from frequenting the spot, but everyone else wonders if all the secrecy is to produce the opposite effect. The enigmatic barista is not only tight-lipped about his recipes, but everything else about him as well. Most people don't even know his name. Try to talk to him, and he'll close up faster than a mousetrap on a piece of stolen cheese. We tried to request an interview, but when we reached out for comment, our calls were ignored. When we visited, we encountered the burly mountain man—all muscle with a thick beard and long hair—and we were asked not so politely to move along. When our reporters attempted to get the public sales records for the coffee shop, they were told that all the transactions had been made under the pseudonym Brian Brown—who no one appears to know. If you ask the barista, residents say he won't utter a word about any of it. Is it all a publicity stunt? It got us to write this article, didn't it? That's all it says," Piper finished.

"He must have shaved for us," Lila teased. But then she sobered. "So nobody knows his name," she said, shaking her head in disbelief, the phone pressed against her ear. "At least nobody who will say anything…"

"He never told you?" Piper asked.

"He may have. When I was asleep, I swear he said it, but I can't remember it. I'd been teasing him for not telling me." She squeezed her eyes shut, willing the moment to come back to her.

"While you were asleep?" Piper asked in a playfully suspicious tone. "Why was Theo with you while you were sleeping?"

Lila laughed. "You know how I get after long days. I dozed off."

"I don't buy it."

"I swear!" Lila said, squeezing her eyes shut in amusement. "Literally, *nothing* happened. I was exhausted. I might have even snored a little."

"Ugh, you have no juicy details?"

"Sorry," Lila replied. She continued to ponder his last name, thinking out loud. "Percy? Parker? I just can't place it."

"Theo Parker, Theo Percy," Piper said, dropping her banter and trying the names on for size. "Something with a P then?"

Lila's thoughts returned to that envelope she'd found in Theo's office. "Hey, I'm going to run into town to see if I can find any answers. I'll go crazy just sitting here."

"Okay," Piper said. "Good luck and be careful."

Getting into Eleanor's car again, Lila went straight to the coffee shop, grabbing the key and letting herself in. "Theo!" she called, every cell in her body on high alert. "Theo?" she said again. There was nothing but her echo. She locked herself in and kept the lights off, rushing back to his office. Shutting the door and locking it, she clicked on the light. She sat down in his chair, noticing that his desk was tidier than it had been yesterday. She flipped through a small stack of papers on the corner next to a cup full of pens—nothing too interesting; mostly the stubs of bills that had been sent off: electric, water, coffee supplies. She set them down, leaning back in the chair, convincing herself that she had a right to go through his files again.

A rap at the front door of the shop sent her bolting to her feet. Her heart banging around in her chest, she grabbed the doorknob to unlock it but then froze. How would she explain being in here? Quietly, she twisted the lock and opened the office door a tiny crack to check who was outside. A man she didn't recognize was cupping his hands and peering into the shop.

When he turned toward the parking lot, Lila bolted from the office, steadying herself as she went to the main door.

"May I help you?" she asked through the glass.

The man swiveled around to face her, holding up an envelope. "I have some papers to deliver to Theo Perry," he said.

Theo Perry?

A warm sensation spread through Lila as she realized that was exactly the name Theo had said. She remembered his quiet voice as he'd told her, "My last name is Perry. Theo Perry." He hadn't thought she could hear him, and she wasn't entirely awake, but she was cognizant enough that his words had roused her into alertness. And Perry had been the name on that envelope in his office. P. Perry—who was that?

"I just need someone to sign for them."

She opened the door. "I can do that."

"Great." He handed her the digital screen and a pen.

She signed her name.

"Thanks so much," the courier said, handing over the envelope.

As he walked away, Lila hurried back inside, locking the door again and rushing through the dark dining area to the office, shutting herself back in. She sat down in Theo's chair once more, holding the manila envelope in her hands.

"So, Theo Perry," she said. "What do we have here?" She fanned the envelope in the air.

Just then her cell phone rang, sending her heart up to her throat. It was Piper.

"Any luck?" Piper said when Lila answered.

"I'm holding an envelope of his that was just delivered to the coffee shop," she said, her voice low even though no one was there but her.

"You're in the coffee shop?" Piper asked.

"Yeah," she replied. "I wondered if I could find anything to figure out where he is. I did find out his name."

"What is it?" Piper asked.

"Theo Perry," Lila replied.

Piper gasped. "Oh my God!" she squealed, forcing Lila to pull the phone away from her head to save her eardrum. "Hang on a minute." Her words were followed by the soft thud of the phone leaving Piper's hand. A second later there was the rustling sound of her returning.

"What is it? You're killin' me here."

"Theo Perry? That's his name?"

"That's definitely it," she told her friend. "But I don't know who Theo Perry is."

"Given the article, it's pretty amazing that he spoke to us as much as he did."

Lila smiled to herself, all the moments she'd shared with Theo suddenly becoming even more intimate. She'd pushed and pushed, but actually, he'd shared more with her than he probably had with anybody.

"If it's the same guy, Theo Perry is the missing son of Smash Perry, the millionaire guitarist for the band Rockford and Smash."

"I know who that is! *Guitar* lessons…" Lila said to herself with a smile. Then she sobered. "Smash Perry's son is missing?"

"It's a very strange story," Piper said. "Nobody's really saying much, but there have been rumors that about three years ago, Smash and his son Theo had a falling out at one of the bars downtown, and the next day Theo was gone. His father didn't report him missing for five or six months. People speculated that Smash had done something to him, since he'd had a few run-ins with the police in his lifetime. When they investigated, there was no evidence of foul play, and they had no leads. He'd just vanished. The authorities decided that the evidence they *did* have suggested Theo left of his own accord, and with him being an adult, the investigation was closed."

"And does that Theo look like our Theo?" Lila asked.

"We've got to get you up to speed on the music industry," she teased. "Yes! Now that I think of it, they look a lot alike. Let me put you on speaker and search for him. I'll text you a photo." Piper hummed from afar as Lila waited.

Lila's phone pinged with the image of a gangly guy in his late twenties. She zoomed in to get a better look at Theo Perry's face. He had the same hair color as the Theo she knew, and it looked like his eyes were also blue. As she studied him closer, something registered. There was a little smirk on the lips of the guy in the photo. The same little smirk she'd seen on her Theo's lips. "He's so skinny... but I think it might be him."

"It's interesting that your Theo suddenly went missing, just like the famous Theo Perry. Seems like this could be his exit of choice: disappear without a trace."

Lila tried to piece together the unanswerable questions she'd had about him. Her mouth dried out.

If this *was* the same Theo, and he *had* chosen to disappear like he had yesterday, did that mean he wasn't planning to return?

"You okay?" Piper asked, pulling Lila from her thoughts.

Lila took a deep breath. "Honestly... I don't know." But if he wasn't planning to return, he'd have no problem with abandoning the envelope that she held in her hand, would he? And what if he hadn't abandoned them and something had happened? Would there be some clue inside? She shouldn't open it—definitely not.

"You should open the envelope that was delivered so we can see what's inside," Piper cut in.

"I can't," Lila said.

"Given the circumstances, I doubt Theo would even care."

"Still, though," she said, noticing the flap was only closed by the envelope's brass clasp.

"What if his life depends on it?" Piper asked.

"Okay, okay," Lila said, giving in. She unclasped the envelope and pulled out a small piece of notebook paper with a handwritten message.

Theo,

You have ruined our family's reputation, and I'll never forgive you for that. If you think you can run from me instead of facing the mess you've made, you've got another thing coming. You've stolen from our family and you've disgraced my name. I've been looking for you since the day you left, and I've got the best people on this case that money can buy. You'd better call me, or I'll be coming to you.

A.

"Whoa," Piper said. "That's heavy."

"Definitely. I wonder what it all means." Lila was at a loss. She slid the letter back into the envelope and snapped the flap shut, setting it on Theo's desk. "Looks like I'm not the only one who needs answers," she said in a whisper.

Chapter Seventeen

There was a knock at the cabin door. Lila kicked the blanket off her legs and set her mug of hot cocoa on the coffee table. She'd been sitting in the living room since leaving the coffee shop, trying to relax and get her head together for her next move, but the mysterious letter she'd signed for and the bits of information she'd gathered that suggested Theo was involved in something possibly criminal kept running through her mind. She'd debated whether to send Theo a text letting him know that she'd figured him out. She'd typed and deleted about three different messages, never sending any of them for fear she'd only push him further away—if he was running away at all. She kept replaying their last conversation and wondering if she'd missed something. Had she said anything to make him want to leave? So many emotions were racing through her. She answered the door to find Eleanor holding a red-and-green Christmas box.

"Your treats," she said, holding out the gift.

"Oh, thank you. You're too sweet. Come in," Lila said, opening the door wider and accepting the box.

Eleanor wrinkled her nose. "It smells damp in here." She unwound her scarf and hung it on the hook by the door. Her boots squeaked against the wooden floor as she worked to slide them off. "It's looking like snow again. I hope the plumbing issue won't impact the warm water in the cabin. If it does, feel free to come over to the main house."

"I'm sure the water will be just fine," Lila said. "Are you too full from baking nibbles to share with me?" She held up the box. "I could make us some coffee. I've got decaf."

"That would be wonderful, dear." Eleanor settled at the kitchen table and folded her hands in front of her. "Any word from Theo?"

"No," Lila replied, not knowing if she should divulge what she might have learned about him. She dared not spread any rumors. It was all just hearsay at this point. "Have you ever heard the name Perry anywhere? I've been doing a little digging and speculating that it could be his last name," she said carefully.

"That would be interesting if it were," Eleanor said. "I have a lodger who comes once a month or so on business. His stays are what have been keeping me afloat recently. Name's William Perry."

"William Perry," she repeated. "Wonder if they could be any relation?"

"He's from Nashville, like you, so I'd have thought Theo would've said something if he were from there as well, wouldn't he?" Eleanor replied. "The man's a musician. He's rough around the edges—he's got sleeve tattoos and spiked hair—doesn't really remind me of Theo." Lila tried to imagine that. She conjured up old memories of her ex, Razz, the last musician she'd been around. His loud, extroverted rants and antics were nothing like Theo's quiet introspective ways. But while he didn't seem like Theo, that description of William did sound a lot like Smash.

Lila got up to make them each their cups with the makeshift French press she'd been using. While she did, she grabbed her phone and opened the search engine, quickly typing in *William Perry*. She coughed to hide her gasp when she saw what popped up:

William "Smash" Perry is an American singer, songwriter, and musician. He is best known as the lead singer and guitarist of the multi-platinum, award-winning duo Rockford and Smash, a Nashville-based country music band in which he also plays banjo and mandolin. He currently lives in Nashville, Tennessee.

Lila navigated out of the page and clicked another with a link to Smash's music. One of his songs began to play while she poured their coffees. It was a rock-based banger with undertones of those familiar hillbilly and blues elements so prominent in this area. As she watched Smash play guitar in the video, the resemblance was uncanny.

It's him, she thought. *Smash is Theo's dad.* She was nearly sure of it.

Putting her phone down, she finished making the coffees, bringing one over to Eleanor and sitting down beside her. She reached into the box of confectioneries and pulled out a piece of fudge. Pinching it between two fingers, she asked, "What does that guy do when he's here?"

"William? He usually keeps to himself; he takes a lot of walks. He prefers to be left alone. But that's just fine with me. He always pays his entire bill in advance, so he can do cartwheels through the yard for all I care." Eleanor laughed.

"How long does he stay?"

"Oh, about a week or so. Sometimes just a few days."

"When is he next due to visit?" Lila said, unable to hold back and feeling a rush of adrenaline at the thought of these estranged people being in such close proximity. Did William know Theo lived in town? He must do.

"He's on tour at the moment, I think," Eleanor said. "Lots of questions..." Her eyebrows bounced up and down with interest.

"Sorry. I just thought they might help me find Theo."

"Have you called the police?"

"I suppose I should."

"So that would bring the total to..." Lila tapped the numbers on her phone screen's calculator. She swallowed. "Twenty-three thousand, two hundred, seventy dollars."

After she'd tried to put in a missing person's report, Eleanor had asked Lila to come over for dinner. Lila had spoken to the police department, but since it had been less than twenty-four hours, and Theo was a grown man, they weren't as receptive as she'd hoped. Not knowing how much she should say about what she knew, she'd left it at that, thinking perhaps she'd try to call again tomorrow.

Apparently, Eleanor had been just as busy making savory dishes as she had been with the desserts.

Eleanor put her face in her hands. "With figures like that, I'll never be able to fix this place up," she said.

Lila peered down at the list of suggested renovations they'd been making together. "We could take off the new carpet."

"I hate to say it, but after the leak, your cabin smells like old socks," Eleanor told her with a laugh. "We need new carpet throughout *all* the cabins really."

"We could leave the exteriors the way they are. Maybe power wash them?"

"The paint's peeling, Lila." Eleanor shook her head, her gray curls swishing back and forth with the movement. "It's no use. I think I need to find a real estate agent."

"Where will you go?"

"No idea. I suppose I'll have to start looking."

"How about Florida? It's warm and sunny all the time."

Eleanor smiled, closing her eyes. "Mm. I could do with the sunshine." But the look in her eyes told a different story. This had been her home with Chester, and she clearly wanted to stay.

"Maybe not Florida," Lila said.

"The truth is that I don't feel like I fit anywhere else." She turned her head toward the Christmas tree, its holiday lights glimmering, and let out a sigh.

Lila sat in silence in her cabin after dinner, an idea brewing, and closed the banking app on her phone as she covered her legs with the blanket on the sofa. What was she doing? Was it too late in the night to make a decision like this? Perhaps she was delirious with exhaustion...

This might have been the most impulsive idea she'd ever had in her life, but everything inside her made her feel like it was the *right* thing to do. Lila had total savings of five thousand dollars, and she was about to sink it all into Fireside Cabins. Perhaps, if she could actually pull off a renovation and Eleanor could begin to turn a profit, she might need someone to work there with her. Lila could imagine herself in Pinewood Hills for sure. It seemed a long way off, given the state of the cabins, but if Eleanor needed a Christmas miracle, maybe if Lila played her cards right she could be exactly that. They wouldn't be able to do everything on their list, but they could do something to get the cabins up and running full tilt again.

Piper's mother had had some landscaping done in the fall, and she'd gotten an incredibly good price. Lila thought it might be worth checking to see if that company would be willing to make the two-hour drive to

Pinewood Hills. She opened a new message to text Piper and realized her friend had already sent her a message. Lila had been so busy with Eleanor that she hadn't seen it until now. It was a link to an article about Theo. She opened it and stared at the photo in front of her—a thinner, lankier, tuxedo-clad Theo with a shiny, sculpted supermodel in a sequined ball gown on his arm. Under the image, it said:

Theo Perry and fiancée Alexa Fontaine call it quits after a rocky year. When asked why the two canceled their 1.5 million dollar wedding, Alexa told us, "He's a complete fraud." Attempts to locate Theo Perry for comment were unsuccessful.

Lila put her phone down and stared at the tree until the lights blurred in front of her. This Christmas was a complete mess. All her friends had gone. She was alone, considering putting herself in the poor house for renovations on a property she had no rights to whatsoever. And she was falling for a guy who, according to the press, was a coward and a fraud—*and* who had totally disappeared on her, without a glance over his shoulder. She chewed on her lip, considering her options. She could pack it all up and head back home, enjoy the Christmas season in Nashville, maybe spend the next few weeks shopping downtown, listening to bands, and getting coffee with her friends... The alternative was painting tumbledown cabins in the freezing cold, feeling lonely and rejected, making regular visits to the local police department to see if they'd found Theo, and having a quiet holiday with Eleanor.

Having spent her young adult life mostly alone, Lila had developed a heart for people. She craved the connection that was stolen from her too early. It was what made her great at her job, and it was how she'd become such good friends with the women in her life. It was also why

she felt the overwhelming need to stay at Fireside Cabins, to keep
Eleanor company, despite the fact that her brain was screaming at her
not to do it. It was her heart over her head this time. It was the season
of giving, after all.

Chapter Eighteen

By six in the morning, Lila had already gotten herself together for the day. She knew people would be lining up at the coffee shop in about an hour, and Theo shouldn't leave his loyal customers high and dry, so she pushed away the sting of his disappearing act, deciding to fill in until she could figure out where he was. She grabbed her coat and headed out the door.

Lila knew it was probably pointless, but she couldn't help but look for Theo as she drove to the coffee shop. Her eyes roamed the barren tree line, the frost-covered medians; she peered over at every shop door and window on the way, scanning faces, just hoping to find him. But it was wishful thinking. If he'd run, he wouldn't be hanging out in the woods.

As she came to a stop in the small lot by the coffee shop, her mouth dropped open in surprise. She snapped it shut, gaping at what was in front of her. "He moves fast," she said out loud, to no one but herself. In the yard leading to the coffee shop, a corporate sign had been posted. The coffee shop was for sale.

Lila got out of the car, the icy wind assaulting her, and went up to the shop, taking the key from behind the *Coffee* sign. She unlocked the door and slammed it shut, causing the Christmas wreath to shimmy back and forth.

"Theo!" she called angrily, stomping through the dining area toward the office, but there was no response, just like before. She peered into the office and gasped. It had been totally cleaned out. All his books—gone. The furniture, the filing cabinet, the envelope—also gone. Turning back, she looked around the place. All the coffee shop paraphernalia was still in place, but his personal things had disappeared: the latest book he'd been reading, which he'd always kept on the counter, the cash in the tip jar, the jacket that had been draped over the chair in the corner of the prep station. The festive greenery was still there, a reminder that the holiday was looming despite the fact she didn't feel a single bit of good cheer.

Feeling suddenly like she was carrying a weight bigger than herself, she slowly climbed the stairs to the little apartment where he'd always retreated, fearful of what she'd see when she got up there. When she reached the top step, her fears were confirmed. The open space was empty, the kitchenette bare, the wood floors swept. Not a stitch of Theo in the space.

Her eyes filled with desperate, frustrated tears as she pulled out her phone, the old feeling of her happiness being ripped away from her when her dad had died swelling in her gut. It was a helpless, angry feeling of being abandoned. She opened up a text to him and typed: *I don't always know the right things to do, and—news flash—neither do you. But I don't run away from people who care about me.*

She stared at the screen and willed the little bubbles to show on her phone, alerting her that he was typing back, but they never came.

"Hello-o!" She heard a woman's voice downstairs. "Anyone here?"

Lila wiped her eyes and squared her shoulders. Then she headed down to the shop to greet the customer.

Evening had brought a chill into the coffee shop. Lila zipped up today's earnings in the empty bank bag Theo had left in the cash register drawer and took it with her. If and when she saw him again, she'd hand it over. He could ruin his own Christmas and hers, but she wouldn't let him ruin the Christmas of all the townsfolk stopping in for their peppermint lattes and caramel crumbles. Even if he was selling the place, she was going to keep it going until the last possible minute.

A few people had asked about Theo and the for-sale sign. She'd brushed off their suggestions that he was planning to sell the lot and close down. She'd kept his office door closed and turned on Christmas music to keep the atmosphere light, and his absence hadn't seemed to be an issue for anyone but her. Turning off the lights, she flipped over the "open" sign to "closed," and locked up.

When she got back to the cabins she went straight over to Eleanor's, deciding to go ahead right away with her harebrained idea, to avoid the thoughts of Theo and his whereabouts that had been on her mind all day.

"I have an idea," she said the instant the old lady opened the door.

"What is it?" Eleanor poked the fire in the old stone hearth with the iron, the flames licking their way up the chimney in protest, sending a wave of heat through the room. She sat down on the sofa, patting the spot next to her.

"What would you say if I told you I found a donor for this place who is willing to invest about five thousand dollars into renovations with no questions asked?"

"I'd say you've had a little too much eggnog somewhere," Eleanor said, with a disbelieving but excited laugh.

"Call me what you want, but you've got it if you want it."

Eleanor gasped, covering her mouth in surprise, her eyes wide. "Who's the investor?" she asked through her fingers.

"Me."

"What? You can't invest that much of your money."

"I can invest in whatever I want to invest in." Lila gave her a big, loving grin. "We'll have to be smart about what we use the money for to be sure we get the biggest bang for our buck. We don't have a ton to work with."

"You really want to do this?" Presley jumped into her lap, purring.

"Yes," she said with feeling. "I love this place—I see so much potential here. And I adore the town. I've toyed with the idea of sticking around for a while…"

"Oh, my dear! That would be wonderful."

"Now, let's get started. Who are we going to get to help us with the exterior?"

"I found a painter who will touch up the cabins for three thousand dollars," Eleanor said, setting the cat down onto the wood floor. Its tail swished back and forth as it made its way over to the fire and curled up on its little cushion there.

"For all the cabins? Wow, that's incredible."

"And a carpenter who will fix my steps and the porch. He wants four hundred."

"Okay, good. We're getting somewhere. We could try to rent a steam cleaner and steam the carpets instead of replacing them. I don't mind painting the walls inside the cabins. How many are there?"

"Five, plus mine. We could just paint the family rooms, since that's what you see when you come in the door."

"Great idea. We could also ask Pinewood Farm if they have any clearance garlands to use. And we could rake up the leaves around the green spaces."

"This is amazing," Eleanor said, wrapping her arms around Lila. "But I'm worried you're spending too much on this. Where are you getting all the money?"

"Don't worry about it," Lila said with a grin. "Merry Christmas."

"Merry Christmas." Eleanor put her hand on her heart, obviously still overwhelmed by the gesture. "Stay for supper," she said. "I'll make us a celebratory feast."

Eleanor had been true to her word, cooking soft-drop biscuit chicken and dumplings, cornbread, and buttery stewed carrots. Lila was bursting full, but Eleanor insisted that she carry a family-sized box of leftovers back to her cabin. She'd spent the whole dinner telling Eleanor about Theo and how she'd run the coffee shop today.

"I can't believe it," she'd said. "Well, actually, from what I've seen of him, I can, sad to say."

Lila could understand her point of view, but she refused to believe Theo would just abandon them. She'd seen another side of him—hadn't she?

As she slipped the key into the lock and let herself in, she took stock of her surroundings, the silence of the cabin making her feel lonely. Just then her phone pinged, and she couldn't deny the fizzle of hope that it was Theo. She had been checking her phone all day, but had had no reply from him. Pulling her phone from her pocket, a mixture of happiness and disappointment simultaneously swam through her. It was Edie.

The text read, *We're doing a group video call. (It was Piper's idea.) Are you free?*

Yes, she answered, amused.

Her phone lit up, and she ran into the living room and grabbed her iPad, opening the app on the bigger device and settling in on the sofa, under the soft glow of the lamp and the Christmas lights.

"Hi!" Piper said from the corner of the screen.

"Hey, everyone!" Lila said, waving to her friends. "Charlotte, are you still in LA?"

"Yes!" Charlotte was all smiles.

"What's that framed behind you? Is that someone famous?" Lila asked.

Charlotte reached around and held up a glossy photo of actress Nikki Mars, signed in swooping script in the corner. "Yeah!" she said from what looked like her trailer on set. Lila could see a tiny tinsel-strewn tree behind her friend. "Nikki signed it for me after I did her hair. She said no one has been able to style it as well as I did, and she's requesting that I do her hair on the set of her next major motion picture!"

"That's amazing," Lila said, delighted for her friend. "You deserve it. You're so talented. I'm thrilled that people are noticing."

Charlotte gave her a giddy little wiggle on her screen.

Lila turned her attention to Edie. "How's the PR business going?"

Edie was in her apartment. She had her hair pulled back, and she was wearing the reading glasses she always used when she was working. "I've been up to my eyeballs in press release verbiage. Don't ask," she told Lila.

"We all felt terrible leaving you," Charlotte said. "And we wanted to call to tell you that we miss you."

"I miss you all too," Lila told them. "I've been deprived, not having our morning coffee. How have I survived without your latest gossip?"

"Speaking of gossip..." Piper chimed in. "You need to dish, right now. We're all dying to hear what's going on with Theo."

Lila set about telling them everything, from the very beginning until her final text. "I think I'm going to go into the coffee shop to run it again tomorrow," she told them.

Piper gave her an empathetic smile. "Lila," she said softly. "Running the shop won't bring him back. It's for sale. He's gone."

Her tender tone cut Lila like a knife because she knew why Piper was approaching the subject so gently. Since her father's death, Lila had struggled with loss. Piper knew firsthand how it had torn Lila's heart out. When she and Razz hadn't worked out, Lila had crumpled into a heap of tears on Piper's bed in her apartment, the ache so strong that she could hardly breathe. All Lila wanted in life was connection and, for whatever reason, it was elusive. And now, when she felt like she'd found someone she was beginning to really *see*—even with his walls up, someone who, in such a short time, had made her feel alive—he was gone.

Much of her adult life she'd been alone, and not of her choosing. Razz had ruined their relationship, her parents had left her, and her friends were moving on. But the coffee shop was a place that made her feel like she wasn't alone. If she kept it open, even just for a few days, it would stop the loneliness and solitude from crushing her.

"I know I can't run the shop with him gone...But I wish I could fix it somehow," she said.

"You're trying to save the world," Edie said, clearly shocked by her statement. "It's too much for one person, Lila. You need to focus on your life and what *you* want. And Theo Perry's not worth a minute of your time," she added. "He's clearly not the kind of person you deserve. Do you really want to get wrapped up in all his baggage when he could be involved in illegal things?"

Lila sat, silent, digesting Edie's comments, when everything in her gut told her that Theo wasn't who they thought he was.

Edie did have a point, but what if there was some other reason for Theo's behavior that they just hadn't thought of? What if they didn't have the whole story?

"Can I ask you something?" Edie cut through her thoughts. "Are you investing in the cabins because you're thinking of staying in Pinewood Hills?"

"I've considered it," she said, honestly.

"And are you staying in the hopes that Theo might return? Because if that's your reason, I have to beg you to listen to me when I say there's more out there for you than that, Lila. You stayed in Nashville for Razz and look at where it got you."

"I've considered staying because I like it here," she said, but Edie's parallel had shaken her. Was she making the same mistake twice without even knowing it? "And Theo probably isn't coming back anyway," she added, trying to convince herself now. But the more she thought about it, the more she realized that staying in Pinewood Hills had nothing to do with Theo. "Being here makes me feel whole. Eleanor feels like family. I love waking up in the mornings, knowing that Eleanor's just across the yard, and I haven't been able to have family close to me in a very long time," she explained. "I fit in here."

Just then her iPad screen lit up with a text that floated right over Edie's face, and simultaneously stopped Lila's heart. It was from Theo. It had flashed up so quickly that by the time she got herself under control, she'd missed it, and now all she wanted to do was open it. She rummaged around the sofa for her phone, but she must have left it in the kitchen.

"You just went ghostly white," Piper said. "What's wrong?"

"I got a text," she said, breathless, her mouth drying out as she got up, carrying the iPad with her on her search for her phone. "From Theo."

"Go!" Charlotte said. "Check it and call us back later!"

The others all agreed, their heads nodding simultaneously. She snatched her phone from the kitchen counter, said her goodbyes to the girls, and then settled back down on the sofa with her phone in both hands. She swallowed, her tummy aflutter with butterflies, and opened the text.

It read simply, *You don't even know me.*

Heat spread over Lila's face and down her neck. All she could do was be honest with him, since that's what she wanted most from him. She returned, *I don't know your favorite dinner dish or what makes your skin boil, but I want to.*

Lila's stomach burned with unease. She had never been so transparent with anyone, but he'd looked so vulnerable at times that she thought he needed to hear she had faith in their connection, and if he'd just let her in, they might find there could be something wonderful between them.

When he didn't text back, she texted again: *Seafood.*

A plume of exhilaration swelled inside her when the bubbles showed on her phone. He typed, *What?*

She replied, *That's my favorite dinner dish—any kind of seafood.*

But he didn't come back, and her heart sunk at that knowledge.

Lila clearly wouldn't get the chance to talk about the sale of the coffee shop, why he was suddenly leaving, what the papers were saying about him, or what the note in his office had meant. She knew she shouldn't waste her time trying if he wasn't willing to reciprocate. She could only go out on a limb so many times before giving up. So she sent one final text and went to bed:

Your life can't start until you let go of whatever is holding you back.

As Lila crawled under the covers in the silent cabin, she wondered if that had been advice for Theo or for her.

Chapter Nineteen

Rex put his little hands over his ears to stifle the loud growl of Judd's tractor. When Judd had heard from Adele that Lila was helping out at Fireside Cabins, he came right away. Lila had no idea that Adele had said a thing—she'd only mentioned it to Adele when she'd put a sign on the coffee shop apologizing for closing its doors. The next thing she knew, Judd was rolling up the hill on his tractor with Rex and his hound dog in the front seat, the large reel on the back of the machine grinding the fallen leaves and snow, leaving green grass in its wake like a colossal vacuum cleaner.

"You reckon Winston can hear anymore?" Rex called out to her over the ruckus. "He sits with my daddy every day and it's so noisy." The little boy had gotten out of the tractor after seeing Lila in the yard, and now the two of them stood in their coats and scarves, warming their hands next to the small crackling fire in the fire pit on the side of the main cabin that Eleanor had lit for them. The flames licked their way into the air, causing the snow on the edge of the fire pit to glisten. "His back legs tapped like crazy when he found out he's gettin' to ride on a Saturday too," Rex continued. "He usually just lays on the floor all day on weekends, waitin' for Monday when he can get back to work with Daddy. He loves it."

"It seems like he does," Lila said with a laugh.

"Sometimes I wonder what Winston thinks ridin' in that tractor."
Lila looked down at Rex. "You're an old soul," she told him after
the tractor had moved further away from them, easing the clatter. "You
think a lot. I can tell."

"I'm always thinkin'," Rex said, kicking a small stone from the patio
into the grass. "Lately I've been thinkin' that I won't get to see Theo
again." His face dropped, his bright eyes clouding. "And my grandma
said she might not get her coffee anymore. He moved, didn't he?"

Lila shook her head, unsure of how to approach the subject.

Rex's lip wobbled. "He didn't tell me bye."

Unexpectedly, tears swelled in Lila's eyes. "He didn't tell me bye
either," she said, attempting to swallow the lump forming in her throat.

Rex pushed a smile across his face. "Maybe that means he's coming
back. Right, Miss Lila?" he asked, his features lifting. "Otherwise, he
wouldn't have left his guitar at my house."

"He left his guitar?" she asked.

"Yeah. He's got lots of 'em, but he said the one at my house is his
favorite, and that's why he let me use it." He folded his arms across his
chest, confusion washing over his face. "I tried to text him yesterday,
but he hasn't texted back."

"Y'all frozen yet?" Eleanor asked from the side door of her cabin,
interrupting them. "I've got hot chocolate, if y'all want to come inside
and warm up."

"Yes, ma'am," Rex replied, his arms dropping to his sides as he ran
to the door.

Lila followed suit, a mixture of emotions swirling inside her. Theo
was kind and thoughtful, and it was clear that he really liked the little
guy. He'd brought Rex his favorite guitar and let him keep it—but

then he just upped and left, without a word, ignoring the poor boy's messages. It made no sense. The line from the article Piper had sent her went round and round in her mind: *He's a complete fraud.*

Rex immediately went over to Chester's guitar, and it was clear that he wanted to stay connected to Theo in his absence. "Mrs. Eleanor, may I take a look at this?" he asked.

"Of course you can," Eleanor said, walking over and lifting it off the stand, handing it to Rex.

Rex sat on the floor and began strumming. He hummed a tune as he did, and Lila stopped still, all her attention fixed on the young boy and his fingers moving on the strings. They were a little clumsy, but that didn't stop the tune from sounding rich and beautiful.

"What is that song?" Lila asked, sitting down by the fire, across from Rex.

"It's something Theo taught me."

"Does it have any words?"

He kept his eyes on the strings as he nodded.

"Will you sing them?"

Rex repositioned his fingers on the neck of the guitar and started over, singing in a sweet little voice.

"There's a light in my soul
When you walk through that door
Your smile so innocent
of all that came before…"

Eleanor came in with their mugs. "That's beautiful," she said, setting their hot cocoa on the hearth and taking a seat on the sofa. "Whose song is it?"

"Theo's," Rex replied. "He wrote it about a few days ago. That's all I can remember. We only practiced it a couple times."

The fact that Theo had these lyrics in his mind took Lila's breath away. Who was he talking about in that song? "And he just wrote it?"

"Yep. He said he wrote it right there in the coffee shop when he saw somebody walk in." Rex started strumming another melody.

Lila swallowed, her breath leaving her. But then she actually considered what she was thinking. There was no way that song had anything to do with her. His disappearing act proved it.

"What other tunes do you know?" Eleanor asked, her gaze fluttering over to Lila suggestively.

Lila dismissed it, taking a sip of her cocoa, focusing instead on the chocolaty cream to get her mind off it.

The front door opened, and Judd popped his head in.

"Come on in," Eleanor said.

Judd and Winston joined them.

"All done," Judd said with a proud puff of his chest. "Not a lick of brush left. With the spring comin', I'd suggest layin' down seed come March or April."

Winston moseyed over to the fire and flopped down in front of it, putting his head on Lila's knee and sending Presley bounding up the stairs.

"Thank you so much, Judd," Eleanor said. "How are you doing?"

"I'm good, I guess," Judd said. "Not much changes around here with most folks, and that includes me." He turned to Lila. "Wish Theo would comply with our way of life. He's always doin' somethin'. Will you tell me if you talk to him?" he asked.

"Of course," Lila replied.

"Appreciate it." He ruffled Rex's hair. "You 'bout ready to go?" he asked his son. Winston popped up and trotted over to Judd's side.

As Judd, Rex, and Winston headed to the door, Judd paused and peered over at the broken window. "What happened to that?" he asked.

"One of the renters' trucks sent a rock up from the drive and it smacked right into the window," Eleanor replied.

Judd rubbed the scruff on his chin. "You make him pay for it?"

"No," she said, shaking her head. "It was an accident."

"You're too nice, Mrs. Finely," he told her as he grabbed the doorknob. Before he twisted it, he said, "I can fix it for you. I'll come round tomorrow."

"That's so sweet of you," she said, her eyes sparkling from his gesture.

Eleanor invited Lila to stay after the others left, and Lila had been delighted to have more time with her new friend. Eleanor felt like the grandmother she'd never had. She and Eleanor worked side by side, rinsing dishes at the sink.

"What do you make of that song little Rex played?" Eleanor asked as she grabbed a towel to dry her hands, the last mug placed in the dishwasher. Presley pawed at the dish towel as it dangled from Eleanor's fingers, and she batted the cat away playfully.

"Theo seems to be very talented," Lila replied, not wanting to admit to herself that the lyrics had been burned into her brain, the tune bouncing around her head ever since he'd played it.

"He wrote it about someone at the coffee shop," Eleanor pointed out.

Lila nodded. "Could be anybody," she said.

"Or *some*body." Eleanor placed a little laundry basket of clean kitchen towels between them on the counter and handed Lila one to fold as she took one herself.

"I don't think it was me." Lila folded the towel in thirds and then in half, setting the rectangular bundle on the counter and grabbing another.

"I think you don't want to get hurt."

"What?" She held the limp towel between her fingers.

"If Theo was writing about you, then that means he left *you* when he disappeared. And that would be heartbreaking, I'm sure." She took the towel from Lila, set it on the counter, and grabbed her hands. "But Lila, his troubles don't have anything to do with you. You were just caught in the middle, that's all."

"Did you know that there are people claiming he's a thief?"

"What?" The skin between Eleanor's eyes folded with a deep wrinkle as her face contorted in bewilderment.

"The press paints a not-so-great picture of him. They called him a fraud."

"Oh my goodness. Do you think it's true?"

"I don't know what to believe anymore. I hear things like those song lyrics and it makes everything so confusing."

"The sad thing is that I thought you were getting through to him, and if that song really is about you, he's missing the best thing he's probably ever been given in leaving you behind."

Lila gave Eleanor's hands a squeeze, considering what she'd said. She thought she was getting through to Theo too, and the frustration she felt that he wouldn't stick around to see things through was eating away at her.

"Do you mind if I head back to my cabin for a while?" she asked. "It's been a big day and both of us could probably do with a rest."

"Of course, dear. Come over any time, though."

"I will." She gave Eleanor a hug. "Thank you."

Lila went back to her cabin, crossing the icy expanse between hers and Eleanor's, and closed herself in to the musty quiet of her living space. The Christmas decorations felt as if they were mocking her with their cheer. If Eleanor had been right, and Theo had felt something for Lila—which she could swear he did—then he had to be pretty selfish to do this to her.

Frustrated, Lila pulled out her phone and texted Theo:

There's a light in my soul
When you walk through that door
Your smile so innocent
of all that came before…
If that has anything to do with anything, come back, Theo. At least talk to me. And, by the way, Rex was in tears because you didn't tell him goodbye.

Her text sat, solitary, on the screen as the minutes ticked by. Nothing. Once again, Theo wasn't answering. She dropped her phone onto the sofa and headed into her bedroom, closing the door and falling onto her bed, biting back the tears.

Having promised herself when she awoke this morning that she'd enjoy the holiday, Lila settled at the kitchen table in her cabin with a warm cup of cinnamon tea and the book she'd brought to read during those long vacation bubble baths that had never materialized, when her phone rang on the sofa. She scrambled over to get it. It was Piper.

"How's it going?" Piper asked when Lila answered.

"We've started working on Eleanor's cabin, and I'm so excited for her. She seems just over the moon about it all."

"That's good..." Piper said. The way she trailed off made Lila wonder if there was more she wanted to say.

"What's up?" she asked, taking a sip of her tea.

Piper took in a breath. "If you want to stay on at the cabins for Eleanor, then that's fine, but don't wait around for Theo. He's a bad egg for sure, Lila."

She set down her mug. "What are you talking about?"

"I was trying to help you figure out where to look for him, and I found another article. Can I read the beginning to you?"

"Of course," she said, already worried just by her friend's tone. Piper gave everyone the benefit of the doubt, so something was definitely wrong.

"Okay," Piper said. "Here goes." She began to read, "*Winding Alley Music, the production company owned by famed musician Smash and his son Theo Perry, has closed its doors for good, leaving all its clients scrambling for new producers. A source close to the family stated that Theo Perry had embezzled from his own company until he'd run it dry, and to cover it up, he shut it down; although no formal charges have been brought against him. His father, and only living relative, who spent his twenties in front of judges for various misdemeanors, declined to comment, although it's rumored that Smash plans to investigate the embezzlement himself. Winding Alley Music was responsible for seven of Smash's hits in the last five years.*"

"Oh my God," was all Lila could say, her stomach plummeting. His last text echoed in her head: *You don't even know me.* How right he'd been...

"I think that family is a mess," Piper said. "Another article said Smash has been in and out of rehab, swearing this last time was the charm... The more I read, Lila, the more I think you need to stay as far away from him as possible."

Was that why his father had been staying at the cabins? Was Smash trying to pin the embezzlement on him? Had Theo gotten wind that his father knew where he was and made a run for it? Her head spun with it all.

"Why am I drawn to the bad-boy musicians," she said, shaking her head.

But all she could think about was the way those blue eyes had looked at her, and the vulnerability he'd shown whenever he'd let his guard down. She had been so sure that this wasn't just like Razz all over again... She thought about Rex and how Theo had given the little boy his favorite guitar. How sweet he'd been to him when they'd taken Rex for burgers. No matter how hard she tried, she couldn't make the pieces fit together.

"Because you like to help people." Piper's answer came after the tick of silence, jarring Lila from her reverie. "But sometimes they just end up bringing you down."

"Yeah," she said. She knew she had to believe this, but she just couldn't—for even a second—conceive that Theo was beyond help. Maybe she was just being crazy. Maybe it was time to get a grip.

"You need to really think about what you want, Lila. You deserve to have a life that *you've* built, a life that you actually desire, because right now, I feel like you're just at the mercy of what has been thrown at you."

"What do you mean?" Lila asked, stunned by her friend's words.

"You live in Nashville because of a guy you followed there, and you work as a waitress because it was the first job you could get when he left you. Now you're sinking all your savings into the cabins, and if you had more you'd put it into the coffee shop, when neither will move your life forward. You deserve better than that."

Out of nowhere, a tear escaped down Lila's cheek. She wiped it away and took in a steadying breath.

"You're so right," she said, the reality of it all setting in.

Chapter Twenty

Lila was officially losing it. Her rent was nearly up, so soon she'd have nowhere to live, she'd given her car to her friends for the foreseeable future, and now she'd just called work and told them she'd quit. Piper's words earlier today had hit her hard, and she'd had to do some real soul-searching, but while her friend had been right about a lot of things, she wasn't on the money with one point in particular. This little mountain town had made her feel more alive than she ever had in Nashville, and she was, against all the odds, considering staying. And not for Eleanor or Theo. For her. As she sat by the twinkling lights of the Christmas tree in the cabin, with the fire roaring and snow beginning to fall on the newly cleared lawn outside the window, she knew in her heart that it was time for a change.

It wasn't like she had much of a life back in Nashville, or barely anything worth returning for. She needed to live in a place where people put relationships first. Trudy and Judd had stopped what they were doing to help their neighbor take care of the cabins; Eleanor had loaned her—a lodger—her car without hesitation; everyone she'd met in town had been more than friendly. Although she had no idea what she'd do for income, where she'd find an apartment, or if Theo would be around... Feeling a rush of appreciation for her new neighbors, she'd made a big pot of stew and called Trudy to ask her, Judd, and Rex over for dinner, and she'd invited Eleanor to join them.

They were at the door right on time. Lila hopped up to let them in and when she did, Rex was standing in front of his parents with an enormous smile on his face. He rushed in and gave her a hug around the legs.

"Hi," she said, backing up with him to let his parents in. "How are you?"

"I'm great," Rex said. "Theo came over!"

"He did?" Lila asked, trying to swallow her shock.

"Yeah! He said he heard I was missin' him. Did he come see you?"

"He didn't." Her cheeks flushed. She took Rex's coat as Trudy and Judd shrugged theirs off, and hung them all on the hooks by the door. Trudy offered a look of sympathy over the little boy's head.

"How long did he stay?" Lila asked, hoping she didn't sound too disappointed.

"Not too long. He said he had to get back to where he was going," Rex told her.

"And where was he going?" she asked, trying not to sound desperate but dying to know. Did that mean he was still in the area?

"He didn't tell me," Rex answered. "But he promised he'd come back to see me as soon as he could."

"That's really nice." So he'd definitely got her text. Which meant that she was able to reach him—if he would ever stop ignoring her. But after hearing Piper's last article and reading the letter in his office, did she even want to? The question hung in the air around her as Eleanor peeked her head inside the cabin.

"Hello-o," she said, pushing it open wider upon seeing everyone gathered inside. "I brought this for you," she said, handing Rex a giant candy cane while balancing a gorgeously festive poinsettia in her other arm.

The child's face lit up as he grabbed it. "Thank you, Mrs. Eleanor," he said, giving her a side hug to avoid the huge plant she was holding.

"You're welcome." Her eyes shone with motherly adoration. "Merry Christmas." Then she turned her attention to Lila. "And this is for you." She handed Lila the poinsettia.

"That's incredible," Trudy said, leaning in to get a better look at its bright red-and-green foliage.

"You didn't have to get me anything," Lila told Eleanor.

"It's only a tiny gesture to say a very big thank you for everything you've done—not just hosting tonight." She tipped her nose up. "It smells divine in here."

"Thank you. I made stew and I've warmed some bread in the oven. Y'all come on in and dish yourselves a bowl so we can warm up while we're talking." She ushered them all into the kitchen, cradling the plant. Lila showed them to the bowls and spoons. Then she took the lid off the pot and stirred it with the ladle, the savory aroma of beef and vegetables floating through the air. "I'll just put this poinsettia in the living room while you all get your stew. Be right back."

Lila went into the other room and set the plant on the floor next to the fire. Then she pushed her feelings of rejection aside and took a quick second to text Theo. She typed: *That was really nice of you to visit Rex.*

Regardless of what Theo had done, he'd been nothing but wonderful to Rex, and Lila was happy that he'd thought enough of the little boy to come see him.

After dinner Judd and his family headed home, but Eleanor had stayed for a cup of coffee. They'd settled on the sofa.

"I'd love to have you work for me," Eleanor said, after hearing that Lila had quit her job. "I just don't have any way to pay you."

"You know I'd work here for free, Eleanor. But I have to eat."

"Pesky hunger. Always ruining everything," Eleanor teased. Then she sobered. "How are you, dear?"

"What do you mean?" Lila asked.

"I mean just that. How are you?"

She wasn't sure how to answer. "I can't complain..."

"You *don't* complain. And that's admirable, but when you told me you'd quit your job, I have to be honest, I thought it was to chase some wild dream you've always had or something fanciful like that. But you quit and don't even seem to know why."

"I quit because I hate that job."

"Then what job would you love?"

Lila chewed the inside of her lip, thinking. "I don't know," she told her. "I'm sort of lost."

"Well, definitely something with people," Eleanor said as her coffee mug met her lips.

"That was one of the only things I liked about waitressing," Lila admitted. "I enjoyed talking to the people I met—I heard about their vacations or why they'd come to Nashville. The nights I had good customers, the time would fly and my shift would go faster." She folded her legs under her and leaned back, holding her cup with two hands to warm them. "I like it here," she suggested.

"If it's people you enjoy, then you wouldn't want to stay around here," Eleanor said with a pout, running her finger around the rim of her cup.

"Why?" Lila asked.

"There's no one here. Look around. We have a few festive events every year, but people don't want to come to Pinewood Hills anymore. They have better things to do." She took a thoughtful sip from her mug and swallowed. "I've been thinking a lot about that as I plan the work on the cabins, spending your hard-earned money. For what? Why am I trying to make this place better when no one visits? Even the coffee shop is closed now. Theo probably couldn't make any money in that location."

"I think Theo is selling the coffee shop for his own reasons," Lila told her. She pushed aside the pang that pinched her insides when she thought of him. "And there's a lot here. The farm is adorable, there are loads of wonderful places to visit, and Main Street is adorable. I truly believe that if you can update the cabins, we could really wrap some solid PR around it, and people would come."

Eleanor smiled fondly at Lila. "You're always so optimistic."

"I see the value in things, that's all. Can I somehow make a living doing that?" She set her mug down on the side table and twisted toward the old lady. "You know when you have a really great cookie dough, and the chocolate chips are right there at the surface? You're sure that it'll make delicious cookies even before it's baked. I can always spot good cookie dough."

"Fireside Cabins are a little low on chocolate chips, then," Eleanor said.

"But the dough's good! We just have to add a little more chocolate."

Eleanor laughed, holding her mug in her lap. "I never discourage anyone who believes we need more chocolate." She patted Lila's arm. "I just hope that paint and remodeling will bring people in."

"I think you could do more than that," Lila said. "You could beef up the trails, add more prominent historical markers, a guided tour, maybe. You could have a gift shop on the premises with trinkets to commemorate visitors' stays, you could reach out into the community and offer the grounds to youth groups for meeting space—maybe even have an after-school club or something. I'd love to volunteer for that. But I'll need to find a job in town first."

"I'll keep an eye out for any jobs that come up, although I wouldn't hold my breath in this small town."

"Thanks, Eleanor," she said. "In the meantime, I'd still like to help you fix this place up any way I can. We don't have to have a grand plan. We can start modest and build as we get more revenue. But we'll get these cabins up and running." And no matter what, she was going to make it happen.

Chapter Twenty-One

Lila shielded her eyes and took a step back to admire the main cabin, her breath puffing out in front of her as the snow drifted down from the heavens. She and Eleanor had spent the last week immersed in renovations, which Lila was thankful for because it got her mind off Theo and the fact he hadn't even tried to make contact. She couldn't believe how much they'd accomplished. After Judd had fixed the window he'd power washed the cabins, and when the painters had tidied up the blemishes with fresh stain, they'd left them all a gorgeous natural wood, their metal roofs with the new greenery and lights they'd added making them look like they were dressed up for Christmas.

Lila and Eleanor used Judd's farm truck to bring back a five-foot Christmas tree for every cabin porch, loading each one up with sparkling white lights and red ribbon. Judd had offered them free of charge to say thank you to Lila for watching Rex. They'd also placed an evergreen wreath on every door and old silver farm buckets of pinecones lining each step.

Christmas music rang out over the hills. Eleanor had dug out speakers that had been used for events in the cabins' heyday, and they'd just finished getting them all hooked back up. The grounds were a blanket of white, the twinkling lights on all the porches like stars in the night sky. They'd shoveled all the walkways and replaced the gravel, lining each one with topiaries, their buttery glow meandering up and down the hills.

"It's amazing," Lila said, taking it all in.

They'd both worked so hard. While Lila had been busy weeding, laying new mulch in the freezing cold, and coordinating the work on the outsides, Eleanor had been inside the cabins, showing the decorators where to focus their attention and cleaning the carpets. Lila had spent some of her money to buy every cabin a tiny Christmas tree for the interior in addition to the full-size ones on the porches, and she'd decorated each one with red beads and white snowflake ornaments, still hoping to push the PR and get a few new lodgers in for the holiday season. Trudy and Rex had come over throughout the week to help Eleanor with the interiors and Judd had been on duty outside.

"It takes the sting off for a minute, doesn't it?" Eleanor said, rubbing her hands together as she admired the scene.

"What do you mean?"

"Well, we've gotten a good start, but we still don't have any revenue coming in. I have to cover my personal expenses, like food and healthcare. There're things like merchant services and the website to pay quarterly; kitchen equipment, new linens for every cabin, business supplies, entertainment—we've made it look great, but we haven't scratched the surface with the rest of it. The thought of selling it now and getting your money back has crossed my mind..."

Lila stared at her aghast, uneasiness swelling in her gut. "Now that we've got the cabins mostly done, we can take a look at the business side of things and make a plan."

"It's all a bit overwhelming. Chester used to take care of all that." She fluttered her hands in the air. "But I won't dwell on it now. We both need to get cleaned up and rest so we can enjoy the beautiful work we've done."

"Maybe we'll get a Christmas surprise somehow," Lila said, trying to be hopeful. "Christmas is full of them, right?"

Eleanor raised her eyebrows and smiled. "You never know!"

Lila was on the sofa, curled up with the afghan, after a long hot bath. She'd soaked in the citrus and aloe bubble bath Piper had left, the zesty scent of it still on her skin. She'd spent the whole time thinking long and hard about what she really wanted in life. What she'd loved about working with Theo was getting to talk to all the customers. She kept wondering if there was some place here where she could do that and be around people, make them feel like they were family. And her mind kept coming back to Fireside Cabins.

She'd started a fire and finished her leftover bowl of stew while she researched on her iPad just to see what it took to run a property like Fireside Cabins. It was an absolutely crazy idea—she had no background in how to run an inn—but somehow she felt compelled to do it. Even if Eleanor were up for it, could Lila somehow take it over? Maybe get a business loan to see them through? Would she be approved for something like that? Probably not. Especially with no job. She could ask her friends to pitch in money... They couldn't sustain it, though. And she would never really want to ask. Even though it seemed completely impossible, she couldn't help thinking that Fireside Cabins had been just waiting for her to come along. And it was the first time she'd considered what *she* wanted, instead of someone else. She just had to figure out how to make it work.

If only she could talk to Theo about it. She closed her eyes and summoned up the image of the little creases that played at the corners of his eyes when he was listening to her, and her chest tightened. It had been over a week since she'd heard from him. He hadn't been to see Rex again. Was he okay? She reached over and grabbed her phone, opening up a text to him, unsure of what she even wanted to say. So much had been left unspoken between them. If anything, she needed some kind of closure. She abandoned the text screen and hit the call button. She'd had enough messaging; she needed to talk.

Lila waited for Theo to answer. She fully expected to get his voicemail, so when she heard the gentle "Hello," in that familiar deep voice of his, her breath caught in her chest.

Lila had two options here: she could yell at him for leaving and not at least warning her first, and press him to explain those letters she'd read, like she wanted to do—or she could follow her gut, which told her something had to be seriously wrong to make him just disappear. She closed her eyes, summoning the feel of his arms around her as they'd slept on the sofa. The tender way he'd held her—that wasn't somebody who was a fraud and a thief. And given how hard it had been to crack his shell, being vulnerable like that surely hadn't been easy for him to do. "I miss you," she said in a whisper. The words fell out of her mouth before she could stop them.

The end of the line was so still that fear shot through her as she sat, worried he'd hung up. She checked her phone screen to see that the line was still connected. Finally, he spoke. "I didn't want you to miss me," he said, and she could hear the ache in his voice. "I tried not to let you in..."

"Why?"

"Lila, you don't want to get involved with me."

His statement sent a tiny wisp of doubt through her mind. Was the bad press about him true? "You're not giving me a choice at all. Why don't you tell me what's going on and let *me* decide?"

"There are things that make what we started between us…impossible. You deserve better."

"Look, is this something about stealing money? Because—"

Theo cut her off. "What did you say?"

"I read an article…Well, Piper read— It doesn't matter. They're saying you did some pretty crazy things. Tell me about what happened with the embezzlement. Are you in any danger? What's going on, Theo?"

"You know…" He trailed off. "I've got to go."

"Wait," she said in a panic, but the line went dead. "Hello?" Nothing. She immediately called him back, her heart racing.

"Yes?" he said, less angrily than she thought he would, but she still felt a wave of relief.

He answered.

"I like to fix things," she said. "That's what I do. You will literally send me to the crazy house if you don't let me help you with this."

"You can't fix *this*."

"How do you know if you won't let me try?" She scrambled for a way to show her solidarity with him, to let him know she could help him deal with whatever this was. What could she offer? Then suddenly, it occurred to her that if she was really on Theo's side, she might want to mention Smash staying at the cabins. "Did you know your dad stays at Fireside Cabins?"

"What?"

"Eleanor said he often rents a cabin here. She didn't know about the connection to you."

"You've got to be kidding me."

"Why?" she asked.

"I heard he knew where I was—that's one of the reasons I left. But I had no idea he'd been to Pinewood Hills before." Then he whispered, "He wants the money. That's why he's here."

"Should you come clean and give it to him?" Even as she said the words, they sounded wrong to her.

The line fell silent again. After an incredibly long pause, he said with regret in his voice, "Lila, I don't think we should talk anymore. I'm sorry."

"Is it because you did it?" she asked, her voice coming through in a crackly whisper, her emotions getting the better of her. "Because if you didn't do it, I don't understand why you won't let me in, Theo." She just couldn't make herself believe that he'd do something like that. She closed her eyes, the phone pressed against her ear, remembering how sweet he'd been with Rex, the way his fingers had rested tenderly in her hand, his safe embrace when he'd taken that horse ride with her . . . She wasn't sure why, but his silence suddenly hit her. "I believe in you," she said.

"What are you talking about?"

She heard him swallow on the other side of the line.

"You didn't do this. I don't believe it. And I need you to tell me what you're thinking," she pleaded.

He cleared his throat. "I didn't take the money. They all think I did, but I've stopped caring what the public thinks. I shouldn't have to prove anything to anyone. And you believed me when I hadn't even defended myself. I'm wondering how you can read me like you do. You're the first person to ever do that."

"I need to admit something to you," she said. "I went into your office, and I found a note about how there's nothing to worry about legally, and no one can be charged with a crime. What was that?"

"What the hell, Lila!" he boomed. "That wasn't something you'd just stumble upon—it was in my filing cabinet!"

"I know. I'm so sorry. I was just curious."

"Those were my personal files. You certainly know a lot about me. Where else did you snoop, huh?"

"Theo. Listen to me, please. I absolutely shouldn't have gone through your things, and I feel terrible to have done it. But that letter sounded like a cover-up of some sort, and I'm telling you that even having read that, I don't believe you've done anything wrong. Because, while I don't know the situation you're in, I know *you*. And I just couldn't believe you'd ever do anything to hurt someone. I'm so sorry I went into your files. I'll never do that to you again. I'll just ask you my questions outright."

There was silence on his end.

"Does your dad know the truth?" she continued. "We need to tell him you didn't take anything," she suggested. "I can find out from Eleanor when he's coming back..."

"Lila! No, no, no. You can't tell my father anything. He cannot know that there's any way to get in touch with me. I do *not* want him in my life, and—believe me—you don't want him in yours. And, as much as it hurts, I can't have *you* in my life either because it's just too risky."

"You're talking in circles," she said, frustrated. "Where are you? I need to see you. I want to talk to you, face to face."

"Lila, let it go."

"No," she said emphatically. "I need to know you're okay."

"If you let me live my life and leave me alone, I'll be okay."

It pained her to hear that. She sat on the line without speaking, trying to keep the tears from forming; the only sound was his soft breath on the other end. If he didn't want her in his life, then she'd have to live with that choice. She wasn't going to beg him. "If that's what you want," she said at last, defeated.

"It's what I want. Goodbye, Lila."

She couldn't bring herself to reply, so she just sat there, the ache in her chest making her feel like she couldn't breathe.

"I hope you meet someone great," he said, his words sounding genuine.

Then he hung up the phone.

Chapter Twenty-Two

The wooden cabin floors were cold under her feet as Lila padded over to turn on the Christmas tree, shivering in the icy air while stifling a yawn. She hadn't slept well at all last night. Instead, she'd tossed and turned, wondering what he'd meant by it being too risky to be with her. She'd thought about everything she'd wanted to say to Theo now that she'd processed everything. It was pretty clear at this point that he didn't want to see her, and Lila wasn't going to try to force the situation. But she couldn't help the ache it caused her.

Lila's cell phone intermittently lit up on the counter separating the living area and the kitchen. She went over to view the notification and realized it was a missed call from Theo last night after she'd gone to bed. With tingling electricity shooting through her, she grabbed the phone and dialed his number. It was early, but he'd gotten up much earlier than this to run the coffee shop, so he should be awake...

There was a click on the line and she stood still, ready to talk. But she stopped short when she heard the automated recording: "We're sorry. The number you have reached is no longer in service. Please check the number and try your call again. Thank you." The call ended.

Lila dropped the phone, her gaze on the window but not processing the view. She felt sick, empty. She suddenly realized how serious he was about not letting her into his life. He didn't want to be found. Defeated, Lila slumped down on the sofa in a daze.

After a few restless attempts to nap, to alleviate the stress and her lack of sleep last night—neither of which was improved by the effort—Lila grabbed her iPad. Overcome by confusion, she decided to do an internet search for Theo, to see if she could get any information that would help her better understand the situation. She typed in his name and scanned the list of articles, clicking on one that interested her: "The End of an Era—Perry Dynasty Collapses."

Lila began reading.

Smash Perry suffers another relapse only weeks after leaving his most recent stint at a rehab facility, which was organized by his son Theo Perry, in his hometown of Nashville, Tennessee. Sources close to the singer tell us he's currently resting in his Brentwood mansion, but it's rumored that he is trying unsuccessfully to get sober at home after a public disagreement with the facility, regarding the quality of his care. Reports suggest that his latest relapse is due to the fact that his only son is being investigated on allegations of fraud. Despite putting out a debut record in his teens, Theo Perry asserts he has no plans to continue the family musical tradition, a claim that has evidently caused a rift between father and son.

So that rift was why Theo didn't want to have contact with his father...But why was his father frequenting Fireside Cabins? Was he looking for the money? She sighed, having got more questions than answers. She rolled her head on her shoulders, trying to let the Christmas lights calm her.

Unable to get this whole thing off her mind, she decided to call Piper to tell her what was going on. She needed to hear a friendly voice. Charlotte was most likely busy in LA, and Edie was less sympathetic over things like this. Piper would listen objectively and give her honest but gentle guidance.

"I keep reading about him, too," Piper said once they were talking. "I'm surprised it's taken this long for people to realize he was living just outside Nashville in Pinewood Hills."

"It is funny that he didn't go very far," Lila noted.

"He's born and raised in Nashville. It's his home."

"Yeah . . ." Lila said. "Makes you wonder if he's still close." She took in a deep breath to keep her chest from tightening, her gaze flickering over to the view out the window of the rolling, snow-covered hills dotted by pine trees. "It could just be wishful thinking." She picked at a loose string on the afghan. "I just want to help him."

"He's a big boy. He can handle it," Piper said. "But you know what I think?"

"Hm?" she said, waiting for Piper's insight.

"I think it's more than wanting to help him. I think you like him. A lot. But I still feel like you deserve better than this, Lila."

Lila didn't answer—she didn't know what to say to that.

"And if it makes you feel any better," Piper added, "I think Theo knows that too, and that's why he's cut the cord. He cares enough about you already to let you go before you get mixed up in his mess."

"What if I can handle the mess?" Lila said. "His life is definitely chaos, but I really don't think he stole the money—I have to believe that."

"How can you be sure?" Piper asked.

"Because everything he's done until now doesn't fit with that. He didn't run away somewhere and live in the lap of luxury. He pulled into himself and moved to a modest town to run an even more modest business. It was almost as if he didn't want anything to do with money." She remembered his intensity when he'd told her, *This is my life. This is it.*

"I think you should just be careful, Lila. Take the disconnected phone as a sign that this is a little too messy to get involved with."

"Maybe you're right," she said, still not really believing it.

"Right, on to something more cheery. How's Eleanor? Has she baked anything delicious?"

"She's always baking something amazing," Lila replied, glad for the change of subject. "She made some Christmas sugar cookies that were out of this world."

"I should've stayed," Piper said. Lila could feel her warm smile down the line.

"There's still time. It looks like I'll be staying awhile... I quit my job."

"What?" Piper said with a gasp. "You finally did it?"

"Yep. My lease is up in a matter of days too."

"You're staying around Nashville, right? Please say yes," Piper said in a pleading whine.

"I'm not sure..."

"Are you thinking of staying at Fireside Cabins?"

"I'd like to." Before she could answer completely, Lila's iPad lit up just as her phone pinged with a text, and she sucked in a breath. "Hang on," she said. "Someone's texting." Her heart pounding, she reached over and grabbed her iPad off the table. When she saw who the caller was, it felt bittersweet. "It's Charlotte," she said, trying not to sound disappointed. "She says she misses me and to call her when I'm free."

"Aw, that's nice," Piper said. "She's been crazy busy. I've hardly been able to talk to her at all. I'll let you go. You can call me back any time. Go ring her."

"You sure?"

"Yes," Piper replied. "I'm going to need at least an hour more so I can convince you to stay in Nashville."

Lila smiled. "I haven't said I wasn't. I just don't know."

"Well, call Charlotte and then call me later so I can talk some sense into you," Piper teased.

"Okay," Lila said with a laugh. "I'll call you later."

They said their goodbyes and Lila called Charlotte immediately.

"Girl!" Charlotte said, without even a hello. "I miss you!"

"What have you been up to?" Lila asked, already in a better mood. Her friend always had that effect on her.

"Well, I got a Haley Russo original for starters."

Haley Russo was an up-and-coming fashion designer in Nashville. Her line was a funky mix of elegance and cowgirl chic, and Charlotte had been dying to get her hands on one of the blouses in last year's line.

"I couldn't believe it. She was doing a runway show out here in LA, and she grabbed me after the show, recognizing me from her debut party in Nashville!"

"Oh, that's awesome!" Lila said, genuinely excited.

"She was thrilled that I'd been following her since the beginning, and when I told her I'd been dying to get my mitts on anything from her line but just couldn't get there before it all sold out, she took me backstage and let me choose something from the model rack."

"Oh my gosh, lucky you."

"Yes," she hissed with excitement. "I got a red sundress with a little slit on the side."

"Sounds amazing. Any chance you can grab me something? Maybe one of her big southern belt buckles with the beadwork?" Lila teased.

"Give me time…" Charlotte said with a laugh. "But that's not even the main part of the story. Guess how I got invited to the show in the first place?"

"Do tell."

"I've become really good friends with Nikki Mars—remember I was so worried about doing her hair? Turns out, all she needed was a little straightener. Anyway, knowing I was from Nashville, Nikki invited me to Haley's show."

"Very cool," Lila told her, folding her legs under her on the sofa.

"Nikki is super sweet. As I got to know her, she told me something and my mouth fell open."

"What is it?"

"Guess who Nikki's best friend was in school?"

"Who?"

"You'll never believe it."

"*Who?*" The suspense was killing Lila.

"Have you ever heard of Alexa Fontaine?"

"Stop it… You're kidding." That name was burned into Lila's brain.

"Let me just give you her full title: Alexa Fontaine, former fiancée of Theo Perry. Better?"

Lila held her breath, the only sound she could hear the buzzing of the lamp beside her. After a loaded moment she asked, "Did she say anything about Theo?"

"Piper told me all about what's been going on with you and Theo, so I poked around a little. I asked Nikki if she was still in touch with Alexa, and when she said yes, I asked if Alexa was still dating that musician's son Theo Perry."

"What did she say?"

"Nikki told me that Alexa wouldn't even speak of him. He completely ruined their upcoming wedding. Her family was toying with trying to sue him for the cost of it—it was *millions*. But she said it's useless because he doesn't have any money anyway. She thinks that's why he was stealing from his own company."

"None of this sounds like him," Lila said, shaking her head in confusion, her heart racing.

"I figured you'd say that, so I asked why he wasn't ever arrested if he stole from his company and everyone knew about it. She said Alexa thinks his dad paid off the police department. They got that new wing at the department, and suddenly the family accountant declared it was just an oversight and paid the taxes, and everything was wiped clear. But Theo's dad cut him off from the family inheritance and he ran."

"Then why would his dad be looking for him now?" Lila asked. It didn't make any sense.

"I'm not sure. Maybe his dad found out he'd stolen more money or something, and he wants to get it back. I don't know."

"This seems so crazy. Why would Theo steal money from his company if he was a millionaire already?"

"Nikki said there have been rumors that Theo overspent extravagantly and ran the family finances into the ground... I think you're too kind, Lila," her friend said gently. "If he cut you off, then it was probably a blessing. Who knows, his phone may have been disconnected—can he pay the bill?"

Lila sat, shell-shocked. She didn't know what to say. Theo sounded worse with every bit of new information she'd gotten. And even though it went against her gut instinct about him, she was at a loss for how to feel.

"So you're telling me that the man we met who runs a coffee shop, gives free guitar lessons, and watches Rex all day and night as a favor—that guy is an overspending, lying thief who stole from his own father? I just don't buy it."

"We don't really know him, do we?" Charlotte said.

Lila shook her head, feeling lost. With a sinking feeling, she finished up the call with Charlotte and walked into the kitchen, thinking, when she noticed a tiny slip of paper tucked beneath a candle on the counter. She picked it up and smoothed it between her fingers. It was the fortune she'd gotten from the confectionery when she'd visited with the girls and Eleanor. Lila scanned the words: *When faced with a choice, choose to believe. It'll change your life.* In that moment the sentence spoke to her—even though there were so many things piling up against Theo, she still prayed by some miracle none of it would be true.

Wanting to go for a walk and clear her head, she put on her big coat and wrapped her scarf around her neck, her mind racing the whole time. None of it added up. Was she in denial? She was a pretty good judge of character, and while Razz had been a disaster, a part of her had known that going into the relationship. But Theo was different. It was as if he had some sort of split personality.

She opened the front door and stopped cold. Sitting on the porch of the cabin, in the freezing temperatures, was a giant Christmas bouquet with at least twenty red roses and sprigs of holly, spruce and baby's breath. It was the most incredible bouquet she'd ever seen. Lila looked around, wondering if the delivery had been to the wrong cabin, but she was sure no one was renting the others. After all, she'd just helped Eleanor fix them all up.

Lila carried the bouquet inside and set it on the kitchen table. She took her coat back off and dropped her scarf in a lump on the chair, before plucking the card out of its little envelope. It read, *You know, you made me like Christmas. And I didn't mean to ruin yours. Enjoy the holiday. Love, Theo.* She held the card to her chest, her skin tingling with joy.

The handwriting looked similar to the scrawl she'd seen on his ledger book at the coffee shop, which meant that he'd gone into the florist's himself... Lila turned the card over and read the name: *Hutton's Flowers.* With a quick search on her phone, she was able to get the address. But then she paused. Did he want to be found? If there was even a slight chance that he did, it was worth trying to find him. She grabbed her coat again and ran out the door, heading straight there.

Chapter Twenty-Three

"I know that it's not usual protocol, but can you please give me the address of the person who ordered my flowers for me?" Lila asked the florist, her heart thumping.

The woman behind the counter shook her head apologetically. "Even if I could, I don't have it anyway," she said. "He paid in cash, and the only contact information I have is Brian Brown, which you probably already know since he was the one who signed the card, right?"

He hadn't even used his real name. Had she really thought he'd give his address? "He actually signed it Theo," she said. "But I guess that doesn't help. Okay, thank you for your time. Sorry to bother you."

Lila pushed aside her disappointment. What had he intended by sending her flowers? Was it a consolation prize—*sorry I won't ever see you again and I feel bad*? Or had he meant something else? Whatever the gesture was, she felt even more confused than before. Realizing that she needed to get out of her head and try to enjoy the holiday, on a whim she decided to stop by the farm on her way back to the cabin. Maybe a nice hot chocolate in the café would turn things around. Trudy and Judd were probably working, and Lila could hear about how they were all doing and catch up on the latest cuteness with Rex.

She needed a friendly face, and the Johnsons were just the right family to lift her spirits.

Getting into Eleanor's car, Lila drove down the main road toward the farm. The snow was really coming down now, a winter storm rapidly moving in. The hills were a blanket of white with little dots of green spruce peeking through, the scenery stretching out in front of her, looking just like a Christmas card. She really did love it in Pinewood Hills. She couldn't wait to have something delicious like a peppermint hot chocolate and cinnamon Christmas roll at the farm. She'd cozy up by the heater and chat with Trudy and Judd until she was dripping in holiday cheer, and hopefully Theo would soon be a distant memory.

Even though she knew better and was trying to put herself in the festive mood, Lila glanced over at the coffee shop as she passed it, despite knowing the for-sale sign would only distress her. But when she caught sight of Theo getting into a red truck, she slammed on her brakes, hydroplaning on the wet tarmac and sliding toward the ditch. The two passenger-side tires skated madly across the surface, locked and helpless to control the vehicle. The growl of the engine as the car came to rest, the tires groaning against the snow bank, caused Theo to spin around. She could see the frustration in the slump of his shoulders as he started marching toward her.

Lila cut the engine and jumped out of the car, her feet sinking into the snow that had piled up, icy clumps of it sliding into her shoes as she trudged toward him. But she barely noticed, the mixture of elation and anxiety overwhelming her and clouding any rational thought she had.

"What the hell just happened? Are you okay?" he called to her, as he peered over her head at Eleanor's car.

His tone was clipped but Lila didn't care. When she reached him, she couldn't help smiling. Instinctively, and despite everything, she lifted her arms to put them around his neck, but he caught them and gently held them by her sides.

"Thank you for the roses," she said, looking up at him and not bothering to hide her affection.

His face softened. "You're welcome."

"Were they goodbye roses?" she asked, feeling the vulnerability in her words.

He stared at her, as if drinking her in, not answering. Did he even know?

"Don't disappear," she said, twisting her hands around and grabbing his. "Let's go inside and talk for a minute."

"I think we should work on getting Eleanor's car out of the ditch first," he suggested.

"It's not in the road. It'll be fine for a few minutes."

Theo clearly deliberated.

"I'm freezing..." she tried.

With a huff, he took her hand. They walked up to the door of the shop and he let her inside, the warmth hitting her like a tidal wave, giving her a shiver as the cold left her. When she'd recovered, she smacked her hands on his chest, startling him. "You shut off your phone," she snapped, everything she wanted to say surfacing at a mile a minute in her head. "Do you have any idea how much I've worried, having no idea if you're okay?"

"The way you care for people is unbelievable," he said.

But she didn't let his statement derail the conversation. "Theo, if you don't want me around, then so be it, but don't just disappear and cut yourself off completely. *Don't* do that to me again."

He locked eyes with her, remorse sliding down his face. "Lila, I didn't intend to meet you, and it's really bad timing..." He tilted his head, seemingly contemplating the situation. For a second she thought the corners of his lips were forming a smile. But then it faded. "I didn't cut off my phone so you couldn't call me. I cut off my phone to keep myself from calling *you*."

A buzz of excitement swam around inside her. "Why stop yourself?" she asked.

Theo slid her coat off and draped it on one of the chairs, then offered her a seat. He lowered himself down across the table from her. "The first time I saw you walk in with all your friends, something about you pulled me in. I had to work to keep my eyes off you. It frustrated me to no end because all I wanted was to be left alone."

"Why?"

"It was easier to avoid getting hurt."

"And now?"

"That's the problem, Lila. I'm not in a position to be what you want me to be."

"And what do I want you to be?" He was talking in riddles.

"Present." He rolled his head on his shoulders, closing his eyes, clearly dealing with some kind of inner turmoil. "I'm so far underwater that I can't focus on anything but myself right now. No matter how much I'd love to."

"You're present every day at the coffee shop," she said.

"I won't be anymore. I'm here because I just met with my real estate agent. He's got an offer on the shop."

"Oh," she said, letting her dejection show. She leaned across the table and touched his arm. "Theo, why don't you tell me what you're going through so I can go through it with you? You don't need to deal with whatever it is alone."

"I don't want to drag you into this."

"You wouldn't drag me into anything. I'd willingly step into it with you." When he didn't answer, avoiding her gaze, she changed course. "We don't have to have a plan right now. And I guess we should get Eleanor's car unstuck before the snow buries it."

"I'm not sure we can get it out of the ditch. You've dug yourself into a pretty good hole. But if you want to try, we can. Worst case, I can drive you home in my truck." He stood up, lifting her coat off the chair and handing it to her. Then he went over to the closet and pulled out a shovel.

Lila wasn't any closer to answers, but Theo had used the word "we," which was a start. She put her coat on and followed him back out into the cold.

When they got to the car, she stopped him. "I'll tell you what. We get this car out and you tell me what's going on. All of it. If the car's stuck, then you're off the hook."

His gaze shifted to the tires, half buried in dirt and snow. "You're always making deals..."

"Do we have a deal?" she asked, ignoring his attempt to sidestep her suggestion.

He shook his head disbelievingly. "Deal."

While Lila got in the car and wound down the window so they could talk to each other, Theo dug a pretty good trench at the front and back of the two stuck tires. Then he stepped away.

"Put it in reverse and hit the gas lightly," he told her.

Lila complied; the engine moaned but the wheels rocked backward a bit.

"Okay, now put it in drive," he said.

Lila shifted.

"Got it in drive?"

Lila gave Theo the thumbs up.

"When you hear me yell 'go,' hit the gas. It's definitely in drive, right?"

She checked again. "Yes."

"Don't run me over."

"I won't."

Theo walked around to the back of the car. "Go!" he yelled.

Lila hit the gas just as Theo grunted loudly, pushing the vehicle. It strained forward, the wheels spewing snow, dislodging itself but not completely out of the dirt. He dug another trench around them. "Let's do it again. Ready?"

Lila nodded.

"Now!"

Lila hit the gas while Theo pushed, and suddenly the car felt light, releasing from its spot and sliding onto the street.

"Oh! We did it!" Lila said excitedly, the idea of having Theo to herself making her nervous and excited at the same time.

Theo rolled his eyes as he came around and got into the passenger seat, winding up the window. "I can't believe I lost another bet." He blew on his hands to warm them up. "Well," he said, "I hope you've got time tonight. You're gonna hear quite a story…"

"I can't wait," she said honestly.

Lila drove off with Theo, and she couldn't get back to the cabin fast enough.

Chapter Twenty-Four

"What do you have to eat at your place?" Theo asked from the passenger seat of Eleanor's car. "I never had lunch, and it's nearly five o'clock."

"I don't have a whole lot," she replied.

"We could grab some dinner and take it back to the house."

"Oh, yes," Lila said, making the turn back toward Pinewood Market. It had a kitchen where they prepared the most delicious-looking meals, and Lila had wanted to try one ever since that first day she'd stopped in with the girls. "We can grab a bottle of wine too, since it's a date," she teased.

Theo raised his eyebrows, but couldn't hide the fact that he enjoyed her banter.

Lila pulled the car to a stop in the lot outside Pinewood Market. The display windows were all aglitter with white lights and tinsel, and "Rockin' Around the Christmas Tree" was playing over the speaker outside. "Do you know what you did that you'll never live down?" she asked with a devilish grin, as they got out of the car and walked toward the store.

He faced her. "There are so many things," he said. "I'm afraid to ask."

"You admitted that you love Christmas," she stated dramatically. "You are in sooo much trouble now."

"Oh no."

She grabbed his hands and lifted his arms, spinning underneath them as if they were dancing in the snow. To her surprise, he gently grabbed her waist and began to sway, taking her hand, pushing her outward, and twirling her back in with perfectly smooth movements. Then he let her go and opened the door.

Flabbergasted, Lila followed him in. "You know how to ballroom dance?" she asked, shuffling up beside him as he made his way to the back of the store. He plucked a menu from the holder on the counter and held it out so she could read it with him.

"My mom made me take lessons as a teenager, before she decided to run off after another lead singer and never come back."

"Oh," she said, her pleasure fading. "I'm sorry."

"I'm not," he said matter-of-factly. "She was a disaster—confusing for a young guy. It took me a long time, and a lot of therapy, to learn that it was her and not me that caused her to leave. But she did give me the ability to dance with you on the front porch of the local market... if that's a good thing," he joked, handing Lila the menu. "I think I'll get the salmon and creamed spinach soup. What about you?"

"The filet with asparagus sounds really good."

"Excellent." He turned to the woman behind the counter, who was clearly trying to figure out his story while she put in their orders.

"So, white or red wine?" he asked, pulling a bottle out of the fridge next to the counter.

"Both," she said with a grin.

He eyed her.

"You said it'll be a long story. We're going to need two bottles."

Theo raised an eyebrow and grabbed a bottle of Sangiovese, setting it on the counter. Then he got out a bottle of Chardonnay. "Both of these too, please," he told the woman, handing her his credit card.

After leaving the market, they made the short drive along the meandering road to the cabin and carried the steaming containers inside. Lila bustled into the kitchen and dished up their dinners while Theo made a fire.

He dropped the last log on the blaze, which crackled and spat, and then dragged a finger along Charlotte's stocking, which was still hanging from the mantel along with the others. "Are your friends coming back?" he asked, on his way into the kitchen to join Lila.

"No," Lila said, trying not to let it get her down. "Charlotte's in LA, and Edie's tied up with some big project at work. Piper probably could, but it wouldn't be the same without all of us."

"You're close with them," he stated, picking up their plates and carrying them to the table.

"Yes. They're my best friends. I don't have anyone else. My parents are both gone, and they're like my family."

He nodded, thinking. "I gave them a hard time, but they seem like good people." He pulled out Lila's chair.

"Wait, the wine," she said, still standing.

"I'll get it," he told her, motioning for her to take a seat. "White or red first?"

"Red, please." She liked this new Theo—dancing, suggesting dinner, lighting fires. She was afraid to blink, for fear she'd open her eyes and realize the whole thing had been a Christmas dream.

Theo poured their wine and handed her a glass, as he sat down.

She took a sip, the rich floral flavor of it making her feel festive. "So, where do you want to start?" Lila asked.

"Are we jumping right into explanations?"

"Yes. I think it's best to get them out of the way first, so I can tell you it will all be fine and we can enjoy ourselves."

"It might not all be fine, Lila," he said seriously. "But I'll let you hear it." He stabbed a slice of his salmon, his jaw clenching as he looked down at it, clearly debating how to begin. "Well, I think the first thing I should tell you is that I'm married."

Lila, who was cutting a piece of her filet, stopped cold. "What?" Amidst all the updates she'd gotten from Piper and Charlotte, this was something entirely new.

"On paper." He took a sip of his wine and leaned on the table. "I was engaged to a woman named Alexa." He took a long, meditative sip. "I didn't want a big wedding. For me, it was about celebrating us as a couple and both of us had families in the public eye, so a huge event would've been a complete circus. We would've had to hire choppers to do surveillance, guards at every drive... It would've been a nightmare."

Lila remembered Charlotte telling her about Alexa's family wanting to sue him for the wedding. "But you planned a big wedding anyway?"

"Yep." He lifted his shoulders and let them fall, doing a little stretch as if to ease his growing tension. "We'd only known each other a little less than a year, but there was pressure from both sides of the family to get married. My dad had invested in a shady business of Alexa's father's—something to do with a real estate development he was heading up. My father had overpromised, and when he couldn't come up with the money, and Alexa had been so intent on getting married, he wanted me to sort of smooth things over by going along with the wedding she wanted. And I didn't know this at the time, but Alexa's father didn't want us out of arm's reach until he had his money. He also knew that my recording studio, Winding Alley Music, was doing so well that he'd eventually get his money back if Alexa and I split, which he'd placed a heavy bet on. He didn't like me from the start because I didn't have Ivy League schooling and a country club card in my pocket. It put a crazy amount of pressure on both of us."

"I can only imagine," Lila said. She added more wine to his glass and then took a sip of hers, the alcohol loosening her tight shoulders.

"We didn't tell anyone, and we ran off to Fiji and got married. I still remember the doubts I had, even as I said, 'I do.' I should've stopped, but I just didn't. When we got back home, Alexa's mother went hysterical and told her it was a disgrace to the family not to have a huge celebration. She really put Alexa through the wringer. And truthfully, Alexa had wanted the big wedding. Looking back on it now, I think she resented me for not agreeing to that lavish ceremony right away. Her mother told us we could still do the wedding and no one would suspect they weren't our original vows. Next thing I know, I'm having caviar tastings and choosing calligraphers for the wedding stationery."

"Wow." Lila couldn't imagine the burly mountain man she knew doing anything like that. "That doesn't seem like you at all."

"It isn't." He took another drink from his glass. "To top it all off, Alexa and I were already drifting apart. The excitement was gone for her, and I got a hard dose of reality when I figured out that she'd never really loved me for me. Once I saw through her, I couldn't bear to pretend. But by the time I realized I was in too deep, I already had a wife and wedding commitments. We were barely even speaking by the wedding, but she refused to cancel—breaking it off would upset a whole lot of people, and ruin her family's reputation. I knew I had to come clean. I couldn't live like that. And I wasn't going to be with Alexa just so she could take half of the business to hand over to her father. Even though, given our little trip to Fiji, that was a real possibility. So I sold Winding Alley Music, and I didn't tell her. I basically gave it away. I didn't need it, and I didn't want my name attached to any questionable business practices. She was furious, claiming she'd never marry a 'washed-up musician,' as she called me. After I sold Winding

Alley, and before the big wedding, I left her, came here to Pinewood Hills, and opened the coffee shop, never looking back."

"So what did she say when you left?"

"I don't know. I wasn't there to see. She'd refused to speak to me until the day of the wedding, when she had to. I told her to have it her way and left her a note." He shook his head, disgusted. "She's been trying to press charges—for what, I have no idea. There are no grounds to press any charges. It makes no sense. I think she just wants to get me in a room so she can give me a piece of her mind, even if it's a lawyer's office. She wanted to sue based on a set of laws called 'Heart Balm' laws that claim that by leaving her before the wedding, I was in breach of contract, and that this breach caused her anxiety and humiliation. Those grounds aren't even valid in Tennessee, but she was using her one-time residence in New York to bring the charges. I doubt they'd stand, but the legal bills for representation would eat away at precious funds. Last I heard, she'd hired a private investigator to find me. She's so bitter."

"My God." Lila couldn't imagine putting him through that. She stared into the fire, digesting all of this.

Just then there was a knock at the door, interrupting them.

Lila chewed on her lip, deciding whether or not to ignore it, but there was another knock, this one louder. "Just a sec," she said, placing her napkin on the table and standing up. "Don't disappear," she told him with a wink.

Lila opened the door to find Eleanor, holding a gift wrapped in bright red paper. "I wanted to bring this over to you."

"Come in," Lila offered.

"Oh my goodness," Eleanor said, as she reached the kitchen table and saw Theo. "Hello! Lila's been looking for you—I'm delighted she's found you. And you two are right in the middle of dinner. I'm so sorry to interrupt." She set the gift on the table.

"I wanted to do something to say thank you for all your help with sprucing up the place. You truly saved the day. And thank you, Theo, for fixing the plumbing. If I'd known you'd be here, I'd have brought you something too." She waved her hands in the air. "I won't stay."

"You're more than welcome," Lila said. "And I'm so happy to help."

She opened the box to find a brand-new Christmas scarf and mittens set. They were made of the softest large-weave buttercream yarn, with little holly leaves embroidered on them. "These are beautiful," she said. "Actually, they're incredible. Where did you ever find them?"

"I knitted them," Eleanor said proudly. "They're my own design."

"Wow." Lila set them back in the box. "You could sell these."

"I'll bet Trudy would like to put a few pairs in the farm's gift shop," Theo said.

"Really?" Eleanor asked. "I can make them in about a week."

"You're so talented," Lila told her.

Theo added, "I'll check with Trudy and get her to call you."

"That's wonderful," the old woman replied, beaming.

Lila's heart was full at seeing the smile on Eleanor's face. Now if she could just find a way for her new friend to keep this place...

Chapter Twenty-Five

"I love it that we've been able to lift Eleanor's spirits at Christmas," Lila told Theo, as they settled in the living room with their glasses of wine after dinner. "It makes me so happy."

"You might be the most kindhearted person I've ever met," Theo said.

"Family is everything to me, and mine was taken away too soon. I think that's why I enjoy helping people. It makes me feel close to someone."

Theo took her hand.

"It's never too late, Theo," she said.

"What?"

"It's never too late to fix things with your family. I wish mine were still around, and I don't want you to regret anything…"

He caressed her palm with his thumb. "You have this innocent outlook on the world, but it's not always as easy as a phone call. My mother abandoned me. And my father… He's a complete disaster."

"Any idea why your dad's been staying here at the cabins?"

"I don't know." He dropped her hand and rubbed his face in alarm. "That's why I left. And why I went dark—to protect you. I saw him slowly drive by the shop, and I knew he'd figured out where I was. I was hoping to spend the rest of my life alone, away from his warped judgment and bad choices."

"What happened with him? Would you tell me?"

"Do we really need to get into it?" he asked.

Lila took his hand again and squeezed it gently. "I think that you have a decision to make here," she said. "If you want to let me in, you have to let me all the way in."

Theo took a drink, then held up his glass of wine and looked at it, as if he were playing for time, his thoughts clearly somewhere else. Holding her breath, Lila realized the full scale of what she'd just said. He could get up and walk out right now, and decide not to tell her. Or he could stay.

When he surfaced again from his contemplation, he began, "I owned the production company with my father and I produced some of my dad's music..."

He was letting her in. The man who hadn't seemed to let a soul into his world for a long time. Unable to stop herself, she put her hands on his face and kissed him, surprising him, nearly knocking his wine out of his hand and making him laugh. He set down his glass, wrapped his arms around her, and pressed his mouth to hers, the feel of his lips like oxygen, filling her and making her feel like she hadn't been alive until that moment. Then he pulled back. "What was that for?" he asked.

"For trusting me," she replied. "Now, tell me the rest."

He rested his hand on her knee. "So, my finance guy asked me one night if he thought I should change the budget to reallocate funds. When I asked him why, he said it would make sense, since we'd been paying three times the normal amount to my dad in salary for the last few months. When I looked at the books, I found out that my father had been signing business checks in his own name."

"Why would he do that?" she asked.

"To fuel his overspending habit. He invested in quite a few shady businesses—I'm not sure he knew that at the time. He felt invincible, like he was made of money, and he overcommitted to these people. When he didn't have what he'd promised, they came looking for him."

Suddenly, it all became clear—the articles, the media painting him as a bad seed... the press had it wrong: none of this was Theo's fault. Everyone had been so quick to blame him, and even she had almost fallen for the lies.

"Why didn't he go to jail for stealing from the company?" she asked.

Theo replied, "Because I had my accountant convert it all to legal income, saying that I'd paid him, and then I paid taxes on his extra income for him. It took every cent I had in my bank account to do it."

"Oh my gosh, Theo. Why did you cover all that up?"

"Because he's a train wreck, but I love him. He's my dad, after all. When I confronted him about his spending and taking the money, he cut me off, and kicked me out of the partnership. When I sold the business, we went our separate ways. I tried to talk to him, but he wouldn't see me." Theo ran his fingers through his hair. "I've dealt with that kind of stuff my whole life, and this was the tipping point. I'd had it. I didn't want any part of it anymore."

"I'm so sorry, Theo," Lila said, her chest heavy with sadness for him.

"When I had no money, Alexa was angry and embarrassed because of the way things had ended, and she spread rumors to all our friends that the family was bankrupt, that she didn't believe I'd had any money in the first place, and that I was a fraud. Alexa threatened that she'd find a way to take everything I had left—even if it was through unnecessary lawyer fees. Me being broke would make it look like her claims about me were true. Then she could save face as the deceived, poor Alexa, and I'd be the bad guy.

"I did an online search and found the coffee shop. It looked exactly like the kind of place where I could disappear. I promised myself that I wouldn't get close to anyone again. Self-preservation, you know? And I make a decent living. I have to have money to live—I won't let her take what I've earned, and I think she's going to try, just to spite me.

"But the big issue here," he continued, "is that if I'm seeing someone while I'm married, Alexa might seize the opportunity to try to win a case against me. The last thing she wants is her reputation ruined. She'll do anything to protect it."

"This is insane," Lila said. She folded her legs under herself on the sofa and sat back on her knees with her glass of white wine in her hand. "You need to set the record straight."

He stared at her fondly. "I wish I could see the world like you do. Just once. I'll bet it's amazing."

"Sometimes, my way of thinking gets me hurt."

He nodded, listening.

"Look, it's Christmas. I don't have a family—I didn't get to choose that—but you do. And I really think you need to talk to your dad, clear things up with Alexa, and if you really want my opinion, you should call your mom too."

"Anything else?" he asked.

"Take the coffee shop off the market and reopen."

"Wow, you want a lot."

"It could be your Christmas gift to me."

"Great. Way to make it difficult."

"I'm not finished," she said, scooting over to him. "I want a big, giant Christmas tree in the coffee shop, and festive music, and reindeer rides..." She reached over him and set her wine down on the side table beside him, before snuggling into his warm broad chest and inhaling his spicy scent. She looked up at him. "And I want us to fill Eleanor's cabins with people, give them horseback riding lessons, cut trees for them over at the farm..."

Theo laughed and then leaned down and kissed her. "I think you might actually be crazy," he said. "But I love it."

Chapter Twenty-Six

Having divulged to Lila that he'd been sleeping in a motel in the next town, Theo had slept on her sofa in the cabin last night. She'd offered him one of the beds in the other rooms, but she'd gone to get ready for bed and when she came back, he'd fallen asleep on the sofa. This morning, she'd walked into the living room, yawning, forgetting for a split second that he was there.

Lila stopped, her breath catching at the sight of him sleeping. The little cabin sofa was no match for his tall stature, one leg stretched out and the other bent, with his sock-clad foot on the floor. His arms were covered up to his biceps with the blanket from the arm of the sofa, and he'd wadded one of the decorative pillows under his head. His eyes were closed, the most peaceful expression on his stubbled face.

Evidently sensing her presence, he opened his eyes. "Morning," he said in a husky voice with a groggy stretch as he sat up. He blinked a few times before his gaze landed on her, drinking her in, a warm smile forming.

Only then did she realize her hair was still drawn up into a haphazard ponytail from when she'd taken off her makeup last night, and she was wearing her red-and-white flannel pajamas with little Christmas trees on them. She pulled the band from her hair and ran her fingers through it, self-conscious.

"Don't," he said, reaching out and taking her hand, pulling her toward him so he could scoop her into his arms. "You're gorgeous." But then he sobered, his breathing deepening as something crossed his mind.

"What's wrong?" she asked.

"You and I can't move forward until I get things straight with Alexa. I've been afraid to serve her with divorce papers because once I do that, she'll try to ruin me. I think she truly believes I lied to her about everything. And the main thing she cares about is her reputation. She won't let me get away with it easily."

"Eventually, she'll want to get married to someone else, and this will have to happen anyway," Lila told him. "You need to talk to her."

"Are you sure you want to get involved with all this? It's not for the faint of heart."

"All relationships have to start somewhere," she told him. "I won't be put off that easily…"

"Relationships?" His smile gave her a flutter.

"What else should we call this?" She waggled a finger between them.

He pulled her into him and nuzzled her neck. "How did I get so lucky? I didn't do anything to deserve you."

She twisted around and gave him a kiss.

Theo stood up, grabbed Lila's hands, and pulled her up. "I'm starving. Let's get some breakfast."

"Where are we going?" she asked.

"To the market to buy ingredients. I'm cooking." He wrapped his arms around her waist, his gaze more delicious than anything he could make in the kitchen.

*

"You haven't lived until you've had my breakfast pizza," Theo teased as he stir-fried the mushrooms, green peppers, and onions they'd bought at the market, tossing them with butter, the savory aroma filling the room. He turned the heat to low. "Would you grab a bowl? We need to mix the yeast with the sugar and warm water." He flipped the bacon sizzling in the pan beside him.

There was something so irresistible about him standing in his bare feet, with Lila at the stove, wiping his hands on the kitchen towel. It was a sight she knew she would crave on those lonely nights by herself. She grabbed a bowl to refocus, so the thought of him being anywhere but there didn't linger in her mind.

Theo mixed the ingredients, causing the yeast to fizz. He added olive oil and flour, dusting the counter with a little more flour. "We just have to knead this," he said, sprinkling salt over the dough and mixing it in. His large hands manipulated the dough easily, forming a neat ball that he plopped onto the counter and stretched out into a circle. "All done. We'll just pop it into the oven for a few minutes while we make the eggs."

When the crust had baked a few minutes, Theo spread pesto over it, and then topped the pizza with bacon, eggs, mozzarella, and veggies, placing it back into the oven.

"What should we do while the pizza bakes?" Lila asked.

"Hm. Maybe this?" He nuzzled her neck, kissing it and giving her goose bumps.

She squirmed away playfully. But then she sobered. "I'm so happy you're here," she said. "I really am."

"I'm sorry it took me so long to get here," he replied. "You should never be alone."

"Neither should you," she pointed out. She'd had to live her whole adult life by herself, and she knew how to do that, but in all the years she'd had to get used to it, it had never gotten any easier. Theo had chosen to be alone, and the idea of that was unfathomable to Lila.

"You should call your dad," she suggested, keeping her expression lighthearted so as not to change the mood between them. "Or let me call him?"

"What?" He wrinkled his nose at her.

"Let me talk to your father. Let me call ol' Smash."

Theo rolled his eyes. "I don't want you to have anything to do with him. I want to shield you from that as much as possible."

"Oh, please. Give me your phone." She reached around to his back pocket.

"No." He laughed again, dodging her, grabbing the kitchen towel and snapping it in the air as if that would ward her off.

"He probably won't even answer. Let me call him!" she said, giggling as she tickled his sides, trying to get at his phone and making him squirm.

Theo playfully defended himself, tossing the towel onto the counter and taking her wrists, using his weight to turn the tables.

"That's not fair," she said, laughing and trying to twist out of the grip of his large hands. His thumbs caressed her skin, sending her stomach into somersaults.

He moved her past the counter and pinned her down on the sofa, hovering over her while gently letting her go. "You're going to have to fight me to get my phone."

"Fine," she said, her muscles relaxing.

Softly, his fingers trailed down her arms, giving her goose bumps. She fought the urge to kiss him, instead reaching around and swiping his cell phone from his back pocket as she slid out from under him onto the floor. She scrambled to her feet.

"Got it," she said, waving it in the air.

"You're not going to let this go, are you?"

"Of course not, it's—"

"Christmas," he said, finishing her sentence. But his face dropped. "It's not going to be all sleigh bells and happy endings, Lila. Life doesn't work like that."

She knew that better than anyone, but she also knew how short life could be, and how important it was never to let things go unsaid. "You might be surprised." She held out his phone. "Call him. I'll be right here beside you."

Theo took his phone and held it in the palm of his hand, staring at the empty screen. Then, to Lila's total surprise, he pulled up the number and hit call.

When someone answered, he said, "Hey, Dad. It's Theo."

Lila sat next to Theo on the sofa with both hands folded tensely in her lap.

"I thought I'd call…"

She'd never seen him look like that before. His shoulders were tight, his jaw rigid, his back stiff. Even when she thought she'd pushed him to the limit in the first days she'd known him, he hadn't had that intense reaction.

"Yeah, I'm still in Pinewood Hills. I'm at the cabins. How did you—Okay." He looked over at Lila. "See you soon." Theo hung up the phone.

"What did he say?" Lila asked. That call had been so much shorter than she'd thought it would be.

"He'll be here tonight at around seven."

"Oh my gosh!" Lila clasped a hand over her gaping mouth. This was the moment when their Christmas could either be really great or completely spiral out of control. And she had no idea which way it would go.

"We have the whole day ahead of us," Theo said, his hands folded as he leaned on his elbows over his empty plate.

"Thank you for breakfast," she said. "You've been holding out on everyone in the coffee shop. With skills like that, you should be making a lot more food than the few pastries you offer."

Lila had been amazed by his culinary skills, having never tasted a breakfast pizza as good as that scrumptious explosion of flavors on the buttery dough.

"Thanks," he said. His smile seemed a little nervous, and she wondered if his father's visit was weighing on him.

"You know what we should do?" Lila asked.

"What's that?" Theo replied.

"We should get your dad a Christmas present!"

He laughed disbelievingly. "This man steals from his own son, kicks me out of his life, and causes me to lose everything I've worked for, and you want to buy him a Christmas present?"

"Do you have any good childhood memories of you and him?" she asked, curious.

"Before my mom walked out of our lives, we were inseparable. He took me fishing, taught me how to change the oil in a car and how to ride a bike ... But when Mom left, everything fell apart. I always used to think the reason she ran off was because I was so much like my dad, and she didn't love him, so she must not love me. I spent my whole life trying to be different from him after that. I got so muddled trying not to be him that I lost who I was. It took me a long time to figure out who I was meant to be. And I'm still learning.

"My dad changed after she left too. He was withdrawn and sad all the time. I spent most of my teenage life with nannies. Between trying to be the exact opposite of him and rarely seeing him, we slowly drifted further apart until, I remember, when I was eighteen, I sat with him at the dinner table and the two of us ate in silence, neither of us having anything to say."

"That's...tragic," Lila said, her heart breaking for Theo. She knew what it was like to live without her father, but she couldn't imagine losing him yet knowing he was still right there within her reach.

"It got better, though. The nanny was training to be a counselor—her name was Janie Simpson. I still remember like it was yesterday. She spent loads of time with me, talking, asking questions, and getting me to think. It was with her that I faced the fact that my mother leaving wasn't my fault. It probably had nothing at all to do with me. Looking back on it now, I wonder how stable she was...If she ever thinks about how she left us, if it keeps her up at night." He took in a deep breath and let it out slowly. "But after I got it all out in our little therapy sessions, I didn't let my mother's actions impact me anymore. And when I came to my dad with the idea for Winding Alley Music, he and I found common ground for a while."

"And then the money issue?" Lila asked.

"Yep," Theo replied. "That was the end of it."

"Have you had any contact with your mom at all?"

"I get a present on my birthday and at Christmas."

"Maybe I should've been more sensitive when I asked you to call your dad," she said, guilt pecking at her. "I didn't know the whole story and I pushed you into seeing him. I'm sorry. Do you feel like you're ready?"

The nerves seemed to emerge again in his smile. "You gave me a nudge, but I had to agree, so don't feel bad." He leaned in and gave her a tiny kiss. "Your heart is so good," he said. Then he pressed his mouth to her ear and asked, "What do you say we go somewhere?"

"For what?" she asked, reeling from the tingles he'd sent down her arm.

"Our first official date."

"Did you just say *date*?" she asked in mock surprise, but unable to hide her delight. "Where?"

"Rock climbing," he said, biting back his amusement.

Her smiled dropped. "Come on. Our first official date will *not* be rock climbing."

Theo gazed into her eyes, his features becoming serious. "Trust me."

She stared at him in disbelief. "It's freezing outside. The rocks will be slippery…"

He took her hands, his gaze locked with hers. "Trust me, Lila."

While her brain screamed out that climbing rocks in the middle of a snowstorm was a terrible idea, her heart reminded her that Theo was asking for her trust.

"I trust you," she said.

Theo leaned in and kissed her softly. Just when she'd taken in the gentle movement of his lips and the warmth of his breath as it mixed with hers, he stood up. "More of that in a little while. We need warm socks, coats, scarves, hats, gloves… With all the trails nearby, I'll bet Eleanor has hiking gear."

"I don't know…" She was still processing everything he was telling her, in shock that she was actually considering this. "Gloves? For rock climbing?"

"You'll see."

"Wait," she said, grabbing his arm. "I thought I wasn't the type of girl you'd take rock climbing. You said so when we first met."

He shook his head. "No, I didn't. I said it depended on the girl as to whether rock climbing was a good idea for a first date. You *assumed* I meant you weren't the type. What I didn't elaborate on then was that it also depends on the guy." He kissed her forehead. "Grab your coat. Let's head over to Eleanor's."

Lila wondered what Theo had up his sleeve. She couldn't wait to find out.

A narrow path led through the woods. It began at the sign where Lila and Theo parked and snaked along the hill in front of her, disappearing between the trees.

"We're standing on a massive slab of rock at the moment," Theo said, slipping on the backpack he'd borrowed from Eleanor and taking her hand. "Let's get climbing." He led her onto the path and into the endless expanse of woods ahead.

As they walked, they got higher and higher, the woods beside the path giving way to a drop-off into the valley below. On the other side of them was a wall of solid rock. Lila kept her eyes on the path with every step. "I'm nervous," she said, her gaze flickering over to the drop-off and then back to the path.

"There's a four-foot bank beside us," Theo said. "It's a long way down, but we've got plenty of room. You'll be fine." He stopped her and came up close behind her. "I've got you," he said, the same way he had on the horse, and she felt her shoulders relax. "In just a minute, we'll be there."

They continued on, the valley below getting further down the higher they climbed through the snowy hills. The snow was continuing to fall, making her fretful. It feathered down around her, landing on her shoulders and in her hair. Her nose was getting cold so she covered it with her mittens, breathing into them to try to generate warmth. Finally, Theo pointed to a hollow in the rock beside them.

"It's a cave," she said in wonderment. She'd never seen a real one before.

"We're going inside," he told her.

"What?" She twisted her head around to make eye contact. She wanted him to see the genuine shock on her face. Bats and other creatures could be lurking in there.

He chuckled. "Listen."

Lila's hearing sharpened as she leaned in toward the cave. She could hear a static shushing sound. "What am I hearing?" she asked.

"Go in and find out," he urged her.

Once she edged in a little bit, she could see light coming from somewhere, so she didn't feel too worried going in, and Theo didn't seem fearful at all. Her curiosity got the better of her and she ducked down, moving into the cave. When she got past the initial opening, the cave widened into a larger space, allowing her to stand up, her eyes adjusting. Lila gasped when the sight registered.

Theo came up behind her and put his arms around her.

They were inside the enormous mound of rock, standing at the edge of a turquoise pool of water that bubbled and fizzed. Lila followed the flow to its source, tipping her head toward the opening in the heavens where the rock gave way to gray skies, the snow filtering in with the light over an enormous waterfall. She watched the snowflakes disappear when they hit the surface of the water. She was so mesmerized by it that she didn't notice Theo had let go of her.

Lila tore her eyes from the magnificent sight to find Theo sitting on a plaid blanket, holding a thermos and two cups.

"Hot cocoa?" he asked.

"Where did you get that?" she asked, sitting down beside him.

"I told Eleanor I was bringing you here."

She smiled.

He unscrewed the lid of the thermos and filled the mugs.

"What is this place?" she asked.

"It's called Pirates' Bash. The story goes that a pirate who'd stolen a ship full of loot hopped on a carriage across country, landing here in Tennessee. He found this place and buried his loot here. No one's ever been able to find it, but in the summer, when the water sparkles under the sunlight, it shimmers gold. It's an old mystery that no one's been able to solve. Some people think it's the way the sunlight hits the wet limestone at the bottom of the pool, but no one's sure." He handed Lila her mug.

"This is incredible," she said, taking off her mittens and holding the cocoa in her hands.

Theo set his mug on the rock floor beside him and leaned back, looking up. "When I first arrived in Pinewood Hills, I needed to escape the noise of my life, so I did a lot of hiking and camping in this area. On summer mornings, before opening the coffee shop, I'd come out here to read. I'd sit with my feet in the water, the birds chirping, the sun just coming up, sending a pink and orange light across the rock. It's so peaceful."

"I can imagine," Lila said. She eased herself back beside him and he rolled onto his side to face her.

"I'm proud of you," he said with a smile.

"Proud?"

"For rock climbing," he replied, his grin widening.

She inched toward him, propping her head up on her hand. "Rock climbing was a little different this time."

"How so?"

"I knew you wouldn't let me fall."

"I'm glad we got back when we did," Lila said to Theo, slipping her key in the lock of her cabin. "The snow is really coming down."

"Is there any wood outside?" he asked. "We should start a fire."

"There's a stack at the back of the cabin," Lila replied.

"Okay," he said as he shut the front door behind them. "I'll get a few logs and make a fire for us."

"That sounds amazing," Lila said. "I'm freezing. It's incredible how cold that walk to the car was after being in the warm cave." She shrugged off her coat and hung it on the hook by the door. "I'll pour us a glass of wine and fix us some lunch."

"Awesome," Theo said, kissing her cheek before heading toward the back door. "Back in a sec."

While Theo got the fire going, Lila made them a couple of sandwiches and poured two glasses of white wine, setting them on the coffee table. She lit one of Piper's candles to send a cranberry scent around the room.

With the flames licking their way up the stone chimney and the snow collecting on the windowsill, Lila switched on the Christmas tree lights and sat down next to Theo, picking up her sandwich.

"Thank you for showing me the waterfall today," she said, folding her legs underneath herself and snuggling up to him.

"You're welcome." He stole a bite of her sandwich.

"Hey," she laughed, pulling it away. "Get your own sandwich. This one's mine." She reached for a glass of wine and handed it to him. Lila was aware she was already under enough of a buzz just being with Theo. She wondered where they'd go from here. "So . . . what are you doing for accommodations tonight?"

"What do *you* want to do?" He'd turned the question around on her.

"Want to stay over again?"

"Yes," he said, an indecipherable look in his eyes. It was as if asking anything more of him than that brought all the uncertainty straight back.

"It's okay, you know," she said. "If you stay, we can still take everything one step at a time."

He nodded. "Think Eleanor would let me borrow her car to run to the coffee shop really quickly, so I can pick up my bag with my toiletries?"

"I'll text her just to be sure, but it's probably fine," Lila said, taking out her phone and tapping away. She got a response immediately. "She says, 'Yep!'"

"Excellent." He set his wine down and grabbed his sandwich as he stood up. "I'll take this with me. Back in ten minutes or less."

She watched him head off, thinking that things could only go up from here.

Lila stood at the front window of the cabin, watching the massive snowstorm unfolding outside under the porch light, Eleanor's tin of cookies in her arms. She ate another salted caramel thumbprint cookie, getting more frustrated by the minute. She wasn't sure if it was the number of treats she'd had on an empty stomach, or the fact that Theo had been gone for over an hour now, that made her stomach ache. They'd missed their window for dinner, and Smash Perry was due to arrive any minute. She had no vehicle and no way to get in touch with him.

Had he slid into a ditch? Was he on the side of the road with a flat tire? The roads were most certainly treacherous...Or did something else happen? She recounted the moments before he'd left, trying to figure out what he could be doing, and all she could think about was the uncertainty she'd seen in his eyes. Surely, he wouldn't have taken Eleanor's car and left town...Would he? But all she had to do was remember the way he'd looked at her with complete honesty, and she knew he'd never do that to her. Which made Lila start to worry all over again.

Before she could ponder any other ideas, a red Ferrari pulled to a stop outside and Smash got out of it. After Theo's story, she didn't even want to think about how that man still owned a luxury sports car when he'd had to steal money from his own son.

He was smaller than he looked on television, a little older. But even his casual attire screamed musician. He had on jeans with a long coat, a stylishly battered and worn shirt under it, and boots. His longer hair gave him a look of ruggedness, and she could almost make out Theo's face in his, noticing right away that they had the same blue eyes. Smash bounded up the steps and knocked on the door. Lila's heart raced, fretting about what might unfold.

What would she say to him? Where was Theo? Lila opened the door.

"Hello," Smash said in his cool swagger. He looked over at the cabin number. "My son Theo said to come to this address. Who are you?"

"My name is Lila Evans," she replied. "I'm renting this cabin, and since Theo is selling the coffee shop, he's sort of staying here."

"Selling the shop?"

"Yes, that's right." She wished Theo was there to intervene, because she wasn't sure how much he wanted her to say. "It's nice to meet you." She held out her hand. He shook it, his face curious. "Come inside."

Piper would die to know that Smash Perry was standing in the little cabin kitchen with Lila.

"Where's Theo?" he asked.

"I'm wondering the same thing. He left a few hours ago and said he'd only be ten minutes or so. He knows you're coming, so I'm not sure what's going on. He was just heading over to the coffee shop to get his bag."

"Hop into my car. Let's go look for him."

She stared at him, hesitant. The next thing Lila knew, she was bundled up and sliding into the soft black leather of the Ferrari, the car purring like a content kitten. She folded her hands in her lap, reluctant to touch anything. Smash put the car in gear and pulled out of the drive, the ride feeling as though they were gliding on ice.

"You know your way to the coffee shop?" she asked.

"Yes," he said.

Lila sat quietly, unsure what to say about the fact that Smash not only stayed at the cabins but also seemed to know all about Theo's coffee shop. But it wasn't her place to ask, so she didn't comment, hoping that they'd find Theo soon.

They drove the dark country roads, the luxury car hugging every turn, taking the curves easily, until they pulled up to the coffee shop.

"Theo's truck is there, but he took my friend Eleanor's car from the cabin." She peered through the passenger window to see if he could be inside anyway, but the shop was dark and there was no car in sight. "Where did he go?" Lila asked, wondering out loud.

"I have no idea," Smash said. "Let's head back to the cabin. Maybe we missed him."

They returned to the cabin, the car filled with a tense silence, and there was still no sign of Theo or Eleanor's car. "Where would he have gone?" Lila asked nervously. "I'm worried."

Smash turned off the engine. "I'll wait as long as it takes."

Lila didn't even want to consider the fact that it could be Smash on her sofa tonight instead of Theo. What had she gotten herself into? She had no idea if he was trustworthy to be around, or what on earth she'd say to him. She would've loved to let Eleanor know, but she wasn't quite ready to admit to the old lady that she'd lost her car...

But as they made their way up to the front door, the crunch of gravel behind them caused Lila to turn around, and to her relief, there was Eleanor's car. "Thank God," she said, delighted to see Theo.

Theo, however, looked like a storm cloud. He breezed past Lila without a single explanation as to where he'd been this whole time, his jaw set and his fists clenched, striding up to his father.

Chapter Twenty-Seven

"What do you get out of it, huh?" Theo spat, his face only inches from Smash's.

Smash stumbled back. "What do you mean?" he asked, clearly confused.

"Let's all go inside," Lila suggested anxiously as she tried to steer them in, shocked by what was unfolding.

Theo didn't move. "Are you getting a cut of the money?" he snapped at Smash.

"What money?" Smash stepped closer to Theo. "I don't know what you're talking about."

"Theo, it's freezing," Lila told him, baffled by the sudden turn of events. "Come inside. Please."

As if just realizing she was standing there, his anger having blinded him, Theo finally made eye contact with Lila. With a resigned look, he headed into the cabin, and Lila and Smash both followed.

"I invited you here to try to make amends and you betrayed me. Again." He pushed against Smash's chest—gently, but enough to show his frustration.

"Son."

When his father said that word, it silenced them both.

Once Smash had seemed to collect himself, he said, "Tell me what you're talking about because I don't have a clue. You called me to come see you, and I was so happy that I canceled my plans for the night immediately and jumped in the car the first chance I got. I've done nothing knowingly to deceive you. So please tell me what's going on."

"About two hours ago, I found Alexa waiting for me at the coffee shop. How would she have known where to find me unless you told her?"

Some sort of realization slid across Smash's face.

"I want to move on with my life!" Theo carried on. "I don't want to have anything to do with Alexa. I tried to outrun her just now, and I nearly drove all the way to the next county until I figured she wasn't going to let me go, so I pulled over and let her say her piece. She's going to actually try to sue us for the wedding, and now I'm going to have to pay a divorce attorney. Thank you very much."

"I met with Alexa's father before you called…" Smash rubbed his forehead in remorse. He turned away and walked over toward the sparkling Christmas tree.

"What?" Theo nearly shouted. He stomped across the room, the tree's ornaments rattling with his movements. "What are you doing, talking to Lawrence Fontaine?" Theo threw his hands up in frustration. "I knew this was a terrible idea, asking you back into my life. You can't just be a father, can you?"

Lila felt terrible. It had been her suggestion to call Smash, and now look what she'd done. Everything Theo had tried to avoid seemed to be happening all at once. She chewed on her lip, wondering what she could say, what she could do, to make this better, but there was nothing. This was all her fault, she thought with a sinking heart.

"When your mother left, I was terrified," Smash suddenly said, turning toward his son.

Theo looked on, bewildered.

"I was terrified that if I was left in charge of you, we'd have a fate like the one we're in now. You were so much more than I ever was... You're so smart, always top of your class, well-read... There were so many people who were impressed by you. My producers would say, 'That boy could be bigger than you if he wanted to be.' I thought if I could distance myself from you as you were growing up, you'd leave me behind and go on to do great things. I didn't see anything good coming of me bringing you up." He stepped nearer to Theo. "I was lucky. I could sing. But you were more than lucky. You had the world at your fingertips."

Smash sat on the sofa and hung his head. Lila wasn't sure what to do, so she lowered herself down next to him. When Theo acknowledged her, she nodded for him to listen to what his father had to say. Theo looked down at his dad.

"I didn't know how to raise a child," Smash admitted.

"I'd think the first step would be to use honesty, something you haven't been able to offer to me," Theo said, sitting down. "Why is that so hard for you?"

"You're talking about the money," Smash said.

"Yes." Theo's frustration was clear.

"I thought I could build your nest egg," Smash explained. "I invested in up-and-coming companies, and I believed in them. That was my fault. They ended up sucking us dry. The investments were a terrible move, but I had your best interests in mind. You talked about how you wanted to expand the business, and I knew how much capital you needed to do it. I was trying to find a quick fix to make the money start rolling in. Before I knew it, I was in over my head." When Smash finished, he looked defeated and tired—nothing like the Smash Perry

Lila had seen on TV. "So when you got upset with me, I took the opportunity to cut ties, thinking you'd be better off without me. And I think you probably are. I'm so ashamed by what I've done. You didn't deserve to have a father who would do that to his son. And I'm so sorry about how the media twisted it all. I should've set the record straight. I thought it would all just fade away. I was wrong. On so many things."

"I don't know what to say." Theo seemed legitimately lost.

"I've lived a hard life, son," Smash said. "And you were running with this privileged, wealthy crowd—a crowd I'd provided for you with the fame that came from my music—but that's not who I am. I came from nothing, and I didn't know how to give you what you need. I failed at every turn."

"All I needed was your support, Dad," Theo said. "That's it."

"I'm so sorry, son."

Theo leaned on his knees, his shoulders slumped, looking wounded. "How can I trust any of this?" he asked, shaking his head. "I mean... You were talking to Lawrence Fontaine today. The father of the woman who just chased me for twenty miles. You got an explanation for that?"

"I do," Smash said.

"Then tell me. I'd love to hear it."

Lila took Theo's hand for support, noting the light tremble in his fingers, betraying his nerves.

"Once I'd done it—once I'd pushed you completely away—I went through different stages of emotions. First I felt a terrible sense of loss. I missed you so much. For a while, I told myself that I'd just have to grieve it, and you were better off without me. Then, when I didn't know where you were, I was worried. I started going to a therapist to deal with the fear. I used what little was left of the sale of our assets and hired a private investigator who found you. I bought a car and started touring again to make money, and I'd come here to Fireside Cabins so I could see you from afar and make sure you were okay. I was biding my time until I felt like I could approach you. I wasn't sure when, exactly, the right time would be—I'd never navigated anything like this before. But I didn't want to upset you, and make anything worse between us."

Theo looked into his father's eyes as if he were just now seeing him for who he really was. "What does that have to do with Lawrence Fontaine?"

"I knew if I ever wanted to make this better, I had to set the record straight with the Fontaine family to get them off your back, so Alexa would quit being selfish and give you the divorce. I had to right all the wrongs, son. Alexa doesn't know that I've been here to see you yet. I thought I could speak to her father first. I told him everything."

"And he must have passed it all along to Alexa. She got straight in the car and came to find me."

"I suppose so," Smash said. "That's too bad. My hope is that he was trying to explain everything to her, and she just hasn't calmed down enough to listen." He got up and walked over to the fireplace, peering into it, his thoughts clearly somewhere else. "I went and did it again. I screwed up, trying to make things better."

Lila finally spoke in a quiet voice. "You're too hard on yourself," she told Smash.

He turned around and offered her a weak smile.

"And, Theo, you've got to face this. If she tries to smear your name, then we'll figure it out, but it won't just go away. And you can't stay married to her forever."

Theo took in an aggravated breath. "Why would I want to put myself in the middle of Alexa's ridiculous world, and get wrapped up in the media circus and negative news coverage that has me painted as some kind of criminal? I was doing perfectly well running the coffee shop on my own and keeping a low profile. I don't want anything to do with that life anymore."

"But you can't start this new life until you end the old one," Lila said.

He nodded reluctantly. "Clearly, she's not going to back down. I knew, dating her, that she had a pretty big bite, and I didn't ever want to be on her bad side. She'll go to the press… They'll have a field day. They'll hound me and make my life a living hell. Not to mention that they will completely overrun this town. I won't even be able to see Rex for fear that he'd be splashed across the inside of some tabloid with stories of being my illegitimate child or something." He ran his fingers through his hair in frustration. "And what will they say when they get wind of us?" he asked Lila. "I won't be able to handle it if they make up lies about you, trying to piece the story of us together."

Just by what she'd seen of him so far, Lila knew that Theo didn't like being in the limelight, let alone a negative one. And his concerns were valid. She'd read enough articles about him to know there was a real possibility that not only his but her own life, and the lives of the people he cared about here, could be altered forever if he confronted Alexa. This was going to be quite a battle, from the looks of it. What a mess. But there was no way around it. They needed to handle this together if they wanted to move forward. And this journey began with Theo and Smash. They had to have time to understand each other first.

"I'm going to go see Eleanor and leave you two alone for a little bit," Lila suggested. "It's been a long time since you were together, and I think you should have some privacy."

"Stay," Theo told her gently.

"It's okay," she said, reaching over and giving his hand a squeeze. "I'll wait for your text." She grabbed her coat and headed to the door. "Listen to each other. You'll figure it all out."

Lila sat at Eleanor's kitchen table, strewn with playing cards, across from the old woman.

"I've got a good hand," Eleanor said from behind her fanned-out cards. Lila looked on as she set two cards on the table. "And I have a pair of twos." Eleanor laid two more cards down.

Lila pursed her lips. "I've got nothing." She drew a card.

"The Christmas tree looks so lovely," Eleanor said. "It should make it really easy to sell when I put it on the market."

"What?" Lila blurted out.

"It's okay, Lila," Eleanor said. "When I sell, I'll get your investment back to you."

"That wasn't what I was thinking," Lila told her, shocked. "You're selling?"

"I know originally I didn't want to sell, but I talked myself into it," Eleanor explained. "I'm getting too old to run this place. The state it was in when you got here explains it all. It might be better if I find somewhere small, where I can maybe get a dog and grow some plants on my porch. A simpler life. While I have a lot of memories here, it just makes sense for me now."

A lump formed in Lila's throat, her emotions surfacing out of nowhere. All at once, she felt the swell of sadness and panic at the same time. That was when she realized that if Eleanor sold Fireside Cabins, Lila's newfound purpose would slide away, out of her grasp, and she'd be left with the same empty feeling she had back in Nashville. She'd quit her job, so she had no income. She'd given up her apartment, so she had no place to live. She'd spent all her savings, and even if Eleanor repaid her like she promised, it wasn't enough to change Lila's situation, or, if she were honest with herself, fulfill her. With Theo selling the coffee shop, and now Eleanor finding a new owner for Fireside Cabins, the comfortable little bubble Lila had just begun to create for herself—the only thing keeping her sane as her friends all went on with their lives—was about to pop. And where would that leave Lila?

"Are you all right, dear?" Eleanor asked.

Lila's eyes filled with tears, beyond her control.

"Oh my goodness. You're not okay," Eleanor said, getting out of her chair and rushing over to Lila's side. "Let's go into the living room, dear. I'll get the box of tissues."

"I'm sorry," Lila said. "I'm just emotional at the holidays." There was no need to make Eleanor feel bad about her decision to sell.

"Tell me, dear. Why?" The old lady took her hand, pulling her up from her chair, and led her into the living room.

Lila plopped down on the sofa. "I don't know where I belong. I'm so sorry! This is ridiculous." She stood up to leave, unsure of where she was even going. "I should go," Lila said. "Theo and his father are in my cabin right now."

"Oh, how lovely," Eleanor said, peeking out the window. "I thought William was on tour."

"I guess not," Lila replied. "I really should get back to them. I was just giving them some time alone." The familiar feeling of not fitting anywhere swelled in her stomach. She wanted to get out of there and figure out what to do next, but she had nowhere to go, no one to really go to.

"You didn't stay very long," Eleanor said. "I feel like I've run you off."

"You haven't."

Eleanor took her hand. "Tell me what's gotten you so upset. Please."

Lila bit her lip, trying to keep the tears at bay. "My friends are all busy these days. And I have no family; it's just me. I've felt more myself here than I ever have before, but everything's changing before I can even have enough time to process my feelings on it all, and I just don't know what I'm supposed to be doing. I feel like I should be running this place with you, which makes no sense—I know. But it makes me whole. When I helped fix up the cabins, I had purpose and I enjoyed it. Now I don't know what to do."

Eleanor stared at her for the longest time. "That's how I felt when I first saw this place. It called to me. I didn't want to let it go, because of that. I was too afraid that I wouldn't know what I was supposed to do next. But the worry of trying to take care of it, and this place practically falling apart, consumed me so much that it just hit me that it might be time to let it go." She patted Lila's hand. "I'm sorry, dear. But someone will buy this place. Perhaps you could work for the new owner."

"Maybe," Lila said, a sinking feeling settling in her gut because she knew it wouldn't be the same without Eleanor. Whatever her future, she knew now that Nashville—and Pinewood Hills—wasn't in it. "Eleanor, could I borrow your car to go back to my apartment for a day or so? My lease is up, and I want to pack some things and get them into boxes. I'm not sure where I'll go, but I won't be living in my apartment anymore, I know that much."

"Of course, dear."

"Thank you."

"You're not packing up your cabin just yet, are you?" Eleanor asked. "I'd like you to stay through the holiday."

"I'd love to," Lila replied, more tears rising up when she considered how grateful she was to have this holiday in the company of her friend.

Chapter Twenty-Eight

Lila stirred, her consciousness pushing through when she didn't feel Theo's warm body around her anymore. She opened her eyes and yawned, assessing her surroundings. Theo smiled over at her from the kitchen, holding a coffee mug, his hair disheveled and his shadow of stubble giving her a flutter.

"Where's your dad?" she asked, sitting up on the sofa, and noticing that she had a blanket over her.

Smash had slept in Charlotte's old room and Theo had stayed on the sofa. Lila had offered him Piper's room, but they'd gotten to talking about how he and his father had begun to understand each other a little more, and ended up getting so sleepy that they'd just stayed there. She'd been so comfortable tangled up with him on the sofa that she'd never gotten up to go to her own room.

"He ran out to get something to eat for breakfast, and then he's stopping over at Eleanor's to get him set up in one of the other cabins. Want some coffee?" His words were casual but he was focusing intently on her, making her forget all about the anxiety of last night for a moment.

"Yes," she said, wrapping the blanket around her and padding over to him.

He pulled out a chair for her at the kitchen table. "I'll get it," he said, pouring her a cup.

"It's not every day I get to have an actual barista in my kitchen to make my coffee," she teased. But his half-smile suggested his musings, and it occurred to her that he wasn't a barista anymore. "Have you thought about what you're going to do with the coffee shop?" she asked.

"What do you mean?" He placed her mug on the table in front of her.

"You won't reopen?"

He sat down. "We've had an offer already."

"Oh . . ." She looked into her coffee, the milky brown liquid circling slowly from the movement of the mug, her future completely unclear. One thing that was certain was that this town was not a part of it. And as she considered this, the thought occurred to her . . . "What's today's date?" She checked her phone and slid it back into her pocket. "I have to move out of my apartment." Everything was crashing down on her at once, and she had no idea what to do next.

"Where will you go?"

"I'm not sure. But I need to box up my stuff."

"I'll come with you," Theo offered.

Perhaps she could put everything she had into a U-Haul, ask Theo to come with her, and then see where the road took them. But she knew that was rushing things. She'd been so busy trying to "save the world," as Edie had said, that she needed the solitude to really think about her own next move, and she couldn't be one hundred percent there for Theo until she'd had some time. When she was packing up her apartment, she'd be back in her reality, the spell of hope and happy endings that Christmas brings pushed out of her sight for a little while. That was the only way she'd know for sure what she really felt in her heart.

*

The car was running outside, as Lila held a small bag of her toiletries.

"Sure you don't want me to go with you?" Theo asked.

"It's okay," she said, drinking in his face and praying he'd still be there when she got back. "I want to do this alone. I need time to be in my head for a little while. It's the only way I'll sort out my thoughts. I'll be back soon, all right?"

"Okay," Theo said, taking her hands. He leaned down and kissed her.

"Will you be all right with Smash?" she asked in a whisper.

"We'll be fine. You positive *you'll* be fine?"

"Yeah," she assured him, although in truth she didn't really know. She wanted to get back into her old life, standing in the middle of her apartment, to see what she felt once all this was out of her grasp. Where would she go from here? The only way to know was to get there.

Lila headed outside and climbed into Eleanor's car. With one last wave to Theo, she pulled out of the drive and left Fireside Cabins, feeling uncertain. Her future was as wide open as the twisting snow-covered roads that led her home.

A few hours later, Lila had arrived. She set a stack of folded boxes against the wall and peered out her Nashville apartment window, Eleanor's car looking out of place in the little parking space at her complex. It was the only reminder of what Lila had just left. She turned away from the view and took in the small space that had been hers over the years. Her refrigerator held magnets from all the places she'd gone with her friends—The Big Apple, Boston, San Diego. The one plant she owned sat looking lonely on the kitchen counter. It always seemed to need just a bit more light than she could provide, no matter where she moved it. The sofa pillows were still squished into an odd shape from the last time she'd sat there, and the living room's wood floors could use a good sweep.

She dropped down onto the sofa, and breathed in the scent of lavender and eucalyptus that Piper had suggested to make the space her own the first year she lived here. Piper had assigned them all scents, telling them they needed something to remind them of what was theirs. Edie's was lilac and thyme, Charlotte had cinnamon and nutmeg, and for herself, Piper had chosen her own blend, which she called "salt and pepper oregano"—an earthy mix of spices and herbs. Piper had been right. Lavender and eucalyptus now reminded Lila of home every time she caught the scent of it—it was the one thing she didn't have at the cabins.

Now that she was home, her trip felt like a dream. She had no idea where to go from here. Nobody she knew had enough money to buy the cabins, nor would she ever be able to convince them to invest in a declining property in the middle of nowhere. The coffee shop was nearly sold, and Theo didn't live there anymore.

It hurt to think that, beyond Theo, there was nothing to take her back to Pinewood Hills. She had made the mistake of following a guy before, but she still wanted to return. She wanted to see the snow-topped rolling hills out her window instead of a concrete parking lot. She wanted to visit Trudy at the farm café and ride horses with Rex. But she wanted more than that. She wanted to sit with Theo at the coffee shop, sipping peppermint lattes together. She wanted to write songs with him, watch him teach Rex how to play a difficult chord on the guitar, take Eleanor to breakfast, learn how to make her favorite peach cobbler recipe. But with the sale of the coffee shop and Fireside

Cabins changing hands, there was no way to make any of it happen. Nothing seemed to be staying the same.

The heating in Lila's apartment was always iffy. Sometimes it would scorch her and other times it would turn her little space into an icebox. Since she'd arrived from the cabins today, it had decided to fry her like a sizzling egg in a pan, which was most inconvenient when she was trying to pack up her things. She'd told the landlord about it when she'd made the phone call to let him know she wouldn't be renewing her lease. She opened the window a crack, the familiar Nashville sounds of country music from the bar downstairs sailing into her apartment.

She'd come a long way since first arriving in the city with Razz three years ago. The sound of the music had been electric for her on that first day they had moved in here. She was wide-eyed and naive, convinced they were on their way to the life she'd always dreamed of. Now the country music was like an old family member, always humming and oddly comforting. It had played through her heartbreak, her trials, and her grief. It had been a constant, watching her grow and change to become the woman packing up right now. She would miss it.

Lila rolled out the bubble wrap she'd had in the closet since before her trip. She'd bought it in case she decided to move, which was telling—like she'd known this day would come along. Placing a plate from her last stack in the center of the wrap, she folded it over, putting another plate on top. All the while, she wondered what she was doing and where she was going. One thing was for sure: there was no good reason to stay here.

She'd checked down the hall to see if Edie was home, but she wasn't. She was probably with her new boyfriend, and Piper hadn't answered her door either. Lila figured it was probably best that they weren't home because she had packing to do, and they would inevitably distract her with words like "cocktails" and "sashimi appetizers," both of which she'd have to lay off for a while since she was now jobless and she'd managed to give away her entire savings. She sat down in the middle of the kitchen floor, cross-legged. Was she losing her mind, adding "homeless" to her list of credentials this week?

Chapter Twenty-Nine

The sun streamed through Lila's bedroom window, waking her earlier than she'd hoped. She'd stayed up far too long, avoiding her growing concern about the future by packing. Over the last two days, she'd gotten the entire kitchen boxed, most of the living room and small coat closet done, and part of her bedroom packed, the whole time considering her feelings for Theo. She missed him like crazy and couldn't wait to see him again.

She and Theo had texted a bit, and he'd told her that he and Smash had spent quite a while talking to each other—something they hadn't done in many years. Theo had decided to meet Lila at her cabin when she returned and tell her all about it. She stood back to survey the nearly empty apartment, all her boxes piled by the door. It was amazing how quickly she could completely leave a place. She got up and headed out to the living area, rubbing her eyes to try to make them focus.

A flash of something shot past her window, grabbing her attention, but when she looked to see what it was, it had gone. The street outside was busy already, the traffic building. She needed caffeine. A nice latte would do her wonders right now... The thought of coffee took her right back to Theo's shop, and she wished she could pass Johnny, the local, as he read his paper with his mug of black coffee, on her way to the counter to put in her order while Theo's blue eyes took her in. She missed it already. For now, she'd go down to the coffee shop on the corner and grab a quick cup.

Lila pulled out her phone and texted Edie and Piper. She'd been trying to get hold of them the whole two days, and she couldn't stay any longer. Eleanor certainly must need her car back. It was so strange that she couldn't get in touch with her friends; it made her realize how quickly things were changing. It seemed like being alone was the theme this Christmas, she thought sadly.

Going into her tiny bathroom, Lila brushed her teeth, washed her face, and combed her hair, pulling it into a ponytail. Then she slid on a pair of her jeans and a sweater, grabbed her coat and keys, and headed downstairs. When she got to the bottom, she pushed open the apartment complex door, the crisp morning air waking her up like a splash of ice water to the face.

As she walked along the busy city street, she thought about how different her life had ended up. Lila had never imagined when she'd gotten in that van with Razz, headed to Nashville, that she'd end up alone, left in a city she didn't really call home, wondering where to go and not having a clue. The one saving grace—and it was a big one—was that she was excited about moving on with Theo by her side. She definitely needed a fresh start. With her apartment all packed up, she was going to make that happen—she just wasn't so sure where they would go or what they would do. And there was a tiny piece of her that wanted to be sure she didn't just run after a guy to the next city like she had with Razz... She felt like things were different with Theo, but how could she know if they actually were? She couldn't bear the thought of making the same mistake again.

Another flash hit her right in the eyes and suddenly a man appeared beside her. "Lila Evans?" the man asked. She didn't recognize him at all, but it was hard to tell with the spots floating in her eyes from the light.

She stopped walking. "Yes?"

"Is it true that you are Theo Perry's mistress?"

"What?" She stared at the man like a deer in headlights, unsure of how to answer further. How did this man know her full name and where she lived? But more importantly, how had he found out she knew Theo? She could barely focus on the man in front of her, all the questions swirling around in her mind. Lila knew she had to stay quiet. She needed to talk to Theo before she said a thing.

"It's been reported that he's been hiding out with you well before the allegations surrounding his embezzlement."

Lila's mouth hung open. "It wasn't *that* long…" The words slipped out of her before she had a chance to stop them.

"So you have been with Theo?"

Shoot.

She shouldn't have said anything at all.

"Where is Theo, Lila? Is he here with you?"

"I need to go," she said, pushing past him.

The man started to follow her, and another flash from across the street blinded her for a second. She was being photographed. Lila weaved in front of a group of tourists and ducked into the alley between the shops, running with all her might to the other side where she quickly turned a corner and headed up a side street. When she got far enough away that she didn't think the man could find her or catch up, she texted Theo and told him what had happened.

He texted back: *Get whatever you need and come back here as soon as you can.*

What if he's at my apartment? she texted.

Just try your best not to be seen. We'll figure it out.

Her heart hammering, Lila ran down backroads all the way to her apartment building and then let herself in through the rear door. She took the elevator up to her room, catching her breath as it climbed the floors. When the doors opened, she moved quickly to her apartment and stopped, her blood running cold.

A note was taped to her front door that read,

Theo is an embarrassment to my family and me. He completely betrayed me and ruined my reputation. The media is having a field day with this. So I won't make this easy on him. You can count on that.

A.

Shocked, Lila ripped the note off the door and shoved it into her pocket. Then she grabbed two boxes of her things and went back down to Eleanor's car. Throwing the boxes into the trunk, she slammed it shut and hurried to the driver's side, her head on a swivel, and locked the doors. Then she put the car in gear and got out of there as fast as she could, the engine revving loudly as she pounded the gas.

As Lila drove, she kept checking her mirrors to be sure no one was following her. Her hands were shaking, her heart beating like a snare drum. She wondered if this would be too difficult for their young relationship, but she couldn't think about that now. She just needed to make sure that she didn't put Theo in any danger with the press or Alexa.

Once Lila was over an hour into the trip, she pulled over at a rest stop to catch her breath. She'd left so quickly that she hadn't even had a chance to see Piper or Edie to catch up. Now she wasn't certain how or when she could get back to Nashville, to get the rest of her things packed up and moved. She'd make Theo go with her next time, that was for sure.

She called him to tell him about the note.

"Alexa was at your apartment?" he snapped. "You don't have anything to do with this!" The anger in his voice was clear. "She's crazy."

"She said you have to fix it," Lila told him.

"How? What does she want me to fix? It's over and done. There's nothing we can do now but move on."

"I have no idea what to do, Theo."

"It's okay," he said, calmer now. "We'll figure it out. Be careful and get here as soon as you can."

Lila ended the call, tears suddenly filling her eyes. This Christmas hadn't turned out at all the way she'd hoped it would. She wiped a runaway tear off her cheek and sucked her emotion back in. There was no time to feel sorry for herself.

Pulling Alexa's note from her pocket, she spread it out flat on the seat beside her, and took a photo of it. She sent it to Piper with the message: *Can you believe this? I'll catch you up later.* With the note still on her seat, she put Eleanor's car in gear, and headed to Pinewood Hills.

When she pulled into the drive, Theo ran out to greet her. He opened her car door, hauled her out, and kissed her lips tenderly, the feel of them erasing any doubt she'd ever had about her feelings for him. It felt so right to be back in his arms.

Theo pulled back and looked down at her. "Hi," he said with a wide grin. "I missed you."

It was the first time she'd ever been told that by someone she was dating, and while it was such a normal thing for people to say, it meant the world to her. She smiled up at him. "I missed you too."

Then a white pop of light blinded her. She heard the purr of a car engine but couldn't see who it was driving up the track and coming to a stop in front of them. Her heart racing, Lila blinked enough to make out a sleek, dark Tesla, the driver's side door opening and long, thin legs emerging from within.

"We're still married, Theo," the owner of the legs said, as the high heels attached to them ground their way toward them.

Lila squeezed her eyes shut and opened them again to find the woman from the photos she'd seen online—Alexa Fontaine—in the flesh. Her dark hair fell in loose shiny waves down the back of her belted coat, and her powder-perfect face was set in a scowl behind her enormous black Prada glasses. Alexa tilted the shades enough for her eyes to clamp down on Lila, appraising her. Then she pushed them back into place with a dismissive and disgusted shake of the head.

"Give me a break, Alexa," Theo said, striding up to her.

She pursed her lips and pushed her glasses onto her head, just to show off an eye roll. "You look like a train wreck. You could do with a shave," she spat. Another white pop went off, and Lila realized it was coming from somewhere amongst the trees behind the cabin. "I'm going to ruin you until the press leaves *me* alone. It's my goal in life to make sure there is enough evidence out there to prove that you and you alone ruined our marriage."

"Fine," Theo said. "They can write whatever they want about me—I don't care anymore."

"The press will have a field day with the angle, 'Theo Perry has gone off the rails and is now shacked up in the sticks, cheating on his wife with a local hillbilly.'"

"Hey, you stop right there," Theo said, sticking up for Lila. The camera went off again from the tree line.

Alexa ignored him and turned to Lila. "If you think you can squeeze any money out of him to get yourself out of your…" She waved her manicured hands around in the air. "*Circumstances*, you're wrong. He's dead broke."

"Alexa, what's going on here?" Smash asked from the porch before Lila could say anything.

Alexa cackled. "Oh, *there* you go," she said to Lila. "A sound investor. If money's what you want, Smash will give it to you—even if he doesn't have it."

"You just sound bitter," Theo said. "This isn't the person I met when we first started dating."

Alexa didn't even flinch. "Likewise," she snapped. "And no, I'm not. You've made me the laughingstock of our social circles. Did you know there was an article in *Music Mag* about my lack of judgment, and how I'm singlehandedly ruining our family empire by the men I choose? They said I was involved and went so far as to say they suspected I'd steal from my own family next!" Her puffy lips began to wobble. "I started seeing someone and on our third date, he canceled. He said he'd heard about my background. And he couldn't risk anyone interfering in his family's fortune."

"Then divorce me," Theo said. "From what you're saying, making me look bad is only going to reflect worse on you. Be the hero and divorce me, and then tell everyone your side."

"Not until you go to the press and explain to them that you stole money from your own company without my knowing, and I had nothing to do with any of this. Until then, I will make your life as miserable as you've made mine."

"He didn't steal anything, Alexa," Smash said, coming down the front steps. "It was—"

"All a misunderstanding," Theo cut in, before Smash could incriminate himself. "Dad took funds from the company as a year-end dividend and forgot to enter it into the books. It was a simple oversight that the accountant found, and tax adjustments were made to correct it. That's all it was."

She eyed him suspiciously. "That's not what the press says, and you certainly didn't tell me..."

"You didn't *let* me. And come on, Alexa. You and I both know what the press can be like. Do you really believe them?"

"I don't believe *you*. Why did you run if you're not guilty?"

"Because I've had it with all this." He waggled his finger between them. "Do you realize this conversation has been nothing but an effort by you to fix your broken reputation? Not even once has it been about you and me. You're angry and hostile because I made you look bad... It's always been about appearances."

"Liar. I married you in some hole of a shack in the sand." She wrinkled her nose in disgust. "That was *not* about appearances."

"I wouldn't call a beachside ceremony under a thatched-roof cabana in Fiji 'a shack in the sand,'" he said, shaking his head, disbelief on his face. "But it further proves my point. Let's end this right now."

She shook her head, slipping her glasses back on. "No. I won't end this until either I prove to the press what a terrible person you are, or you tell them yourself. You won't get a single signature from me on any divorce papers until you say that I wasn't involved, admit your cover-up, and face criminal charges for embezzlement. And in the meantime, if I can make them see how you completely deceived me, maybe they'll listen to me when I say I had nothing to do with any of this."

The camera in the woods went off yet again.

"At least I've got photos to prove my story now," she said, nodding to the invisible paparazzo before opening her car door and getting in. The engine of her Tesla revved and she pulled away down the drive.

Lila sat in her cabin, physically shaken by the altercation with Alexa.

"This isn't how I'd planned today to go," Theo admitted. "I told you she wouldn't play nice."

Smash had gone to his cabin, probably to give them time to talk, and the two of them were sitting in the silent cabin, the fire barely flickering, an icy chill snaking around Lila's ankles, giving her a shiver.

"It's really okay, though. She can't hurt me any more than she already has."

"Can I ask you something out of curiosity?" Lila said, still trying to make sense of what had happened.

"Anything."

"Who are Brian Brown and P. Perry? I saw the names on an envelope in your office."

"Brian Brown is just a name I made up to try to hide away from everything. But now I realize that I can't escape it. I need to face it. And P. Perry is me—Paul Theodore Perry."

She offered a weak smile, glad to know his whole name and also that there were no more questions, but the whole ordeal had her head pounding.

"I think I need some time to process this," she said. She needed to clear her mind and get some rest so she could think straight.

Theo gave her hand a supportive squeeze. "Okay," he said. "Dad and I will go to his cabin to give you space." He looked uncertain, and she wondered if he'd been just as shaken by Alexa's visit.

"Thank you," was all she could muster, completely exhausted by the day.

"I'll text you from Dad's phone so you have a way to get ahold of me if you need me."

Lila nodded.

"I'm so sorry, Lila," he said, but she stopped him.

"I just need some time." She tried to focus on Theo but the pain in her head was now piercing.

Theo stood and gave her a soft kiss on the cheek. Then he let himself out, leaving her alone in the cabin.

Getting up, she let herself into the bedroom. As she sank down onto the soft mattress, her thoughts were still going a mile a minute. Her face was probably going to be plastered across magazines and online. Who knew what they'd say about her? Despite the fact he didn't want to be, Theo was a public figure, and people were interested in his life. Even if he could get Alexa to agree to a divorce quietly, it would most likely be a messy one. She worried Alexa would draw it out just for spite, and spread rumors about them because Theo would never admit to the press what she wanted him to admit—he wasn't a liar. While Theo had tried to warn Lila, the enormity of the situation really hit her now. Was she really ready for all this?

Chapter Thirty

Lila had slept from the time Theo left all the way through the night, and she'd spent the whole day walking around the cabin on autopilot. She'd gotten ready, made coffee, turned on the Christmas lights, thrown a log into the fire, and settled on the sofa, her mind completely empty of solutions. She hadn't moved from that spot except to nibble on some leftovers, but her appetite was nearly nonexistent.

As she watched the sun set out her window, her eyes on the pink haze peeking through the gray clouds rolling in, she knew she had no way to fix this. She and Theo would just have to endure his divorce together and face whatever came their way. Would their new relationship be able to withstand this level of anxiety? She had no answers. No answers, no place to live, and no job—her life in boxes sitting in an apartment she still hadn't totally moved out of.

Breaking the silence, Theo burst through the door. "I know you want to be alone," he said. "But I need you to get into my truck and come with me."

"Why?" she asked.

Theo took her hands and pulled her to a standing position. "Trust me." He walked her to the door and handed over her coat.

"Where's Smash?" she asked, slipping on her boots, confused by his behavior.

"You'll see." He opened the door and they headed to his truck, where he motioned for her to hop in. "I've been busy…"

She'd never seen him this happy and animated. His fondness for her radiated from his face as he looked at her, her worries disappearing in that moment. She realized that in their short time together they'd shared more of their thoughts and feelings than she and Razz ever had. Despite what lay ahead of them, he'd broken his walls down and let her in. That meant everything. "Aren't you worried at all about Alexa?" she asked.

"Nope. I don't care what she says about me or us. I've got my attorney working up the divorce papers." He put the truck in gear and pulled out of the drive. "I've also got him filing restraining orders against her for both you and me, along with the divorce paperwork."

Theo drove the short distance into Pinewood Hills with an enormous smile on his face.

"What is up with you?" Lila said with a laugh.

He glanced over at her happily. "Well, I had something I wanted to show you when you got here yesterday, but Alexa put a slight kink in my plans." He pulled to a stop in the parking lot of the coffee shop.

"What are we doing here?" Lila asked. The lot was full of cars, the windows twinkling with Christmas lights from inside. The for-sale sign was gone and the coffee shop had a new sign on its roof. Painted on a long plank of white-painted wood in black letters, it said, *Fireside Coffee*. She'd been so consumed with her thoughts that she'd totally missed it when she'd driven by yesterday. "Fireside Coffee—like the cabins?" She twisted toward him, excitement bubbling up.

"Eleanor suggested it," he said with a smirk. He put the truck in park and ran around to her side, opening her door.

Lila got out and gasped when she realized what was positioned to the side of the building. "Is that a sleigh?" she asked, pointing to it. "A sleigh pulled by reindeer?"

"It's what you wanted, right?" He took her hand and led her to the front door, opening it for her.

Christmas music poured through the doorway as she entered, and she found out why the parking lot was full. Every table was filled with people, drinking coffee, eating cakes and pastries, while Smash strummed a guitar as he sang the lyrics of the festive tune on a makeshift stage in the corner. He paused to wave to her from beside the biggest Christmas tree she'd ever seen. It was brimming with white lights and sparkling ornaments.

Theo whispered into her ear from behind her, "I didn't sell the coffee shop. I never agreed to the offer."

She turned around. "I wasn't serious when I said I wanted all this," she said, soaking it all in.

"It doesn't matter. I'd give it to you anyway." He took her hand. "Come on. I'll make you a coffee. I have almond milk…"

Lila grinned, emotion tickling her throat. When they got to the counter, something occurred to her. "Oh, did you find the money I left in the drawer?"

"Yes, what was that?"

"I worked here for a day after you left. I felt bad closing up on everyone."

"I thought I must have left it," he said, laughing. "It paid for your reindeer rides."

Lila laughed along with him.

Theo grabbed a mug and gave it a spin in his hand. "Guess what else I did."

"What?"

His face sobered, his eyes on her. "I called my mom."

"You did?"

"Yeah. She told me she felt terrible for leaving me. She was so young and stupid—her words, not mine. And she's wondered about me." He smiled. "She worried that coming back into my life would just make things more difficult, but I told her that was absolutely not true." He set the mug under the espresso machine. "She said she's coming for a visit on Christmas Day. Would you stay too, to meet her?"

"Of course! Oh, that's so wonderful!" Lila threw her arms around him and squeezed his neck.

"Thank you for showing me that I needed to do that."

"How did I show you?"

"I see how you love people and how you always want the best outcome for them. I had things to say to my mom that I hadn't said, and you showed me that I needed to get it off my chest, to make things better. And it has."

The bells on the door jingled, pulling Lila's attention toward them.

"I hear there's a Christmas party goin' on," Judd said, wearing his denim overalls and filling the doorway with Trudy and Rex, who was holding a guitar case as big as he was.

Rex set the case down, broke free from his mother's hand, and rushed over to them, wrapping his arms around Theo.

"Hey, buddy," Theo said. "Missed ya."

"I brought my guitar, just like you said," the little boy told him, pointing back to the case.

"Excellent." Theo beamed at Rex. "We'll do our thing in a bit, but first I need to get your order and then I want to show Lila something. I've got hot chocolate with whipped cream and sprinkles," he told Rex, his eyebrows wiggling with excitement.

"Yes, please!" Rex said, jumping up and down.

Judd was already talking to Johnny over by the stage, and Trudy had made her way to the counter to take a look at the menu.

Theo pointed to the large, circular table up front. Eleanor was beckoning her over, a box wrapped in sparkly silver paper with green-and-red bows on the table next to her. "Head on over, Lila," he said. "I'll make your coffee."

She crossed the busy room and gave Eleanor a hug. "I'm glad you came out," she said over the Christmas music, before she was distracted. "There's a Christmas candle with a holly ring in the center of this table. I've never known Theo to be a decorator."

"Yes," Eleanor said with a jovial chuckle. "He picked them out himself."

"Theo?"

"He said you gave him a reason to care."

She looked over at Theo. He was behind the bar, running the espresso machine and carrying on a conversation with a customer. Just the sight of him felt like home. She looked around at all the faces, the Christmas decorations, the many cups of coffee. Adele waved from a nearby table, and Lila waved back. It seemed like the entire town was there.

"What's this?" she asked, placing her hand on the beautifully wrapped gift.

"It's for you," Eleanor said.

"Who's it from?"

Eleanor smiled. "Everyone." But then with a big smile, she added, "Theo helped to design it. Open it up."

Lila pulled the ribbon free, the bow coming loose. She let the ribbon fall to the table.

Theo came over and sat down. "One lavender almond milk latte," he said, sliding the cup her way.

"Thank you," she said, her heart full at the sight of the contentment on his face. He looked so different to her now from when she'd first met him. His features had a lift to them that they hadn't had before, his eyes bright, his whole body more animated. He was like a totally different man. "Eleanor says you designed this gift," she said, holding the present.

"It's true. I can't deny it." He sent a little grin over to Eleanor. "Open it."

Lila slipped her finger under the tape and pulled it away, ripping the paper and discarding it. Putting the box down, she lifted the lid. She pulled back the tissue paper, and peered down at the T-shirt in front of her. In glittering letters, it said, *Home is where the heart is.*

"That is very true," Lila said. "Home is most definitely anywhere the heart is." She pulled the shirt out and held it up.

"And you've got a home here with us if you want it," he said.

Lila hugged the shirt to her chest.

"You didn't get to wear the Girls' Week shirt very long," he said. "Charlotte tells me you all usually wear them at least a few times during the vacation."

"Charlotte told you that?"

"Mm-hm," he said, nodding.

Just then, someone covered Lila's eyes with cold hands, the very unique scent of Piper's salt and pepper oregano tickling Lila's nose. She pulled free and turned around, her mouth dropping open.

Piper held out her arms for a hug, along with Charlotte and Edie. All three of them were wearing matching T-shirts with *Home is where the heart is* on the front. Lila stood up and threw her arms around them, the women huddling in a giant group hug.

"What are you all doing here?" Lila said with a squeal.

"In all of this, *you* haven't really had a Christmas," Edie said. "So instead of going our separate ways for the holiday, when Theo called to tell us what he was planning, we all jumped in the car—your car—and headed back to Fireside Cabins. We've been here since yesterday, waiting for all this!"

"Is that why you weren't answering my calls?"

"Yes!" Charlotte clapped her hands, bouncing up and down. "Our week vacay starts today."

"We've got loads of fun in store," Piper told her. "So put that shirt on!"

Lila slipped the T-shirt over her head, covering the long-sleeved knit shirt she'd put on this morning, and sat down as the girls all took a seat in the empty chairs at the table.

"You all enjoy your coffees," Theo said. "Rex and I have a song to sing." He got up from the table and stepped onstage, beckoning the little boy to the front. Rex picked up his giant guitar case and lugged it up to the stage, opening it, and pulling his instrument out. He twisted the knob on the microphone, lowering it like a pro, while Smash stepped off the stage and took Theo's seat at the table.

"Ready to sing our song?" Theo asked Rex.

Rex nodded and found his chord.

"This one's for Lila," Theo said.

Lila couldn't take her eyes off them, her heart pattering at the idea they were actually playing something for her.

Theo and Rex began strumming a familiar tune together, and it was only a few lines in when Lila realized it was the song "What Are You

Doing New Year's Eve?" As Theo sang, his voice sounded so good—like his dad's, but younger and deeper. He locked eyes with her and smiled.

"What *are* you doing New Year's Eve?" Charlotte asked into Lila's ear. "Looks like Theo wants to know."

Lila couldn't hide her smile. It was so festive and wonderful with all her friends around her that she'd almost forgotten the drama Alexa had caused. She'd worry about it later—they'd figure it out, and no one here would give a hoot what the press said about them. She was going to take in all the love that surrounded her right now. Today was the first time it had really felt like Christmas.

Chapter Thirty-One

Lila held her hot cocoa with both hands to keep them warm, the jingling of bells filling the air. She and Theo were bundled under a thick fur blanket in the sleigh as snow fell down all around them, the reindeer's hooves click-clacking on the road under a now inky sky.

"You've completely changed your tune since I met you. What happened? Did a Christmas tree bonk you in the head?" she teased.

"No," he said, pulling the blanket up to their chins. "I just realized something."

"What's that?"

"I realized that the whole time I was running away from you, I felt hopeless and empty. I thought I'd gotten used to that feeling, but it hit me a hundred times harder leaving you. And when I saw you slide into the ditch, it was like my world had come back. I didn't want to admit it at first, for fear I couldn't make it work. But then when you left to go back to Nashville, I knew I couldn't spend another second away from you, and all I wanted to do was show you how I feel."

She wrapped her arms around him and gave him a kiss. "So where do we go from here?" she asked.

The reindeer had circled around on its short path and pulled to a stop, the driver maneuvering the sleigh off the road and parking it under an old oak tree covered in white lights, which snaked from its trunk to the tip of every single branch.

"Apparently, not too far," he joked, pointing to the shop in front of them again.

Lila laughed, letting the question linger.

Theo took her hand and stood up, guiding her to join him. He looked at her meaningfully with those deep blue eyes before pointing to the mistletoe dangling from a branch above them by silver ribbons. "Where do we go from here, you ask? Anywhere we want." Theo took her face in his strong hands, leaned in, and pressed his lips to hers. The cold of the night under the falling snow faded away in the warmth they shared in that place, and as they stood in the curling sleigh draped in garland and ribbon, Theo's soft lips moved on hers, his hands traveling down her neck, trailing her arms, and grabbing onto her waist. Her life had never felt more complete than it did right then.

She pulled back to look at him, the twinkling lights like stars above them. "This is the first time in my life I've truly felt what it's like to have a Christmas with a loved one. Thank you."

He grinned. "*Loved* one? You mean girls actually like an old scrooge like me?"

"Well," she said, grabbing his hands and intertwining her fingers with his, "depends on the girl."

Theo laughed, pulling her into him and brushing her hair away from her face. "Your Christmas isn't finished." He kissed her once more on her icy nose. "Adele is watching the shop for me, and the girls and my dad have gone back to the cabins with Eleanor. We've got some things waiting for you."

Lila didn't need any more than what she'd had already. She realized that she didn't require a place to call home—she just needed a person who felt like home. Anywhere she went with Theo would be perfect because he was there, and any future she faced would be okay as long as they could face it together. She couldn't imagine what else Theo had in store for her because, as he held her hand to help her out of the carriage, she already felt like he'd given her everything she'd ever wanted.

The fire roared in Eleanor's fireplace and the Christmas tree glistened in the corner of the living room. Eleanor had made a circle with a mixture of the furniture and kitchen chairs to give everyone a place to sit. Everyone seemed to have something ready to show her. Edie was in a chair with her computer, Charlotte had a pile of large, glossy posters turned over on her lap, and Piper was holding an envelope. Eleanor had some sort of paperwork in her hands, and Smash held his checkbook.

"What's going on?" Lila asked.

"We all have presents for you," Piper said.

Charlotte stacked the posters in her hands. "I'll go first," she said. She turned one of them around. "'It was an advertisement poster for a concert.

Lila read it out loud. "'Paul Switzer to play live at Fireside Cabins for a Christmas show like no other'?"

"Paul Switzer is the lead singer of the Misfit Junkies," Charlotte explained. "They just hit number one this month with their song 'Christmas and You.'"

"I know, but they're playing at *Fireside Cabins* next week?" Lila asked, totally confused.

"Yep," Charlotte said. "It's part of our concert series. We've also got..." She shuffled the posters, showing each one. "Country music greats, pop sensations, and even a songwriter night."

"I've got a date set to play," Smash chimed in proudly.

"I'm still selling, but more on that in a minute," Eleanor explained. "I've been busy talking with Edie. The empty field between the cabins is a perfect place to hold concerts. The natural rock in the hills makes for flawless acoustics, and we can set up benches on the incline. Judd found a way to anchor them in the ground."

Edie cut in. "It's all part of the new PR package I've given Fireside Cabins. I went ahead and used the photos from the shoot we did with Eleanor, and then I took a few more. Have a look at the website." She turned her laptop around and brought it closer to Lila. Edie clicked the *About* page in the navigation.

Eleanor's beautiful photo came up with a little paragraph of history about her and Chester, and the cabins. But it was the larger font centered in the middle that caught Lila's eye. It read, *Passing the torch.*

"Read it out loud," Edie suggested.

"'The future of Fireside Cabins is bright with the announcement of our new operator, Lila Evans...'" Lila looked up. "What?"

Eleanor held up the stack of papers she was holding. "This is the sales contract for Fireside Cabins."

Smash held up his checkbook. "I just did a tour to raise enough money to pay Theo back for all that I took from him. But he said he didn't need it. And someone else did. So Theo and I have decided to buy a resort..." Smash opened the checkbook and ripped out a check, handing it to Eleanor. "It's the escrow payment. I'm finally investing in something great," he said.

"You're buying Fireside Cabins?" Lila asked, in shock.

"Yes. But I need fantastic people to run it, and I thought you and Eleanor together would be the perfect team."

Theo pulled out a little Christmas bag and held it toward her, the gift hanging from his finger. "You'll have to work the cabins sometimes, Dad. Lila's going to be busy with the children."

"Children?"

Piper giggled. "We told him how much you love working with kids."

He pushed his finger forward and she lifted the gift off of it, pulling out two keys.

"One key is to your cabin, which will be completely remodeled to your specifications, per our budget," Edie said. "The other key is for the Children's Cabin that we'll be using for after-school care for underprivileged children. They'll come here for activities, and also learn how to run the grounds so that when they get older, they'll have work experience and we'll offer them a job if we have one, or find them a job that uses those skills. There will be tutors for homework and activity directors for our new ropes course, hiking trails, and off-campus outings—whatever you want to plan."

Lila put her hand over her gaping mouth, tears filling her eyes.

Piper held up her envelope next. "Looks like I'm the last one to share my gift," she said. "Smash and I called some national media outlets and let them know where Theo was."

"What?" Lila asked, aghast.

"We gave them exclusive interviews with Smash and Theo. We told them that Theo hadn't done a thing wrong—that everything people had written about him and Alexa were all rumors, and they could be the first outlets to break the real story straight from Theo and Smash's mouths. And we also told them how Theo's been in Pinewood Hills, living among friends to escape all the drama, which is where he'll be staying to run the coffee shop and help underprivileged youth. The press is running the stories starting next week." She handed Lila the envelope. "Here's a list of all of them."

"When I first told Nikki Mars about this, she called her attorney Trevor Michaels, who was so interested in this case that he's going to take it on pro bono," Charlotte told her. "Mr. Michaels says this one is huge, and that he could go after Alexa for slander."

"But I told him not to do that," Theo added. "He can threaten it to keep her quiet, but all I want is a divorce. Remember the photo you took of the note on your door that you sent to Piper? That was all we needed to keep Alexa quiet and get her to comply." He grinned.

Lila twisted in her chair to face Theo. "Do you think she'll try to bother you?"

"I know Alexa," he said. "And her main motivation for all this is clearing her reputation. Once my name is clean in the media, she'll let it go. And she knows that if she doesn't, it's her own reputation on the line."

Lila was stunned.

"What about you, Eleanor?" she asked. "Are you okay with all this?"

"Absolutely," she said. "Tell her my role, Smash."

"Eleanor will stay on with us and be our resident historian," Smash said. "She's going to be in the new gift shop on the premises, and she'll narrate the three-dimensional video history in the new wing we're building."

"It's very cool," Edie added. "When guests take the tour, they'll begin in seats in a state-of-the-art viewing room where the history of the area is projected on all the walls around them, taking them from the first settlers to the modern resort where they will be spending their vacation."

"Nikki and I are gathering a production team to shoot the footage right now," Charlotte added.

Lila's mouth dropped open and Edie added, "It's all part of the renovation and updating package."

"And when I'm not working, I'll be baking homemade treats to offer all the guests," Eleanor said with a smile. "I've already got some special recipes planned for when we all gather for our Girls' Week every year." She winked at Lila.

Happy tears pricked Lila's eyes. "We're still doing our Girls' Weeks?"

"Of course," Charlotte said. "All families get together at Christmas, don't they?"

Lila sat by the fire, the stockings dancing back and forth as the heat wriggled its way toward them, the tree alight with glittering festivity. She realized that her final Christmas wish had come true. She looked around the circle at these people who had become her family. It turned out that this wouldn't be her last big Christmas after all—and it would certainly rank up there with one of the best Christmases ever.

Epilogue

Presley the cat darted across the newly fallen snow in the yard, as Lila tipped her head up to view the enormous gold star on top of the Balsam fir. It towered over the outdoor concert area at Fireside Cabins as the orchestra took their places for their first annual winter concert, a charity event Lila had started, all proceeds going to local underprivileged children. Over the last year, she'd seen her after-school and job-training program balloon to eighty-five kids, a group of them working tonight to get the concert underway.

Theo came up behind her, wrapping his arms around her, his hands on her belly bump that was getting bigger by the day and kissing her neck, his breath near her ear, giving her a shiver. After eight months of marriage, they'd decided it was time to add to their little family. She wound her fingers through his and leaned into him, running their fingers over the bump. She and Theo were having a baby boy. They'd decided to name him William after his grandfather.

"It all looks amazing," Theo said into her ear. "But not as amazing as you."

She twisted around and kissed him, his affection coming through in the softness of his embrace.

"I love you," he whispered, peering down at her as if she gave him breath.

"It's a full house tonight," Eleanor said, walking through the line of outdoor space heaters and past the wall of poinsettias lined along the exposed rock of the hills behind them. "You've done an amazing job, Lila." The old woman gave her a hug as she looked around the space in wonderment, her eyes glistening. "I never thought I'd see anything like this in my lifetime. Every cabin is full, every seat at the show already paid for; I'm doing double the merchandise orders than I had six months ago to keep the gift shop stocked; Gingerbread Mama's had to take over the baking—I can't keep up!"

Lila gave her a big squeeze, but it wasn't as easy as it had once been, with Lila's belly in the way. "It wasn't only me—we have a lot of people to thank," she said, just as Smash walked up to the three of them.

"I hardly recognized you," Eleanor said, running a motherly hand along Smash's tuxedo jacket. He was clean-shaven, had gotten a haircut, and he was barely recognizable in his spruce green bowtie.

"I can clean up every now and again." He bent down and raised the leg of his tuxedo trousers, revealing a shiny pair of black cowboy boots. "Even got me some new dress shoes," he said with a wink. "And I've got a little something planned."

"Oh?" Lila asked. "What's that?"

"Wait and see." Smash and Theo shared a conspiratorial look.

"Hi, Theo!" Rex said, running toward them down the center aisle between the red velvet-cushioned benches. He looked absolutely adorable in his miniature tuxedo with a cranberry tie and cummerbund, his guitar case slung over his back. "I'm ready!"

"Sshh," Theo said dramatically, eyeing Lila as if she couldn't see it. He gave Rex a wink, making him giggle.

When everyone had taken their seats, the orchestra tuning their instruments, Lila stood at the back, feeling so proud of all she'd been able to be a part of so far. The tours of the grounds were pulling in visitors beyond just the cabin renters, they had a waiting list for vacation reservations, and they'd become so popular that Theo and Smash had considered building out into the hills a bit more, to add a few luxury cabins to appeal to those looking for wedding venues and engagement spots. They'd hired a full-time chef and had a five-star restaurant on the premises, as well as a little red barn that served local beer and wine.

"Let's get to our seats," Eleanor said, taking Lila's arm.

"Our seats?" Lila questioned. She'd planned to watch from the back to allow all the seats to be used by the visitors.

"Yes, ma'am," Eleanor replied. "Front and center." She led Lila to the very front row and gestured to a couple of open spots next to Trudy and Judd. Charlotte, Edie, and Piper, who were visiting for the week, had also settled in beside them.

Lila took a seat, Eleanor sitting down beside her, just as the orchestra became quiet. Smash, Theo, and Rex walked out on the stage, standing behind three microphones. Smash lowered one for Rex. There was a noticeable excitement buzzing among the crowd as they realized that Smash Perry had taken the stage.

"What are *they* doing?" Lila asked. This definitely wasn't what she'd had planned.

"You'll see," Eleanor said, an enormous smile plastered across her face.

"Hello, everyone. Thank you for coming," Smash said into the microphone. "We know you came for classical Christmas music, but we wanted to start off the night with something for our host. Lila Evans, this is for you."

Rex took the mic, to the hush of the crowd. And a cappella, he started to sing, his little voice echoing beautifully through the hills.

"There's a light in my soul
When you walk through that door
Your smile so innocent
of all that came before…"

Suddenly, the orchestra set in, accompanying them as Theo sang a new verse she'd never heard until now, the other two harmonizing:

"I wonder how I'll ever be
All that you deserve
When everything you are to me
Is all I need and more.

You are my wish, my hope,
My future and my faith
That there is more to this world
Than just the dreams we chase.

You taught me how to love,
And showed me what was real
And for the rest of my life
I'll tell you how I feel…"

As the orchestra continued to play, Theo walked down from the stage and took Lila's hand, guiding her up the steps in front of the audience. Her three girlfriends cheered from the front row. "Lila and

I got married in a private ceremony at our favorite waterfall," he told the onlookers. "But that meant that I never got to do this in front of a crowd." He turned to Lila. "I love you with everything that I am." Then he dipped her back into his arms and kissed her to the cheers of the audience.

Lila knew right then that this was the second-best Christmas she'd had, and she had a feeling it was also just the beginning of an exciting future packed with special holidays and happy memories that would fill her heart.

A Letter from Jenny

Hi there!

Thank you so much for reading *Christmas at Fireside Cabins*! I really hope you enjoyed Lila and Theo's story and found it to be a heartwarming Christmas escape!

If you'd like me to drop you an email when my next book is out, you can sign up here:

www.itsjennyhale.com/email-signup

I won't share your email with anyone, and I'll email you only when a new book is released.

If you did enjoy *Christmas at Fireside Cabins*, I'd love it if you'd write a review. As an author, hearing wonderful feedback from readers is as exciting as unwrapping the perfect Christmas gift, and it also helps other readers to pick up one of my books for the first time.

Still craving a little more holiday cheer? Check out my other winter novels: *Christmas Wishes and Mistletoe Kisses*, *It Started with Christmas*, *A Christmas to Remember*, and *Christmas at Silver Falls*.

Until next time!

Jenny xo

Acknowledgments

A bucketload of gratitude must go to Oliver Rhodes for his guidance and direction over the years. He is the one who first breathed life into this career of mine, and I am who I am professionally because of him.

To my fabulous editor Christina Demosthenous, who is always there with the best suggestions. I am so lucky to have her on my side.

I am thankful every day that I found this amazing publisher, Bookouture, and that I've been able to grow with it. A big thank-you to the team for all the behind-the-scenes action that is required to get my books into the hands of readers.

And I couldn't do any of it without my family. To Justin, who listens to all my ideas and keeps the household running while I'm facedown on my computer, I am so grateful. To my kids, who share in my excitement every day and ask, "How many words did you get today?" I thank you too!

I'm blessed to grow in this field, and I couldn't do it without lots of prayer and faith. What a ride!

About the Author

Jenny Hale is a *USA Today* bestselling author of romantic fiction. Her novels *Coming Home for Christmas* and *Christmas Wishes and Mistletoe Kisses* have been adapted for television on the Hallmark Channel. Her stories are chock-full of feel-good romance and overflowing with warm settings, great friends, and family. Grab a cup of coffee, settle in, and enjoy the fun!